THE AMISH
Ballerina

THE AMISH
Ballerina

Richelle Brunstetter
with Wanda & Brunstetter

BARBOUR
PUBLISHING

YOU are the reason we do what we do here at Barbour Publishing. We promise that we will always use our God-given talents to produce content with you in mind—and that we will remain biblically faithful, no matter what.

Thank you for being the heart of our business.

The Amish Ballerina ©2025 by Richelle Brunstetter with Wanda E. Brunstetter

Print ISBN 979-8-89151-197-2

Adobe Digital Edition (.epub) 979-8-89151-198-9

All rights reserved. No part of this publication may be reproduced or transmitted for commercial purposes, except for brief quotations in printed reviews, without written permission of the publisher. Reproduced text may not be used on the World Wide Web. No Barbour Publishing content may be used as artificial intelligence training data for machine learning, or in any similar software development.

All scripture quotations, unless otherwise noted, are taken from the King James Version of the Bible.

Scripture quotations marked esv are from The ESV® Bible (The Holy Bible, English Standard Version®). ESV® Text Edition: 2016. Copyright © 2001 by Crossway, a publishing ministry of Good News Publishers. The ESV® text has been reproduced in cooperation with and by permission of Good News Publishers. Unauthorized reproduction of this publication is prohibited. All rights reserved.

This book is a work of fiction. Names, characters, places, and incidents are either products of the author's imagination or used fictitiously. Any similarity to actual people, organizations, and/or events is purely coincidental.

Cover Design: Kirk DouPonce, DogEared Design

Cover Model Photographer: Richard Brunstetter III

Published by Barbour Publishing, Inc., 1810 Barbour Drive, Uhrichsville, Ohio 44683, www.barbourbooks.com

Our mission is to inspire the world with the life-changing message of the Bible.

Printed in the United States of America.

Dedication

To Kristyn Miller and the Royal Spirits Drill Team. Thanks for the helpful information you shared about the various aspects of your drill team. No doubt the joy you impart on others must also be felt by every team member while performing at various benefit functions and other important events.

And be not conformed to this world: but be ye transformed by the renewing of your mind, that ye may prove what is that good, and acceptable, and perfect, will of God.
Romans 12:2

Chapter 1

Shipshewana, Indiana

Arie Kauffman rushed out of the back room, clutching a box of merchandise to fill the barren shelves throughout the gift shop where she worked part-time. She placed the box near one of the display tables and took hold of as many bars of scented soap as she could handle, piling them up like a bricklayer constructing a wall.

A job like this is best done when there are no shoppers, Arie thought. *If I don't do it now, more people are sure to come in here soon, and then I'll need to be free so I can offer them help.*

"You want me to assist you with restocking the shelves, Arie?"

Arie looked over her shoulder at Barbara, who managed the store and currently stood behind the checkout counter. "No, I've got it," Arie called in response. "Besides, we've been very busy here today, so it would be good if you remained free to take care of the register if anyone else wanders in."

Barbara fussed with the ties of her *kapp*. "True, but I feel bad having you do the hard work around the shop while I stand here and watch."

"Trust me, I prefer doing this. In fact, I've had plenty of practice in my parents' general store."

"Right. I forgot about that." Barbara slumped forward against the countertop, propping her head up with her palms. "When summer ends, will you be leaving your part-time job here and looking for something full-time?"

"I'm not sure yet. I mean, having my own money instead of depending on my parents for expenses is a *gut* thing."

"*Jah*, it is good, but there's a way around that without having to put in any work. You could always rely on Edwin's financial support once you two are married."

Arie frowned. "If we should decide to get married, I would think we could rely on each other, because I could keep working until we have children."

In that moment, the front door opened, and a gust of heat followed, along with several people. Arie reached for the now-empty box and sprinted to the supply room at the back of the store to get some more products.

In any case, I wouldn't want to burden Edwin. I know he'd be an amazing husband, and if we should get married, I would want to be a supportive wife to him, whether it be to help with our finances or as a homemaker.

Arie backed against the wall, her gaze flitting amid the boxes. As much as she longed to stay in the back room to be alone with her thoughts for a while, Arie knew she had to go back out there and put on the most cheerful demeanor she could muster. Given that the souvenir keychain display was empty, Arie opted for a box of replacements.

Reentering the establishment's main section, Arie threaded her way through the cramped aisles, greeting customers who either had sauntered up to pay for the delights they had gathered around the shop or who stared at the items on display with looks of intense concentration. While some returned the favor, others did not even make eye contact with Arie. Which was fine, considering all that mattered was finishing the task at hand without a hitch. She knelt down with the box and dug out the keychains, then proceeded to hang each one on the hooks.

"Mommy, can I have a lollipop? I like the orange-flavored ones."

Arie's ears perked up, and she peered toward the front counter, where a young English girl with her auburn hair worn in a bun at the back of her head stood near her mother. Balancing on one foot, and then the other, the child pointed to the lollipops displayed nearby.

"No, sweetie," the woman answered with a shake of her head. "You've had a treat already today, so no candy right now."

The child's shoulders drooped as she lowered her head a bit, but she gave no argument.

Arie's gaze went to the young girl's waistline, where a beautiful, ivory-colored tutu stuck out from underneath the girl's hoodie. A twinge pulled at Arie's heartstrings, and she struggled not to stare.

Everything reverted back to normal as the mother and daughter left the shop, but Arie's thoughts stayed frozen, even as she kept scooping out more keychains.

Why was the girl dressed like that? Arie pondered. *I know Lorrina's ballet classes are similar to school days, and they resume after summer. So the girl is either enrolled in a summer program or just having fun wearing a tutu.*

Arie found herself whisked away to when she had been ten years old and had observed her first and final ballet performance. Lorrina, her neighbor and friend, had a recital at the Goshen Theater and had invited Arie to go with her. Knowing full well that her parents would be against it, Arie had told Lorrina's mother that she shouldn't go. But Lorrina's mother had insisted, and the next thing Arie knew, much to her disbelief, she was in the backseat of her neighbors' sedan. She'd had no idea what to expect when they arrived at the theater.

Arie remembered as clear as day how the voices from the audience in the auditorium had surrounded her as they made their way past rows of red folding chairs in one of the upper balconies. When she'd settled in her seat, the noise failed to quell the thoughts whirling in Arie's mind. However, the racket that rang in her ears came to a standstill once the lights lowered and the curtains on stage parted.

Arie jolted as someone nudged her shoulder. She raised her chin to see who had done it and realized it was one of the other gift shop employees, Abigail.

"You seem to be in the middle of something, Arie, but if you'd like to go home now, I can take over."

After gathering her bearings, Arie sprung up and nodded. "Jah, I think that'd be okay. *Danki*."

Abigail smiled. "No problem at all."

"Lorrina, your Amish friend is here!"

Lorrina Moore curled her fingers under the tiny rodent that scuttled across the surface of her desk. "All right, Quillace, time to go back in your home. There you go." She set her hedgehog on the padding of his cage, fastened it, and then turned to face her mother. "Mom, she has a name, you know."

"But I'm sure you knew who I meant without me being specific." Mom tossed her silky, black ringlets over her shoulders. Lorrina had always envied her mother's pretty hair.

"I would've known for sure if you had said her name."

"Well, whatever." She jerked down the cuff of her blouse and tilted her head. "I let her in, and she's waiting downstairs for you."

"Okay, thanks, Mom."

Lorrina's mother folded her arms and stepped out of the room without saying anything.

Lorrina blew out a puff of air. *I don't understand why Mother refused to say Arie's name.* She shrugged. *Oh well, tomorrow Mom will act as if nothing happened—just like she usually does.*

Lorrina's heart rate soared as she bounded down the stairs. With the help of her socks, she glided down the hallway to the front door, where her friend Arie stood near the entry table.

Lorrina ran to Arie and pulled her into a hug. "Good to see you."

Arie returned the hug. "I'm glad to see you too."

Lorrina stepped back and took her friend's hand. "Come on, let's go upstairs to my room."

Lorrina glanced over her shoulder once, just to be sure that Arie had followed her up the stairs. Once they entered her bedroom, Lorrina patted the mattress and told Arie to take a seat on the edge of her bed. After Arie sat down, Lorrina marched up to her desk chair, swung it around, and plopped down, facing her friend.

"I haven't seen you in over a week, so catch me up." Cupping her elbow, Lorrina tapped her earring loop. "How are things at the gift shop?"

"It's going okay. With the flea market happening every Saturday and the large number of tourists during the summer, it can get a little crazy sometimes."

"I hear you, which is why I prefer to stay home and away from the crowds in town. That is until summer ends, or I go on vacation somewhere with my folks and we become crazy tourists."

"And how would you go about that?"

"Wearing outlandish attire, claiming to speak some foreign language, photographing everything in sight—mostly food—and so on." Lorrina swiveled her chair a smidge. "Exploring an unfamiliar place can be fun if done mindfully."

Arie twiddled the loops of the paper bag she had placed atop the skirt of her dress's scarlet fabric. "How about you, Lorrina? Anything new, other than vacation planning?"

"It's basically the same old thing. My mother is keen on the idea of me landing an opportunity with one of the elite performing arts companies. She pushed for me to attend the School of American Ballet and their summer program, and I had to put my foot down again and tell her I didn't want to go."

"You telling her that probably didn't go over too well, did it?"

"No, it did not. I've told Mom countless times that the chances of me being considered are slim, even with my ten years of dance experience. I wish she could've kept an open mind and accepted it when I said that I'd much rather become a dance instructor instead of a performer." Scuffing her chair closer, Lorrina rubbed her hands together. "Speaking of dancing, are you ready for more practice today? That's the reason you came here, right?"

"Lorrina, the main reason I wanted to visit you was because I hadn't had the chance to in a while." She gestured to the paper sack in her lap. "And I've brought you something." Arie rose from the mattress and handed Lorrina the bag.

Lorrina grasped the straps and slipped her hand inside. As soon as she felt the shape and density of it, she knew what the object was. She lifted it out and opened the waxed paper covering, releasing a familiar floral scent that lingered in the room.

"What? No way! They sell hydrangea soap at the gift shop?" Lorrina squealed. "You're too sweet. Thank you, Arie."

"You're welcome. I'm glad you like it." Arie offered Lorrina her usual dimpled smile.

"Like it? I love it. I'll have to drop by and get more one of these days." Lorrina laid the soap bar on her desk, spun in her chair, and wrapped her fingers on the armrests. "Anyway, am I getting the wrong impression, or do you no longer want to learn ballet?"

Her friend shrugged. "I don't know for sure, Lorrina. There's a lot that I'm not sure about right now."

"I understand. Simply put, you've shown much improvement over the years. If you quit dancing now, it'll be a shame that your talents will go to waste."

When she saw her friend's hunched shoulders, downcast expression, and pained hazel eyes, Lorrina regretted the words that seemed to have fallen out of her mouth of their own volition.

"I'm very sorry," Lorrina spluttered while twiddling with her necklace. "I worded that wrong. What I meant was, while I've been delighted for the opportunity to teach you, I realize it must be frustrating not to be able to share what you've learned with others."

"I expressed my interest in ballet years ago, and my parents turned it down because it's worldly."

"Well, you can always go with me to my dance studio in Goshen. I'll be starting my final year of ballet at the end of August." Her chest swelled as she unabashedly stared at her wall of ballet portraits taken over the years. "Whoa, ten whole years. I can't believe I've been dancing for that long. Where'd the time go?"

"I'd love to go along with you, but my parents weren't too thrilled when they found out your mom brought me along to your dance recital. Ballet was not a part of my upbringing, and

I've never been able to perform in a tutu. Simply a long dress when no one's watching. Even if I took classes now, I don't think I'll ever be as skilled as you or the other dancers."

"It's never too late to begin learning ballet, Arie. You've got potential, and as much as your parents won't admit it, you're an adult now and should be allowed to at least try. You got a job at the gift shop downtown, right?"

Arie nodded.

"So you could afford to take one class every week, and on the days when I don't have anything scheduled after school, I can still teach you. You have the resources to give it a shot, and I will be there for you no matter what."

"I don't think it's worth the risk."

"There are repercussions for every decision in life. Even working at a gift shop, something's bound to go awry when you least expect it. Isn't it worth taking the risk rather than regretting not experiencing dancing in a ballet studio?"

Arie smirked, and the dainty mole near her Cupid's bow rose like the sun. "You know, my parents warned me that you'd be a bad influence."

"The only person who'll have a bad influence on you is yourself." Lorrina winked.

Her smile grew more defined, but gradually it lessened. Arie sighed and knitted her brows. "Edwin's already considering joining the church soon, and if he knew about this, I doubt he would be for it." She lifted both hands and let them fall in her lap. "It's for the best, I think."

Lorrina slumped against her chair's cushion. *Poor Arie. I admire the dedication she feels toward her family, but she needs something in her life that is personally rewarding. What if Arie is intended to be a dancer, but she will never know?*

As Arie strolled along the driveway, the heap of pebbles beneath her sandals shifted with every stride. The breeze rustled among the branches above her, and birdsong filled her ears as she approached the property's fence line. She cast a quick glance at her parents' store, then the barn across the way.

Maybe I should keep my job after summer's over. It gets a little too chaotic at home, and even if it's only for a few hours, working at the gift shop is the only time during the week I get to spend away from my family. She leaned against the fence. *Is that selfish of me, though, since my parents depend on my help here? And what about Edwin? I've not been seeing him very much, except for Sundays. Considering how busy he's been at his job and the drill team he's involved with, maybe that doesn't really matter.*

Her attention flickered to the barn once more, and she sighed. *Not yet. First, I have to go see if Mom or Dad needs me for anything.*

Arie headed to the general store owned by her parents, where they sold clothing, kitchenware, and other household goods. A few vehicles were parked out front, and two horses and buggies stood at the hitching rail. The commotion of people milling about the store greeted her after she'd tugged the door handle and entered. The midday sunshine flowed in through the store's skylight, cascading onto the shelves and the epoxy flooring they had recently installed.

"There you are, Arie!" Her mother's voice resonated from the front counter, as she circled around and approached.

Arie's stomach roiled like winds in the waters of a pond. "*Wie geht's, Mamm?*"

"All's good so far." Mom tilted her head. "You're back an hour later than usual. What took you so long?"

Arie had to use all of her resolve to resist buckling under the pressure of Mom's penetrating gaze. It didn't help that her mother's dark brown eyes almost matched the shade of her pupils, making it indiscernible at times how dilated they were. Arie knew she had to drum up an answer fast, because if she mentioned being at Lorrina's house, her mother would go off on a tangent about why Arie shouldn't be friends with her.

"The gift shop was swamped today because of the flea market," Arie asserted. "So I had to work harder and more efficiently this morning to keep up with all the shoppers."

Mom's nose freckles darkened. "Oh, that makes sense. One of these days, I should visit the flea market and spend some time browsing. Of course, I'd have to convince your *daed* to close the store on a Saturday."

Thank goodness Mom found the reason I gave her about the gift shop being busy acceptable. I didn't have to lie to her either, which is good. "Anything I can do around here today to help out?" she asked.

"Since you're so willing to help, I've got a few tasks for you to carry out. Firstly, I need you to restock the shelves near the front of the store. I've already opened up some boxes in the back room."

Oh, yes, I'm so eager to unload more boxes. Rather than demonstrate her dismay aloud, Arie clenched her jaw and cracked her mother a grin. "I'll get right to it, Mamm."

Although Arie wasn't looking forward to doing extra work, she felt fortunate to shift her attention elsewhere. She moved on to where the recent shipment of boxes had been stowed, then brought out an inventory of canned goods and began unloading. As she eased into the rhythm of her routine, Arie recalled something her mother had often told her when she expressed her discontent with things.

"Happiness is the fine art of making a beautiful bouquet from only those flowers in reach," she mused.

Even if that quote wasn't from her, it still holds true. There's a standard notion of what happiness looks like, but in all actuality, happiness is more about the things we have than the things we lack. Twisting her mouth, she clenched the can in her hand before lining it up on the shelf. *I know this is true, but why do I still feel so frustrated? Could Lorrina be right about my desire to be a dancer? Would ballet bring me the happiness and fulfillment I desperately seek?*

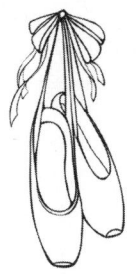

Chapter 2

Lorrina squirmed on her seat in the pew while waiting as the church elders distributed communion trays, row by row, to those seated in front of her. Now that they had finished passing the platters and carrying the wafers, they were serving the grape juice. The sound of the organ up on the platform reverberated throughout the sanctuary, and a handful of the congregation hummed or sang along with the hymn. She looked over at her mother, who had not spoken to her since the previous day. Mom's gaze was fixed toward the podium where the pastor stood.

When one of the elders reached their row and handed her the tray of juice, Lorrina tweezed out a plastic cup and passed it to her mom. Lorrina figured out an approach to cut the tension while holding the small plastic cylinder between her fingers.

"Mom," Lorrina muttered. "Do you think they reuse these cups?"

Her mother's face flickered a meager smile. "Lorrina, don't ask questions like that," she whispered.

"Like what?" Lorrina's father interjected quietly, while pushing up his thin-framed reading glasses.

Mom leaned over to Dad and repeated what Lorrina had said. "No, they don't do that. Well...maybe they could."

"Peter," Mom tittered, covering her mouth.

Lorrina did her best to repress her snickers, and she noticed that even her parents struggled to contain their laughter. However, her mother delivered a slight finger raise, followed by a modest "*shush.*" This was understandable, given their juvenile behavior during church service. It was a good thing they sat in the sanctuary's last few rows toward the back.

The organ music stopped, and the pastor spoke into the microphone mounted on the podium. "We read in 1 Corinthians 11, verses 25 through 27 (ESV) that Jesus took the cup after the Passover supper and said: 'This cup is the new covenant in my blood. Do this, as often as you drink it, in remembrance of me.' Then Paul observed, 'For as often as you eat this bread and drink the cup, you proclaim the Lord's death until he comes. Whoever, therefore, eats the bread or drinks the cup of the Lord in an unworthy manner will be guilty concerning the body and blood of the Lord.'"

The pastor raised his focus from the Bible lying before him. "We evaluate ourselves for this reason. Please, as you lower your heads in prayer, look within and address what needs to be cleansed."

Lorrina closed her eyes in prayer as the preacher requested the congregation to pray over the cup. She pondered in her heart whether she was worthy of taking communion or if there was anything she should pray about or confess before partaking of the elements. As much as she felt grateful that she and her mother were back on speaking terms, the real issue lurked beneath the surface, and it was only a matter of time before it flared up again. Lorrina hoped they could find a resolution, but how could she settle their dispute if her mother wouldn't hear her out?

Lorrina crossed her ankles and sagged against the pew, darting a peek at Mom. *When I get home, I'm going to have a talk with her and try to make things right.*

Grasping the reins, Arie rode with Edwin along the expansive field, their horses' hooves in tandem as they trotted side by side. The clouds above scuttled along, as if trying to keep up with them.

After church service and the noon meal that followed were over, Edwin had suggested that they venture out on the scenic backroads and spend some quality time together. All for the idea, Arie had headed home with her family, filled with enthusiasm while waiting for her boyfriend to arrive so they could get a move on before the afternoon sun set over the community.

"Isn't this the most breathtaking location there is, Arie?" Edwin asked, slowing his horse near a thicket of wild roses.

Arie matched his pace and narrowed her eyes. "You say that wherever we go."

"That's the point." Averting his gaze, Edwin's face reddened. "Because when we're together, everything around you is *wunderbaar*."

Even though it was kind of corny, Arie's heart swelled at her boyfriend's sincerity. "That was a sweet thing to say, but you're very silly, Edwin."

"I meant it. That's why I have high hopes about what the future holds for us."

Arie managed to chuckle, but no matter how hard she tried to immerse herself in the moment, Edwin's words dissipated in the midst of her thoughts. She couldn't ignore the pestering notions that led her off the beaten path.

Am I truly ready to give my life to the church like Edwin is? Edwin is quite aware of who he is as a person, whereas I am not so certain. Arie's spine tensed as she gripped the reins, her nails burrowing into her palms. *Even though I love him, the thought of being with Edwin forever causes me to feel like I want to flee. Wouldn't my uncertainty tear him down? He should be with someone who is sure of themselves, someone as passionate and driven as he is.*

A sharp pain struck her left side above her chest. Arie pressed her hand there, allowing a blast of air to pass between her chapped lips. Her ribs felt like they were hugging her lungs, impeding the passage of oxygen. She tried to ease her nerves as best as she could, yet her breathing was labored.

Aster reared up, and as she dipped her head, the mare's canter changed to a gallop.

"Arie!" Edwin hollered. "Where are you going?"

Feeling as though she was in a stupor, Arie scrunched her cheeks and squinted her eyes as she tried to make sense of what was unfolding. Once she snapped out of it, Arie instructed her mare to slow down. But Aster pressed on, quickening her pace, and Arie's pulse accelerated in time with her horse's hooves striking the ground.

She tugged on the reins and gave Aster a slight inclination of her head, and the mare went in the appointed direction. They continued to turn in a loop until Aster gradually slowed down. Arie let out the breath she held onto and managed to ease her horse to a halt by leaning back and drawing the reins to her torso.

Edwin caught up, dismounting from his horse. "Are you all right?"

"Jah, I think so." Arie moistened her lips. "For some reason, my *gaul* doesn't want to listen to me."

"You know how horses can be when they're given the opportunity to roam." Leading his horse, he sauntered up and smoothed his fingers over Aster's grayish-white coat. "How often have you been riding your horse?"

Arie hesitated. "It's been a while, but I've been so busy, and I do let her out in the pasture when I return home from work."

"All a horse needs is to feel free. Otherwise, they'll feel cooped up, and they may not want to listen anymore. If you bring her out here more often, she'll be attentive again. It could also be from nervousness, which horses can sense, and it might make them anxious as well."

"You certainly know a lot about horses, Edwin. More of an expert than I am, that's for sure."

"Hey, don't sell yourself short, Arie. You're an excellent horseback rider. You're simply working out the kinks a bit. Getting back in the saddle, as they say." Edwin jested. "With the proper guidance, even the most rambunctious horses can listen. Isn't that right, Daisy?" He patted his horse's neck.

Daisy, Edwin's beautiful horse, whinnied and raised her head. He wasn't wrong, since Daisy was sometimes a mischievous creature. Arie had taken in some of the horse's antics when she went over to see Edwin at his parents' home. As they were all outside feeding the horses, Daisy had nipped his mother's kapp and taken off with it. Needless to say, they'd had to chase the mare down. It was no wonder his mom, who had owned the horse before Edwin, gave the stinker of a mare to her son. For whatever reason, Daisy was fond of Edwin, and Arie couldn't comprehend how such a seemingly tame horse could create such mayhem.

Arie leaped from her horse and landed on the balls of her feet, bending her knees. She kept her hold on the reins as she patted Aster's neck. "I think I need a break from riding before we head on back."

"That's fine with me." Edwin swept his sandy brown bangs away from his brows. "Are you sure there isn't anything you want to get off your chest?"

"What do you mean?"

"Don't know. These days when we're together it seems like you're staring off somewhere else."

Her sight veered to the horizon in front of them. "I just have a lot on my mind, is all."

"Wanna talk about it?"

Arie shook her head. "I'm sure it'll sort itself out." She turned to face Edwin again, noticing how his blue eyes glistened in the sunlight filtering through the canopy of trees above them. "But danki, Edwin, for checking on me."

He stepped forward and drew Arie into his arms. "I'm here for you, even if you feel like you can't tell me what's bothering you," Edwin assured, his gravelly voice settling her nerves.

Sighing, Arie laid her head against his chest. *All I do is worry about everything, all the time, even over the littlest of things*, she thought. *And now I'm causing Edwin to worry. I really need to work on hiding the stresses in my life. Either that or I have to come up with some way to lessen my stress so there's less to worry about.*

Something skidded across Arie's forehead, and she knew right away that it wasn't Edwin's doing. His dark-haired mare had joined them in their intimate moment. Arie wondered if Edwin's horse might be a bit jealous of the attention he'd been giving her instead of the mare.

"Daisy, no," he scolded. "You goofy gaul. Back off now." He pushed the horse's nose away from Arie.

"Daisy might be jealous, Edwin." Arie brought a hand to her lips.

Edwin let go of Arie and stroked under his horse's chin. "There's enough room for both of you in my life."

Don't be so sure of that, Edwin, Arie thought. *You might be better off with the horse providing the tenderness you need rather than me. If you knew my secret longing, I doubt that you'd even want to be seen with me.* The fact that his horse intervened was fortunate. Arie found some solace in diverting attention away from herself.

"So, what about you?" she inquired. "How are things going at work?"

Edwin winced. "Oh, don't get me started on that."

"I'm guessing Markel did something he wasn't supposed to do."

"Easy guess, given that he does it almost every day."

Edwin continued to express the displeasure he felt with his job, while Arie did her best to be an attentive listener. As he continued to speak on the subject of his brother, Arie's mind wandered once more.

I love hearing Edwin share his interests with such confidence, but I wish I could do the same. Maybe I should just tell him what I've been doing for the last eight years. Since we started dating, I've tried my hardest to hide it from Edwin. But if I decide to set my desire for dance aside, does it even matter if I tell him?

Back home, Arie directed her horse into the appropriate stall. Through the barn's gable vent, she could see the radiant splendor of the golden hour. Most of the horse's care had already been handled, so Arie went to replenish Aster's water and provide her some hay to chew on. Then she fetched the curry comb to loosen the soil from when she had rolled on the ground.

"I'm sorry for not giving you the attention you deserve." She ran her fingers gently between Aster's eyes several times. "I'll try to make time to take you riding more often. At least a few times per week. Sound good, girl?"

Aster snorted and nudged against her palm.

"Okay, it's a deal." Arie winked and gave the horse a few tender pats.

Being in solitude and brushing the horse's mane made Arie feel the most at ease she had felt all day.

After putting the comb back on the top shelf, Arie became aware that she ought to help with supper preparations inside the house. But she remained stationary awhile longer, and even though her stomach felt ready for food, she had a hunger to move about. The more Arie marinated in her pool of thoughts, the more she was determined to take the plunge.

Okay now. . . Arie shook out her legs while taking a deep breath through her nostrils. *If I'm going to do this, I should make sure to warm up properly.*

Arie ambled up to the unused hitching post near the stalls, which she'd repurposed as a makeshift ballet barre. She raised her hand to the barre, spun, and touched her heels together into first position. Arie bent her knees, keeping her feet planted on the ground, and rose back up. After a few pliés, she lowered even farther into a grand plié. She held that position for a moment, feeling her hamstrings ignite within her upper legs.

Arie rose from the ground, her back straight, and shifted into second position. She resumed her barre warm-up, stretching her extremities. Once she finished, her arms led the way, and Arie arched her feet with each stride. Moving about the barn, Arie recited a ballet pattern Lorrina had her practice, striking her heel above the ankle.

"Piqué arabesque, cross, glissade, leap."

She raised her rear leg and arms, shifting all her weight to her standing leg on relevé. Arie then crossed her back foot forward, pushing off the soles of her feet to glide over the concrete flooring.

At long last, she catapulted herself into a massive leap. Arie's chin shot up toward the barn ceiling, transfixed by the satisfaction of achieving antigravity and then dropping back down to earth.

Arie pivoted around and repeated the motions on the other side. After that, she improvised by pointing her foot, raising onto her tippy toes, executing sharp chaîné turns, and spotting the inner barn's apex as she whipped around and around. Then she bent her knees and sprang to her feet, picking up her back leg into a pirouette. Arie twirled once, brought her foot behind her, and concluded with arms outstretched. She felt invigorated, and took in a massive breath despite the dust in the air she'd stirred up.

With her head tilted back, Arie grasped her sides and observed dots in her field of vision. Her sole acknowledgment of her performance came from a locust fluttering its wings, which sounded like a thimble-sized person clapping. Nevertheless, she curtsied to her applauding witness.

"What are you doing, Arie?"

Dread prevailed, and she stiffened. How much did Arie's mother see of her performance? How would she explain herself? Arie's gaze strayed to the floor, where she perceived a black piece of fabric near her toes. It was her head scarf. While she'd been frolicking around the barn, Arie had been unaware that it had slipped off.

"Picking up my scarf, Mamm." After yanking the scarf off the floor, Arie flicked it up to show her mother and then turned to look at her. "I'd just gotten back from horseback riding with Edwin."

"But about thirty minutes ago, I saw you and Aster out by the fence." Mom's lips curled into a pucker. "And you look a little flushed."

So much perspiration had collected under Arie's clothing

that she felt as though she had been out in a downpour for too long. "J–just taking care of Aster, and I got a bit sunburnt today," she stuttered while glancing down at her shoes. It was agonizing waiting in silence for her mother to respond. Arie couldn't help but wonder whether Mom relished having the power to exert authority over her.

"All right, Arie. But I need help preparing supper, so no more dillydallying."

When Mom was no longer in view, Arie collapsed to the floor. *That was a close call. Like I already told Lorrina, keeping this secret is too risky. And yet, dancing always makes me feel so much better. Greater than all the other things I do in my life.* Arms encircling Arie's legs, she brought her knees to her chest. *Will I ever be able to give this up and settle down to join the church?*

Chapter 3

BANG! BANG! BANG!
Edwin roused from his deep slumber and groaned. With fluttering eyelids, he lifted his head off the bed.

"Up and at 'em, Edwin!"

Edwin staggered to his feet, and his eyes widened trying to focus in the dark room. He fumbled for his bedside table's flashlight, and when Edwin found it, he clicked it on and aimed the beam toward his alarm clock.

Three o'clock? Dad is hammering on my door so early—why? Edwin stooped over to have a closer look. *Wait, the skinny arm isn't going around anymore.*

"Good golly!" Edwin exclaimed. "Be right out, Dad!"

He hastened to get dressed, his arms flailing while slipping into the sleeves of his shirt and trousers.

I can't believe I slept in. I always wake up before everyone else in this house. What's the matter with me? Edwin groaned, and with his socks in tow, he plopped onto his bed. *Markel's slackness had better not have rubbed off on me.*

Edwin hurried out of his bedroom, fiddling with the buttons on his shirt collar with one hand as he sped down the hallway.

He directed the flashlight's beam toward his father, being mindful not to cast it squarely in his face.

"I'm sorry for waking up so late, Daed."

"Late?" His father's forehead wrinkled. "What are you talking about, Son?"

"Weren't you pounding on my door not long ago?"

Dad wrapped a finger around the long, coiled hairs sprouting from his beard. "I did, but not because you're late getting up."

"What time is it then?" Edwin questioned.

"A little after four. Is there no clock in your room?"

"Jah, but it needs new batteries. If I didn't sleep in, then why were you at my door so early?"

"I will need you for something outside later today but figured with your other chores that you normally do after work, it would be good to get an early start on those things this morning." The skin constricted around his dad's aquamarine eyes. "Your mother isn't feeling well, so I'm sure she'd appreciate it if you went out to the garden and harvested the strawberries, cauliflower, and the newly grown zucchini. She's hoping to do some canning soon."

"Mamm's sick?" Edwin rubbed at the itch on his eyelid. "How serious is it?"

"Given what she went through last night, I think she caught the flu bug that's been going around. I'm letting her have some time alone so she can rest without being disturbed."

"I'm sorry to hear that."

Nodding, Dad crossed his arms. "So, could you get the fruits and veggies for your mother from the garden after you get home from work today?"

"Couldn't you have asked Markel to do it?"

Almost as if it were a dreadful skit, right on cue, the bedroom door in front of them swung open, and his older brother emerged from the darkness. Heaving out a lengthy yawn, Markel scratched at the upper leg of his pajama pants.

"*Guder mariye,* Markel."

"Morning, Dad," he replied in a weary tone, while raking a hand through his matted hair. "Is breakfast ready yet?"

"We're fending for ourselves with whatever's in the kitchen. But first, you need to go back in your room and get dressed. We have a big day ahead of us." Dad skirted around the bend of the hallway, withdrawing from view.

"Wait, why are we fending for ourselves?" Markel asked.

"Mamm isn't feeling well," Edwin responded.

"Oh, I wonder what she caught. Hopefully it isn't contagious, 'cause I sure don't have time to be sick."

Edwin clenched his teeth as he looked at his brother from the corner of his eye. *You might not want to be* grank, *but I bet you'd like to use the excuse of being sick so you could avoid having to work today.* Edwin felt inclined to share his thoughts out loud, but he kept his mouth clamped shut. Well aware that his father was within earshot, Edwin knew he'd get scolded for any unkind remark he might make about his older brother.

Markel backed away from Edwin, stepped into his bedroom, and shut the door. The walls at the end of the hallway were lit by with a faint yellow glow, indicating that Dad had turned on the gas lamps in the kitchen and living room. Edwin subsequently followed the light source and trailed into the kitchen, where he found Dad reaching for a mug from one of the upper cabinets.

"So, what are we doing today, Boss?" Edwin inquired, tucking the flashlight into his trouser pocket.

"Residential work in Middlebury. We got a service call for

shingle removal, and I need you and Markel to make it out there with the driver in a timely manner. Since I need to look after your mother and catch up on paperwork, I'll join you both on the jobsite later when I can." Dad went over to the cupboard where the lazy Susan sat and stooped down to rotate it until he found his jar of coffee grounds. He pushed the cupboard door with his foot and positioned the grounds on top of the counter. "Want any *kaffi*? There's plenty to go around."

"Maybe after I come back in. I'm trying not to drink coffee right after waking up because one of the customers we worked for last week mentioned that waiting approximately an hour before consuming caffeine was a good idea for anyone who likes to drink it."

Dad's chin jutted out. "Why's that?"

"Cortisol levels in the body need time to spike before they begin to drop. That's what I heard anyway."

"Yeah, well, don't believe everything that comes out of someone's mouth." His father cranked the stove's knob to ignite the flame inside the gas burner.

Markel lurched into the kitchen entrance, slumping against the doorframe. "Alrighty. . . I'm heading out to get some chores done." In an instant, Markel jerked open the back door and took his leave.

"Yep, and you'd better hurry out to the barn too, Edwin." Dad gestured to the door, which Markel had left partially open.

Edwin meandered toward his boots, which were close to the rear entrance. When he arrived, though, Edwin was perplexed since his work boots weren't where he normally placed them. "Hey, Daed?" Edwin called over his shoulder.

His father emerged from the kitchen and ambled over to him.

"What's the trouble, Son?"

Edwin gestured to where the boots should have been. "My work *schtiffel* aren't sitting here."

"They are probably in your bedroom, right?"

Edwin gave a quick shake of his head. "No, I never take off work boots in my room."

"Really?" Dad questioned. "I thought you did."

"Markel does, even if they're dirty. That's not what I do, though."

"You should go look there anyway. You probably put them there and just forgot."

Edwin's stomach quivered a smidge at his father's suggestion, but in spite of that, he sprinted back to the hallway and bounded up the stairs to his bedroom. The vein in his forehead throbbed as he inspected every square inch of his room. Edwin knew deep down that he hadn't taken them off in here, but to satisfy his father, he searched anyway. Even when he was out of it, longing to collapse on his bed and avoid talking to anyone for the rest of the day, Edwin always removed his boots near the back door. It was completely nonsensical for Dad to think otherwise, especially after Edwin had made it clear that he never took them to his room.

They couldn't have simply vanished into thin air, Edwin reasoned. *And I doubt that anyone would walk away with a pair of work boots. Unless. . . No. No, he didn't!*

Edwin hurried out of his room and darted across the hall to the door of the room where he believed his boots had been taken. He grabbed the knob, twisted it, and entered Markel's domain. Edwin could have missed the door altogether if it weren't for the flashlight guiding him. The floor in his brother's bedroom was strewn with garments, heaps of paper, piled-up boxes, and all of Markel's footwear in the corner.

How can someone live like this? With a *tsk*, he stepped gingerly across the room to sort through the pile of shoes. *This mess is an accident waiting to happen. Broken bones or fire hazards—it doesn't matter—someone, like Mom, if she came in here to gather laundry or clean, could get hurt.*

Edwin spotted his brother's boots nestled with the other shoes he wore, yet Markel had been wearing boots when he went out the door moments ago. The boots his brother had put on were Edwin's footwear instead.

Edwin picked up Markel's boots, marched out of his brother's room, and then raced downstairs and into the living room. He found his father seated on the couch, sipping from his steaming coffee mug.

"Oh, good. You found your boots, Edwin. I told you they'd be in your room."

"These are not my boots. They're my *bruder's* boots, which I found in his room. How did Markel not realize he had put my boots on instead of his? I'm a whole foot size larger than him, not to mention that my work boots were downstairs and his were in his room."

Dad grunted. "You can tell him he's wearing them when he comes back in. It's not a big deal though."

"It is when you say, 'Look for them in my room,' but your other son keeps shoes in his bedroom and assumes that the pair near the back door are his."

"That's between you and Markel. Talk to him about it. And you have other shoes you could wear, right?"

"Jah, but they're old and not in the best shape anymore."

"Whatever. Just find something to put on your feet and go do what needs to be done outside."

Dad rose from the couch with his mug and dawdled out of the room, leaving Edwin holding his older brother's tattered boots, patched up with layers of glue around the soles. *No wonder he took my schtiffel,* Edwin thought. *I bet he's just too cheap to buy a new pair. Or maybe Markel doesn't have his head on straight this morning and didn't pay any attention to what he'd grabbed up to put on his feet.*

Fantastic way to begin the day! Edwin exhaled as he carried the boots out of the living room. *But at least I have drill team practice to look forward to later, which will take my mind off what will undoubtedly transpire at work.*

At last, the sun crested above LaGrange County. Arie had been commuting from her household chores to her parents' store today, as she hadn't been called in for work at the gift shop. She stood beside the flowerbed and went around with her shears, severing branches from the shrubs and trees that flanked the front yard.

Maggie, her younger sister, skipped along the graveled pathway. She headed from the chicken coop, carrying a woven basket around her forearm. Right away, Maggie took notice of Arie and hustled over, her round face displaying an enormous grin.

"Hey, *Schweshder!*" she exclaimed, mixing an English word with one that was Pennsylvania Dutch.

"Hi, Maggie." Arie waved, then continued snipping away at the branches. "How'd it go gathering the eggs?"

The basket, bursting at the seams with nicely shaped, pale brown eggs, was raised to her sister's head. Her brunette locks, which were closer to the color of ink than chestnut, gleamed in the direct sunlight. "Good, I got plenty of 'em too."

"I see that." Arie winked. "Nicely done."

"*Danki.*" She arched up onto the balls of her shoeless feet before sinking back down in the grass. Then Maggie's demeanor stilled. "What are you doin'?"

"Shaping the rosebushes. I'm trimming them back because they started getting out of hand."

"Does it hurt the roses when ya do that?"

Arie shook her head. "It actually allows them to flourish. It's more like giving the bushes a haircut—you take off the split ends, allowing for plentiful growth that isn't unkempt."

"Just like when Daed and Rudy get their haircuts."

"And you, because while we may have long hair, even our lengthy strands need to be clipped a bit every now and then to remove the dry, split ends."

Maggie giggled and gestured to the shaded plant adjacent to the enormous hydrangea bush, with its petals tinted green. Every limb of the relatively little plant was covered in rows of red heart-shaped flowers.

"Those are pretty." Maggie continued to observe the plant, crouching alongside of it with both hands on her knees. "I like those *blumme*. They look like hearts."

Setting her shears on the mulch, Arie shed her garden gloves and laid them beside the tool. She then strolled up to Maggie and, lowering to meet the flowering plant at eye level, she plucked one of the hearts.

Her sister stood up and stared curiously at the flower in Arie's palm.

"They're called bleeding hearts. And actually, my friend Lorrina showed me something neat about the blossoms. The flower is more than just a heart when you turn it upside down and then peel back the petal here." Arie revealed the flower's inner structure by folding down a portion of the petal. "See? Somewhere inside the heart lies a girl. Her head is located here, and her arms are there, gripping what appears to be a frock while she does so. She kind of looks like—"

"She's an Amish girl wearing a pretty red dress."

"Jah, an Amish *maedel* in a *frack*..." Arie's sentence trailed off, gazing down at the blossom in the palm of her hand.

She gave a fleeting look at the barn before diverting her focus away from it. Earlier, Arie had gone over there with her father and brother to tend to Aster's needs, along with tidying up certain areas of the barn. After almost exposing her secret in front of her mother, Arie had refrained from dancing in the barn for the past three days.

There are moments when I wish I was in Lorrina's shoes, Arie mused. *Having a mother who encourages your passions and doesn't make you hide them out of fear must be nice. I really wish I could've grown up with ballet as a child, but instead, I'm simply an Amish girl with no talents.* She held up the bleeding heart. *An Amish girl wearing a very plain dress.*

Maggie nudged her arm. "Is something wrong, Arie?"

Arie's lips quivered as she feigned a smile while peering down at her sister. "I'm thirsty and in need of some water, so I'm gonna head back to the house. Do you want my help sorting the eggs, Maggie?"

The child bobbed her head and grinned up at Arie. "Jah, please."

The late afternoon sun peeked through the curtains and spilled onto Lorrina's comforter, which she had been lounging on with Quillace nestled in her lap. The rambunctious little rodent had run out of energy from exploring Lorrina's bed. He yawned, retracting his lengthy tongue and furrowing his eyebrows.

"It's probably time for you to take a nap." She tapped Quillace's underside before sweeping him up. Lorrina brought him over to his cage, petting the top of his head tenderly before extending her arms to set him on the padding. When his nose twitched in response, she grinned.

Lorrina returned to her room after washing her hands in the bathroom sink. Once she'd sat back down on the bed, Lorrina heard a light tapping on the other side of her door.

"Lorrina, I need to speak with you," her mother called.

"The door's unlocked, Mom. Come right in."

The door opened, and her mother entered the room. "I was hoping you'd come downstairs and clean the dishes. I need you to do that."

"Do you need me to do it, or are you asking me to?"

"I am asking you to, so you need to go do it now." Frowning, Mom's gaze flicked to the ceiling fan above them. "By the way, I informed your father that you no longer wish to do ballet, and we agreed not to have you resume dance in the fall."

"What?" Taken aback by her mother's revelation, Lorrina's chest hitched. "Mom, why would you do that?"

"You made it pretty clear, and I was listening, so no more ballet for you, Lorrina."

"I—I didn't say I no longer wanted to dance." Lorrina nearly choked on the tears clogging her throat.

"That's not how I remember it. Besides, having you continue with your lessons serves little purpose if you're not going to take it seriously. In fact, it's pointless." Lorrina's mother punctuated her words with a finger pointed at Lorrina.

"How is me wanting to teach dance pointless?" Lorrina held up her hands, pushing against the illusionary barrier in front of her. "Look, I'm trying to be practical, Mom. And I know full well what I want to do. Why can't you understand that I know what's best for me and be encouraging of my decisions?"

"You think you know everything, Lorrina, but I've been on this planet far longer than you have. So, you're going to waste all of your potential on settling to be a teacher, so that someone who you teach can take your place?"

"Not likely," Lorrina refuted. "As I've told you before, it's nearly impossible for the majority of dancers to join the New York City Ballet. It's an unrealistic goal for me, Mom, and I don't want to waste my time trying to pursue something I do not even want."

"You've already squandered time by taking lessons in the first place." Her mother gave a huff and cocked her head to one side. "I can't believe this. You're throwing everything away that your father and I have done for you."

With spittle gathering at the outer edges of her mouth, Lorrina raised her voice. "I'm not throwing away what I've been taught by—"

"Don't yell at me. I've had it up to here with you, Lorrina. You don't care how your poor mother feels or how heartbroken I am that you're treating me this way."

It felt as though a swarm of moths had taken up residence in Lorrina's stomach and was working their way out. She yearned to surrender and let go of the bottled-up sorrow that flared within her, but she held herself in check.

"I told you, I don't want to dance professionally. How many times do I have to repeat myself before you get it?" Lorrina wailed. "Why are you disregarding what I'm saying? Don't you care how that makes me feel, Mom?"

"Do not turn this around on me," Mom shot back, her tone now blustering. "What I'm saying to you is not hurtful, Lorrina. As a mother, I'm doing what's best for you, and as such, you should be courteous and not constantly talking back at me." Like a weapon, she thrust her finger at Lorrina once more. "You're very, very disrespectful."

"I'm just trying to say that—"

"This discussion is over." With a lift of her shoulders, Mom clutched the door's handle and pulled it open. She turned her head to look at Lorrina with slanted eyes. "If you want to think practically, you ought to consider another path. You have one more year before you graduate high school to figure it out."

A feeling of heaviness lingered after Mom left the room, and Lorrina brought her palms to her forehead, squeezing her eyes shut as she dragged her fingers past her temples and vowed not to cry.

"Did that actually happen?" she muttered.

With her stomach wrenching, she rolled onto her side, hoping the discomfort would subside. However, it was on the verge of boiling over, and despite Lorrina's best efforts to choke back her emotions, they triumphed. She let out sobs that only she could hear.

Why does it wind up this way every time? she wondered. *I've tried everything to let her know where I'm coming from, but each time, I've only aggravated the disparities between us. Am I wrong for not giving Mom's desire for me to dance professionally a chance? Despite my best efforts to consider things from her perspective, I can't seem to justify her trying to make me do something I don't want to do. I just want to move forward from this, and I want to be honest, but my mom doesn't seem to want that for me. Maybe I'm in the wrong for causing my mother's unhappiness. Maybe I'm an ungrateful daughter.*

Lorrina's sobs subsided. *My mother doesn't understand how I feel, but she's right about one thing—I shouldn't have yelled at her. How do I make things right between us now?*

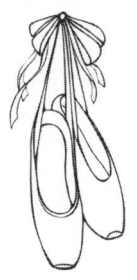

Chapter 4

Lorrina, sprawled out on the lawn and rested her novel on the soft grass beside her. Gazing toward the branches above, she saw limbs swirl in the gentle breeze and welcoming flickers of light seep through the tangled leaves. In that instant, a piece of paper-thin birch bark flittered down and landed on her cheek, right under her left eye. Lorrina flicked it off, seeking to calm down while relishing an ideal summer day. Despite her best efforts and the pleasure of being outside, however, she couldn't bring herself to relax and rest her mind.

Lorrina had not spoken to her mother since their fight the previous evening. She continued to think about the argument, but as much as the scene kept repeating itself—like pressing the snooze button on an alarm clock—Lorrina wasn't sure what to do next.

Though I doubt she's doing the same for me, I'm trying to figure out where she's coming from. Lorrina sat up, leaning against the base of the tree. *If I apologize, she'll either push for it once more and we will argue again, or I'll give in and do what she wants in order to keep things peaceful. Even though I don't want that, I also don't want to have an unbearable relationship with her.* She curled forward and rested her chin on her arms. Her focus on the lawn and home began to blend together, similar to an oversaturated watercolor painting.

I love Mom, and I'm sorry for making it worse by upsetting her. But am I wrong for not striving to become a professional dancer? Sure wish I knew why Mom doesn't seem to get that, despite my clear indication that it's not what I want. She just keeps on pressing so hard for me to do something I have no desire for, with no understanding of my desires at all. Maybe what I want doesn't matter to her. Is it possible that Mom might be trying to live her life through me? When she was a young woman, could she have wanted to be a dancer, but something held her back so that she couldn't achieve her goal? If so, maybe it was a financial matter.

Lorrina's right-hand fingers beat a rhythm against her chin as she continued to mull things over. *Maybe my mother's parents disapproved of her desire to make a career out of dancing. If she even had such an inclination.* The fact was, Lorrina's mother had never discussed much about her childhood or young adult life with Lorrina. Maybe she was ashamed of some things or found it too painful to bring up the past—especially if her mother felt cheated out of something she'd wanted so badly. *But then if that's the case, Mom should allow me to make my own choices.*

Lorrina heard footsteps from behind the tree, and she hesitated, supposing it may be her mother. If it was, she felt sure her mother wasn't seeking a reconciliation. Lorrina winced, anticipating the hammer that might be about to strike her emotions once more.

"May I join you?"

The resonant voice above her certainly wasn't her mother's. She glanced up and smiled when she saw her father's face.

Rubbing her eyelids, Lorrina sat up.

"Your mother told me that you had a big disagreement with her," Dad said, stooping to the ground, though his legs wobbled as he positioned himself.

"I did," Lorrina murmured.

"How are you feeling about that?"

"Horrible." She pinned her arms against her stomach. "What else did she say?"

"She said you were having one of your outbursts again, and that she had never yelled at either of her parents in such a disrespectful way." He folded an arm over his chest. "And I know it's not true at all. You should've heard how she spoke to your grandparents when they were opposed to her marrying me."

"You did go on to get married anyways."

"We did, but not before I insisted that she apologize to them for her outburst. We've done our best to make it work for us, and you, Lorrina. We've always strived for and wanted you to have the life neither of us grew up with."

"I do value the sacrifices you and Mom have made." Lorrina swallowed. "The big problem for me is that Mom believes I should pursue a career as a professional ballerina. When she came into my room and told me you both had agreed not to have me attend dance anymore, I felt enraged and said things to her that I now regret."

Her father's jaw dropped. "Your mom never mentioned anything about that to me."

"It doesn't surprise me. She tries to make it seem like my reactions are uncalled for and stem from nowhere. When we fight, I always feel guilty for attempting to defend myself."

"What'd you say to her exactly?"

"I asked why she couldn't be understanding and encouraging of my decisions, and I told her that joining the New York City Ballet was an unrealistic goal. I've expressed that to her before, but it doesn't seem like she wants to accept it. She told me that taking ballet lessons to become a teacher was pointless, so I became angry and allowed my emotions to take over."

"You're free to stick to your convictions, Lorrina, and you were right to defend yourself against your mother's pressure to do what you aren't comfortable with. But it sounds as though you spoke to her in a blunt and condescending manner."

"What else was I supposed to do? I really didn't want to offend Mom, but things just got out of control and we both said some things we shouldn't have." She looked at her father and blinked in succession. "I suppose she's expecting me to apologize?"

"Apologizing should only be directed at what you're at fault for. Was it appropriate to yell at your mother?"

Lorrina wiped her clammy palms along the fabric of her sweatpants. "No, it wasn't."

"How you go about standing up for yourself does matter, and inferring that your mother doesn't care for you isn't how to do it. She cares very much about you. You can disagree with her while still being respectful. You can't alter her view on how impossible it is to dance professionally, so just keep doing what you want to do without fretting over changing her mind."

"She wants me to find something else to do this coming fall instead of ballet. I love dancing, Dad. It's gotten me through some trying times, and I don't know what I'd do without it." While speaking, Lorrina's voice faltered, despite her best efforts to steady it. "That's why I'm so passionate about sharing it with others, because it can give them a proper outlet—and a sense of accomplishment and self-worth too. The career aspect can be demanding at times, as well as sometimes hazardous, and I want to stay grounded."

They sat in silence for an extended period, and while Lorrina was curious about her father's thoughts, she preferred to sit in stillness, listening to the rustling leaves above. She started to fiddle with the book's spine, feeling the ache in her throat lessen.

Dad gingerly patted her shoulder. "I'm the one who pays for your classes, and I will tell your mother that you'll keep dancing once summer is over."

"Really, Dad?" she sputtered.

"Only if you apologize to her for where you went wrong during your disagreement. Because, while your mother may be stern on the outside, she believes she's doing it for the right reasons." He pinched at the stubble on his chin. "Mom sees major potential in you, Lorrina. So much so that she's told me that she believes you would stand a chance at making it in one of the elite dance studios. That's why she's pushed for it."

Lorrina shook her head. "But that isn't what I want."

"I know, and I'm sure you'll be a fantastic teacher, so don't worry—I'm here for you."

"Thank you, Dad."

"You're welcome."

He rose from the yard and offered a hug, welcoming her with outstretched arms. Lorrina leaped to her feet, embraced him, and rested her head on his shoulder.

I'm grateful that Dad is in my corner. Tears welled up in Lorrina's eyes. *If he had agreed with Mom, I don't know what more I could have done or said.*

The lead rider's shrill whistle pierced the atmosphere, and Edwin and Daisy followed the other riders and their horses along the rail. As they went, his horse trotted behind the rider ahead of him. Edwin relaxed as the air rushed at him, helping him unwind from the day's pressures. The horses moved briskly, and he felt the force of the air catching in his ears.

When the whistle blew again, Edwin closed his right rein and leg, causing Daisy's shoulders to make a flank turn toward the middle of the gated area. All the horses shifted their formation from nose-to-tail to abreast, maintaining a lope pace while doing so.

Edwin looked around at his team members as he rode alongside them. For a few years, he had been a member of an independent group consisting of eight young Amish men and women. Reuben Yoder, Edwin's best friend, had founded the team. It had taken them many months to flawlessly execute their coordinated maneuvers, which he'd written out for the team members every year.

It all began when Reuben had witnessed some of the drill team events in Ohio. He'd had an unforgettable visit, observing the riders and their horses coordinate such a thorough routine. Intrigued, Reuben reached out to the leader of that team for various patterns. Upon his return home, he'd gotten the plans for it underway by seeing if anyone else would be interested, beginning with Edwin. Reuben had a glint in his eye that showed he was determined to share the drill team with the community, and Edwin supported him in recruiting members so they could form a group. While some riders were unsure, others had shown interest and curiosity during the young people's gatherings. After those who had been willing to be part of the group became accustomed to rehearsing, a few other young Amish people indicated a willingness to join in. Although there had been a few adjustments in the composition of the team since its founding, the majority of the members remained.

THE AMISH BALLERINA

Reuben blew the whistle twice, signaling the rehearsal's conclusion. All of the riders stopped their horses, and Edwin eased Daisy to a full halt, rewarding her with a pat. It seemed so unreal to him that they had trained outside for two hours and it was already seven o'clock in the evening. However, sunlight cascaded on his friend's homemade arena in the late afternoon, which would not be the case once autumn arrived.

"Excellent work, everyone," Reuben announced as he dismounted from his horse, Scout. "I feel that we are ready to contribute our routine at the Millers' charity event for their son's recent lengthy hospital stay."

A pair of riders had gone on home, so practice was officially over, but the others lingered for a while along the fence, watching their horses roam around the arena, free to frolic as they chose. Edwin knew they had put a lot of effort into their practice today, and based on prior experience, he was fully aware that he'd be feeling it tomorrow.

And tomorrow, I still have work to look forward to. Edwin rolled his eyes. *I think Dad mentioned we needed to order more pens for the business to hand out to customers, so it's a good thing I already took care of that. But I still need to fill out the time cards for the work Markel and I put in this week, even if I don't consider what he did as real "work." Bare minimum maybe, if that.*

"Hey, Edwin," Reuben greeted, drawing Edwin out of his contemplations. "Got a minute to talk?"

"Jah, sure. What's the trouble?"

"No trouble, really. Even though I've been loving what our group has accomplished, I think there's more we could do to improve the visual appeal of our patterns."

Edwin edged a little closer. "What'd you have in mind?"

"I have a vague idea, but not a roadmap, unfortunately."

He drawled his words, flailing his hands in tandem. "Hear me out, okay?"

Edwin nodded.

"My *aldi* told me about her cousin, who's involved in a group in Ohio. However, they do more than what a conventional drill team does, and what she described to me piqued my interest."

"Oh? What'd your girlfriend say?"

"Said her cousin is supposed to visit Indiana later this year, and I think it would be beneficial to have her here to teach us a couple of things. It could really spruce up our performance, drawing more attention from people, particularly for the charity events."

"So, what is the—" Someone hollered for Edwin from the other side of the arena.

Edwin looked and was surprised to see his horse galloping all about, kicking up the sand in the arena, while the other horses either minded their own business or parted ways when Daisy came too close.

"Is Daisy okay?" Reuben questioned.

"She's getting antsy and probably wants to go home."

Daisy sprang over the fence, touched down, and bounded toward Edwin. The mare approached him with a firm shake of her head. Daisy slowed down in response to Edwin's call to stop, but she still pursued him, looming over Edwin when she was right beside him. Blowing a gust of moisture-laden breath on his scalp, the dark-haired mare nudged the crown of Edwin's head.

Reuben chuckled. "That gaul of yours is a beast, Edwin."

"Jah, I know," Edwin murmured, patting Daisy's neck. *Sometimes I wonder if I exercise authority over Daisy or if she has power over me.*

Brenda's nose scrunched as she sliced through the skin of the plump tomato that rested on the cutting board. It felt like winter slush between her fingers, albeit not frigid to the touch, as she steadied the tomato as far away from the knife's blade as she could. The juice and seeds leaked over every inch of the cutting board's surface.

It always amazes me how tender tomatoes can be, Brenda thought. *It's a fruit by definition, so why can't it be as firm as a lemon?*

Arie bolted through the back door and into the kitchen with rasping breaths and bulging eyes. She slammed it shut, leaning against it as if she expected a herd of cattle to break in.

"What's the matter, *Dochder*?"

"The wasps." Gasping, Arie gestured toward the door. "They're swarming the hummingbird feeder."

Brenda continued to dice the tomatoes, transferring the watery slices to the neighboring bowl as the cutting surface grew too crowded.

"Can't we move the feeder somewhere other than the back porch, which is so close to the door?"

"When I am sitting outside having tea in the morning, I get to watch the hummingbirds up close. I can also get to see them flutter by the kitchen window. Isn't that wonderful, Arie?"

"Yes, it is, but that isn't the point. The wasps appreciate the nectar in the feeders as much as hummingbirds do. Aren't you concerned about the birds getting stung, or me, yourself, or my younger siblings?"

"Arie, breathe. Don't be so dramatic. I've sat out on the porch many times and never had a problem. They enjoy the sugar water, and if there are a few hanging about, it won't cause any harm."

"Mom, there's more than a few out there right now. Come see for yourself."

"I'm in the middle of cooking." Brenda scrunched her brows,

trying to figure out what to do next. "I understand you have an irrational fear of bees, but the rest of us don't."

"It's not all bees. Honeybees are fine, and so are bumblebees." Arie frowned. "Wasps and hornets are not."

"What's up with that, anyway?" Brenda questioned, dumping the chopped onions into the heated olive oil in a pan on the stove.

"Mamm, did you forget? When I was younger, I climbed into the rafters of the unfinished chicken coop and got chased by a whole swarm of wasps."

"I do remember, but you weren't seriously hurt, and I figured you would've moved on from that by now." Brenda raised the wooden spoon she'd placed on the counter earlier and gave it a quick, sideways flick. "You're bigger than wasps, Arie. They're tiny pests that you can swat at if they invade your personal space."

"I suppose." Arie dangled her hands at her sides. Her jaw slacked, then she tilted her head. "What are you making, Mamm?"

Brenda held up the bowl of sliced tomatoes for her daughter to see. "Tomato soup."

"From scratch? Buying a can would be simpler, wouldn't it?"

Brenda clasped the spoon as she went to the stove and sautéed the onions. "Am I not allowed to make things from scratch, Arie?"

With palms raised as she faced Brenda, her daughter said, "I didn't mean it that way. I'm sorry. It's just that you have many irons in the fire, so wouldn't preparing soup from scratch add to your already heavy workload?"

"It does, but it also takes my mind off of all the work in the store or the chores around the home. Finding something you are passionate about will help you avoid becoming overwhelmed by all the other things you need to do." She added some minced garlic and blended it with the onions. The tantalizing fragrance rose from the pan, and Brenda swept a hand, directing the scent toward her face, and took a whiff.

"I understand where you're coming from, Mamm."

"What do you mean?" Brenda peered up from the garlic and onion crackling in the pan's oil. "What are you passionate about?"

Arie's eyes expanded, darting around the kitchen for a moment. Her brows wrinkled as she hooked a finger along the neck opening of her dark blue dress. "I do like horseback riding," she replied.

"Hopefully not in the same way as your boyfriend. What Edwin does with the drill team is much too reckless." Finally, she hauled the bowl of tomatoes to the stove and combined it with the other contents in the skillet. "By the way, some tomatoes that have gone bad are on the end of the counter. You can feed them to the chickens if you like. I've already removed the stems."

Arie's lips quivered as she gave a meek smile. "Okay, Mamm."

Gathering up the tomatoes on the counter, Arie veered to the door, parting it a crack, and peered out the gap. After a few seconds passed, she flung it open and, in one rapid motion, stepped out and shut the door behind her with such force that it caused the wall hanging adjacent to it to slide down on its hook.

That girl has a tendency to get quite worked up over the littlest things. Brenda groaned, turning the knob on the stove to lower the heat and covering the pan with a lid for the ingredients to simmer. *Just like when I was her age. Yet she wonders why I said it'd be better to keep working at home. Arie seems to be doing well at the gift shop, though. She hasn't brought it up much, which is a good sign. It's great she's off doing her own thing. I'm not sure what I'll do when she gets married and moves out, however. While Arie is diligent and obedient, Rudy has to be given some prodding before he'll actually do anything around here.*

Flustered, Brenda brushed aside those troubling thoughts, choosing to occupy herself by rinsing the dishes she'd used for preparing the soup. *I couldn't be more thankful that my daughter will no doubt end up marrying a dedicated young man and joining the Amish church, as she is leading by example for her siblings.*

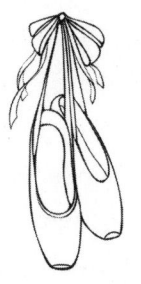

Chapter 5

Grabill, Indiana

EDWIN WAS ON THE JOB site, along with his brother Markel and a few additional laborers who were partners in his father's roofing company. They were non-Amish employees who drove the work truck and contributed to additional construction work. The combination of exhausting labor and humidity caused Edwin's skin to trickle with sweat.

Their roofing crew, albeit small in comparison to some other companies in the area, was efficient, taking only a couple of days to replace a roof on a standard-sized home. They hadn't yet finished tearing off the entire roof on the house they'd spent the majority of the day working on, but they intended to return the following afternoon after installing gutters at another neighboring residence. Since there was a significant likelihood of a downpour that evening, they set down tarps to protect their project overnight.

Having extra hands made the task less daunting, especially when their father was not present for the entire time. He had been spending most days at home with their mother, who had yet to recuperate from her ailment. Whatever bug she had seemed to be hanging on, yet the rest of them hadn't caught it. Edwin had hoped she'd be able to recover from it soon and that her illness wasn't anything serious.

They loaded up the tools needed for the job they had to go to first thing in the morning, then scooped up the leftover scraps and tossed them into the trailer. The ladder was one of those items that hadn't been transported to the rig. When Edwin rounded the corner at the entrance of the house to see what was causing the holdup, he spotted Keaton tapping his foot below the ladder.

"Where's my brother?" Edwin questioned.

"I've been waiting for him to make his way down, but he's still up there." Keaton fiddled with his shirt pocket. "He said he forgot to put his hammer back on his belt."

That's strange, given that he should have it on by now, Edwin thought. Cupping his hands around his mouth, he shouted, "Markel! Hey, we're leaving!"

Edwin called his brother's name again and again, but he got no answer.

"Could you steady the ladder for me?" he asked Keaton. "I'll see what's taking him so long."

Edwin scaled the rungs of the extension ladder, ascending the right side of the house. When he stepped off one of the upper rungs and onto the roof, there lay his brother beside the dormer with his smartphone mere inches from his face.

"Markel!" Edwin yelled.

Markel jolted, and his phone slipped from his grasp. It nearly struck the rooftop, but he snagged the device before it made contact.

"Don't scare me like that, Edwin. Dad paid a lot of money for these phones to use at work, and you can imagine how upset he'd be if it plunged off the roof and broke."

"I believe he'd be more irate knowing that you've been on your phone while he's not here."

"I'm only on it for work-related stuff, same as you." Markel grunted.

"My phone is in Keaton's truck in the glove compartment, not in my pocket. Look, it's the end of the day, so I'll let this go. I'm trying to keep things civil, Markel. Don't give me a reason not to, okay?"

With a sigh, Markel straightened his legs, supporting himself by pressing a palm against the roof's slope. Standing upright, he shoved the phone in his pocket.

When Edwin and his brother climbed back down, the ladder was loaded into the rig, and he spread his arms heavenward. A few droplets of rain hit Edwin's scalp, and he looked up to see the sun peeking through the clouds and more steady drops landing on his scalding skin.

"We got a sun shower, Edwin." Keaton wriggled his caterpillar eyebrows. "Right before the end of the day too."

Edwin cracked a grin. "It's a good thing we laid those tarps down."

As much as Edwin looked forward to returning home and getting a good night's sleep, his day wasn't over yet. He hadn't seen his girlfriend in a while, and it had been a rigorous and lengthy week. Edwin intended to surprise Arie by showing up unannounced to invite her to have supper at his house Sunday evening. Even if they were only going to spend a few minutes together, he was optimistic that Arie would be thrilled to see him after so long.

Shipshewana

Arie watched her two siblings hop up and down on the trampoline in the side yard. Rudy and Maggie were in stitches, bouncing around as she carried on sweeping the storefront porch. On the nights when the wind had picked up, leaves and other debris were strewn throughout the walkway leading up to the store.

For a while today, Arie had been worried regarding the weather, especially since Maggie had helped her hang their laundry on the clothesline beforehand, by reaching into the basket and then handing the items to Arie that needed to be hung. In the middle of it all, it had begun to drizzle. The shower had only lasted a few minutes, however, so they'd continued to remove the rest of the garments from the woven basket and secured them on the line, with the hope that the sun would come out soon and everything would dry before the end of the day.

Arie's nose crinkled when she stared up at the porch's support beam and saw webbing entwined with finch feathers and the husks of beetles. Raising the broom above her shoulder, she swept the edges until they were free of any filth or threadbare webs. Even though Arie was almost done with this task, she had further work ahead of her, and it seemed like there were not enough hours in the day.

"Don't, Rudy!"

Arie snapped her head toward the trampoline. She caught sight of Rudy shoving Maggie, causing her to topple backward and onto the trampoline's mat.

"Rudy," Arie exclaimed. "*Halt, das geht zu weit*! Did you hear me, Rudy? I said, 'Stop, that's going too far.'" She abandoned the broom in the yard, while rushing over to the trampoline. Arie figured it'd be safer than leaving it beside the storefront, where someone could trip over it. Fortunately, Arie's younger brother's focus diverted to her by the time she reached the trampoline frame.

Rudy crossed his arms and looked at Arie with a frown. "Why am I in trouble? She bumped into me first."

"It looked to me like you pushed Maggie, and that was not a nice thing to do," Arie scolded.

He shook his head. "Huh-uh. She kept bumping me when I was tryin' to jump."

"I didn't mean to, Rudy," Maggie whined.

"I think she did it on purpose." Rudy looked at Arie, as if directing his next comment to her. "Not only that, but our little sister's rambling is grating on my ears. It ruins my fun having to put up with her being so annoying."

"I am not annoying." Maggie hunched over. "Stop bein' so mean to me."

Rudy leapt and landed next to Maggie, then bent over her, while the trampoline rattled beneath them. "You can't make me. I'm bigger than you are."

"That's enough, Rudy. Personal space," Arie stated firmly.

He exhaled a rasping breath, followed by a caustic remark. "You know why our parents named you Maggie? Because you squawk like a magpie."

Arie's tolerance was thinning as she scowled at Rudy.

"What? It's only a joke. It's not my fault you don't see it as one."

"Do you know why our parents called you Rudy? Because you are quite rude."

Her brother flinched, and his jaw dropped open like a drawbridge.

Maggie brought a hand to her mouth, as if trying to muffle her giggles. The child's petite hand failed to conceal her split grin, though.

"That's not funny," Rudy protested.

Hands raised to her hips, Arie said, "Maggie is laughing, so she must think it was a little funny."

"It's not to me."

"Interesting that you don't find your 'joke'"—Maggie inserted air quotes—"humorous when it's at your expense. Maggie didn't find what you said to her funny, so knowing what it's like to be on the receiving end, do you believe teasing your sister is hilarious?"

With a wave of his hand, he gave the most off-kilter smirk. "It's the gift of giving, not receiving."

Arie inhaled forcefully through her teeth. "I think it's best to refrain from playing on the trampoline for now. Maggie, please go check to see if the clothes we hung earlier are still damp. I know you can't reach the line, but you can feel the bottom part of the clothes and towels hanging there. If they're dry, let me know so we can take the laundry down, then fold everything and put them away."

Nodding, Maggie clambered to her feet and slid off the trampoline.

Arie gazed up at her brother after her sister had left for the house and was no longer within earshot.

"Rudy, I'm sorry for making a joke from your name. That was irresponsible of me, and two wrongs don't make a right. It would be appropriate for you to do the same for Maggie and apologize to her."

"Jah, except for one thing. I'm not sorry, 'cause she ruined my time on the trampoline, and then she bumped into me." Rudy's lips curved downward. "Maggie's not getting an apology for something she had coming."

Rudy sprung from the trampoline, and after touching down

on the grass, he started across the yard, away from Arie. Seeing him run off without any regard for his actions caused Arie's blood to boil. If she'd behaved with such defiance and carelessness, her parents would have delivered a sharp reprimand.

What's been going on with Rudy lately? Arie wondered. *He and Maggie used to be close, and while they had their moments of getting under one another's skin, it wasn't until recent months that he began to be more confrontational with her.*

Arie wandered back over to where she had dropped the broom. *I tried to bring it up to Mom the other day, but all I was met with from her was "It's just sibling rivalry." That doesn't excuse him from belittling his own sister. Maybe I'm overly concerned about this. Besides, I'm not their parent—I'm their sister, so if anyone should handle this situation, it's Mom or Dad.*

Her eyes flitted to the phone shack, which was situated at the brink of their driveway, right beside the mailbox. She considered Lorrina, and while being an only child may have been pleasant in some ways, it also must have been lonesome at times.

I really don't know what'd be preferable, Arie wondered, carrying the broom with her to the phone shack. *Perhaps a bit of loneliness would do me some good. Lorrina thrives on interaction, whereas I can do without it.* She shrugged her shoulders. *Well, sort of, anyway. As long as it's not too demanding, I like spending time with people.*

Within the confines of the modest wooden building that housed her family's telephone, she yanked the folding chair away from the wall, planting herself on it and scooting to the phone on the built-in desk. Before Arie had gone out to sweep the store's front porch, Mom had asked her to check for messages on the answering machine, which she devoted herself to doing next. But Arie felt obliged to contact her friend first. That way, if her mother questioned where she was, Arie could merely reply that she had been checking messages. She dialed Lorrina's number and pressed her ear to the phone's receiver, listening for her friend to pick up.

"Hello, Arie?" Lorrina answered. "Is it really you?"

"Jah, it's me. Are you busy right now?"

"I'm actually in the middle of getting ready to go out, but we can keep talking for a while. I'm pretty confident in my ability to multitask. It's nice to hear from you again, Arie. What's up with you? Do you need to talk about something in particular?"

"No, not specifically. We hadn't spoken in a few days, and I just wanted to give you a call. So, you mentioned going out? Out with friends? Another date?"

"Yes, I have a date, and I'm in a frenzy."

"How come?"

"I had an encounter at the grocery store."

"Oh, and how'd that play out?" Arie asked.

"You know how I'm obsessed with those California rolls in the freezer section?"

"Uh-huh."

"As it turned out, so was this guy named Casey, who was already in the aisle when I arrived. Downside? There was one package left on the shelf, but he generously offered it to me. So, as a thank you for allowing me to have the frozen sushi I sought, I offered to go with him to Miso Japan in Goshen for some fresh sushi."

Arie shook her head. "I don't know how you could ask a stranger out on a whim like that. I knew Edwin from my church district, and he was the one who asked me out. Without him, I'd probably have no boyfriend right now."

"Yeah, I highly doubt that. You're a catch, Arie, and it doesn't mean anything that I go on dates. I'd rather go on multiple dates with one person than with many. I'd rather be in a relationship like you and Edwin."

"We haven't gone out as often as we used to." Arie gulped down the lump that was forming in her throat. "Anyway, how'd it go with your mom? You brought up your disagreement when we last spoke. Did anything ever get resolved?"

"I said I was sorry for yelling at her. It's all I can ask for now that we've gone back into a somewhat normal pattern around here."

"You showed maturity by responding in that way. Did she apologize for pressuring you?"

"Not exactly. She said 'sorry if I hurt your feelings.' In any case, I said I forgave her, and that was pretty much it. I can't ask for a sincere apology if she doesn't feel it. Otherwise, it's not from her heart." Arie heard Lorrina smack her lips before continuing to speak. "I can't expect her to apologize if she sees nothing wrong with attempting to coerce me into professional dance. All I can do is take ownership of where I went wrong, and if she feels that she needs to apologize, she will."

If Lorrina's mother is anything like Rudy, she won't ever apologize to her. Propping her chin up with an arm, Arie said, "Honestly, if I'd grown up in your house, I might have considered pursuing a professional ballet career."

The other end of the telephone fell silent, and Arie regretted the words that had slipped from her lips.

Arie's nose tingled with heat. "I—I'm not saying that you should pursue a career in ballet. I'm sorry. I might have, though, since I'm already doing what my parents expect of me right now. That's the difference between you and me. You push back, and that's admirable."

"Hey, Arie? Are you certain that you don't want to come to my classes and at least observe?"

Pausing, Arie took a deep breath of the hot, humid air that had built up in the phone shack. She felt the perspiration seeping through the fabric of her dress. "It wouldn't be good. My mom almost found me dancing in the barn recently, so I've been avoiding it altogether."

"That isn't fair. She should at least allow you the right to try it, and you shouldn't feel like you can't." Lorrina's usual crisp tone grew more dulcet. "I'm really sorry you're having to go through this, Arie. Just keep in mind that I'm always a phone call away, and I'll be there for you through whatever trial you're faced with. That's a promise from one friend to another."

"I appreciate that, Lorrina. Danki."

"For the hanky," Lorrina chirped.

They chatted for a bit, although most of the topic turned to Lorrina's date and her expectations. Eventually, Lorrina said she had to go, so she bid Arie farewell.

Arie clicked the button to disconnect the call. She slumped flat on the desk, folding her arms and tucking in her head. She longed to get some shuteye and felt tempted to nap in the thermal mass of the phone shack for a brief period, at the very least until she'd come to grips with the expectations that awaited her. It felt good to remain here a few more minutes. She tilted her head and glimpsed out the windowpane. In the distance stood the barn, beckoning Arie to come once more.

Edwin approached Arie's home and stepped onto the porch. The sound of a *hum* whizzed past his ear. He geared to the noise and saw a wasp circling the hummingbird feeder as it descended from the canopy's hook. Edwin eyed the striped insect as it hovered above one of the spouts, but it didn't take long to lose interest in the depleted feeder and take off.

Having the feeder so close to the house is practically inviting wasps to take up residence on the porch, he determined, recalling that the last time he'd been on the back side of this house, he'd seen a hummingbird feeder near the porch there too. *Free food and rain protection provided.* Edwin swiped a knuckle across the front door's panel and then rapped wholeheartedly.

Arie's father opened the door and poked his head through the gap before emerging from the threshold. He quirked his eyebrow and greeted, "Ah, Edwin. So nice to see you."

Edwin tipped his straw hat. "Evening, Mr. Kauffman."

"I'm surprised you're here. Arie didn't mention that you'd be stopping by for supper."

"Not tonight. Just wanted to talk with her briefly before heading home."

"Arie's not in the house, so she's probably out in the barn." Arie's father shifted his stance. "She's been horseback riding as of late, whenever she's not working at the gift shop or helping around here. Did you have something to do with that?"

"I might've played a part in it," Edwin admitted. "I did say that it would be a really good idea to go horseback riding more often. Despite what she thinks, Arie has a handle on it."

"That's good. You're an encouraging person, and she needs that, because Arie can be hard on herself. Though I'm not sure why."

Shrugging, Edwin pointed with his thumbs in the direction of the barn. "Well, I'm going to see her now, and then I'll be heading on home."

"All right, Edwin. Hope your mom gets better and we see her at church this Sunday. I know my *fraa* misses their after-service talks."

After waving goodbye, Edwin scampered down the porch steps and headed for the barn across the way.

Passing the building's lower siding, Edwin parted the breezeway entrance and sauntered in. The tart scent of the freshly cut hay pervaded his senses. Edwin passed the hayloft ladder at the gable end of the barn, but Arie was nowhere to be found. He wondered where she'd gone, as he hadn't found Arie around any of the horses' stalls either.

Thump! Thump! Thump!

With a lift of his chin, Edwin realized there was something causing the noise overhead. *She must be rearranging things in the hayloft.*

Edwin reached the ladder and mounted the rungs gradually. When he crested the last one to the loft, Edwin stopped dead in his tracks. With her back to him, he watched in awe, as Arie pushed off the floor and practically flew through the air in succession. And they weren't ordinary leaps. They were magnificent, and her limbs were extended and straightened like a swan's wingspan. Her movements were dainty in flight, but when she landed on her feet with bent knees, they struck against the hard wooden floorboards beneath her. She stretched up on her tiptoes and crossed her ankles every time she took a stride. He couldn't have imagined that his girlfriend had been capable of such motions. Edwin's breath stalled as he tried to comprehend what he laid eyes upon, but it was too jarring to even put into words.

"Arie? What is? What?" He coughed, unsure whether his voice had been loud enough for Arie to hear.

She swiveled around, her formerly elegant composure evaporated, leaving her face contorted and her shoulders slumped. Stammering, she asked, "H–how much did you see, Edwin?"

"Enough for my face to be looking like this." He gestured from the neck up with flailed-out fingers like a handheld fan. "Wa–was that some kind of a dance you were doing?"

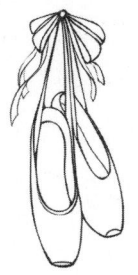

Chapter 6

THE TEMPO OF ARIE'S THROBBING pulse rose to a crescendo. *This is it*, she thought. *I'm done for. My cover is blown, and I can't recover.*

She collapsed atop a bale of hay and stroked its pliable fibers with her numb fingertips. With every inch of her skin engulfed in an opposing sensation, it was the one form of solace Arie had at that moment. The entirety of her stature flared in warmth, no longer able to bear the expression she had seen on her boyfriend's face.

I can only imagine what Edwin's thoughts are. Shutting her eyes, Arie envisioned the hayloft's walls altering and folding in on her. *Everything got ruined by me. I should've had more self-control and not given in to the urge to dance.*

"Woah, Arie." Arie heard Edwin's voice draw near, and she felt his hand brush against her shoulder. "Breathe in and out slowly. You can get through this."

She sucked in a great deal of oxygen and then blew it out. Arie continued to regulate her lungs, and after a while, she grew a bit more comfortable. She blinked and directed her gaze on the dress's crease along her lap, while seeing Edwin in the corner of her eye, but not daring to look at him.

"Do you need anything? Water, or maybe some food?"

With a faint crackle, Arie straightened her back, rolling her shoulders forward as the sweat down the sides of her neck cooled. "No, Edwin, I'm feeling better now. I just needed a little breather."

"You had jumped around a lot, and it probably took a lot out of you." He withdrew his hand and settled beside her. "If you don't mind me asking, what kind of dancing was that?"

She fumbled with her fingers, dragging them to her knees. "It's ballet."

"How long has this been going on?"

"My English friend, Lorrina, has been teaching me to dance since I was ten," Arie admitted.

"Eight years, then?"

"Jah, but it's been less frequent in recent years. I wanted to do more at first, but when I asked my parents if I could register for lessons, they both balked at the idea. Mom and Dad took issue with me and Lorrina hanging out for that reason. I didn't want to upset them anymore, so. . ."

"So you kept it a secret?"

Nodding solemnly, Arie finally gathered the courage to turn so she faced him directly. "I'm really sorry, Edwin. I considered telling you, but I decided against it because I'll soon be joining the church, and then dancing won't be a part of my life anymore. But I should've told you anyway. You must be mad at me for this."

"I'm not mad at you. Dumbfounded, but not angry. I understand why you kept it hidden. You wouldn't be allowed to dance after joining the church, and you didn't want anyone to think you were abandoning your faith." His forehead wrinkled. "You don't want to leave the Amish community, right?"

"I just said I'm planning to join the church, so no."

"What about the drill team, Arie?" Edwin's blue eyes broadened. "We learn various routines and perform them at local events. Since there is sometimes music, it's sort of like dancing. And it wouldn't be considered dancing, so you wouldn't have to do this in secret. Our team could always use another horseback rider."

Arie flinched. "My parents would never allow me to do that either."

"Yet, you're performing ballet in the barn."

"It's not nearly as risky as riding a horse. I have full control over myself while I'm practicing ballet, but with my horse, Aster, there's a disconnection. Besides, Edwin, there really isn't any dancing involved with horses, and that's what I enjoy doing."

"Indeed, it isn't the same thing. I was trying to present an alternative." He grunted, lifting his straw hat and sweeping his fingers through his tousled caramel-colored hair. "I'm sorry. The truth is, I'm afraid if you put your desire to dance ahead of our plans to join the church, I might end up losing you to the ways of the modern world, Arie."

"You won't. I've made up my mind, and I'm willing to give up ballet to be with you. I just need to get it out of my system is all. Please don't say anything, Edwin," she implored. "If my parents knew I'd been going against their wishes, they'd—" The last of her words faded in the depths of her throat. Arie's stomach twinged at the prospect of the consequences. "I don't want to let them down. I've already let you down with my *dumm* decisions, and I'm sorry. I have no idea what to do about any of this."

Silence hung between them, causing Arie to be overwhelmed with queasiness. She wanted to cry, but she was reluctant to force her emotions on Edwin. Even though she was unaware of what was going on within his unspoken thoughts, it had to be far worse for Edwin than it was for her. Arie knew she was asking for too much. He was most likely considering leaving and calling it quits.

"Okay, Arie. I won't say anything about what I witnessed here today."

"R–really?" she sputtered.

"Jah, really. I promise, as long as you agree to tell me the truth from now on. I don't want you feeling like you can't tell me anything." He twiddled with the brim of his hat. "I'm worried about you. I want to do everything in my power to support you in any way that I can. Even if all I can do is lend a listening ear when you want to talk."

"I'm sorry for worrying you, Edwin. I'll try to be more honest from now on—about my feelings as well as my decisions."

"Okay, good to hear."

Arie kicked her right heel against the bale of hay. "I forgot to ask, what'd you come over here for? You know, before all of this occurred?"

"I wanted to see you, of course." Taking a deep breath, Edwin slouched over. "But I can't stay long since I need to head back home soon."

"Then I won't keep you."

"Arie, would you like to join me for supper at my parents' house this Sunday evening?"

"Is your mother well enough for company? I didn't see her at church last Sunday, so I figured she must still be under the weather."

"She's moving around more now, but not quite out of the woods. We can find something else to do after church. All I really want is to be with you, Arie."

"Even after discovering my biggest secret?"

Edwin snorted. "You give the impression that you've committed a crime when you haven't. Though I'm not sure how to make sense of it all, I am willing to try."

"Thank you again, Edwin." Arie smiled, then nestled against her boyfriend's shoulder. "I'd like to spend more time with you too."

Edwin leaned over and pressed his lips lovingly on her forehead. Arie was convinced that Edwin would have ended their relationship over this, but she hadn't anticipated such a wonderful outcome. He must have a great deal of faith in her to believe she would give up dancing so they could be together. Part of her felt relieved, but an inkling of discomfort lurked in the depths of Arie's soul that she had trouble discerning.

The sun cusped on the hills of the farmlands that bordered the route to the home of Edwin's parents. His home wasn't far from where Arie lived with her family, so it wasn't a long walk over to her place. Pausing for a moment, he spun around toward the Kauffmans' property and caught a glimpse of the cupola atop the barn in the distance. The day had begun as predicted, so to walk in on Arie and witness something she'd kept from him had established a few concerns in his mind.

I sensed something was up before today, but I never expected her to be dancing, Edwin thought, scuffing the bottom of his boot along the ground. *Not in a million years. I'm no expert, but the way Arie sprang up in the air suggested that she'd been practicing diligently. She appeared very lovely while dancing and assured of herself even. Arie must really enjoy it.*

His face flushed at the memory of seeing her move around in that manner. Her elusive presence and fluid motions in the hayloft had captivated Edwin. In that instant, his reverie prompted one sole notion: "There's no way Arie would give up something she's so devoted to," he murmured. That thought alone caused Edwin to worry.

What if she doesn't truly love me and is only with me because it appeases her parents? Arie appeared sincere when she said that she hadn't been dancing much either. She's been exceptional at hiding it this entire time, or maybe she abandoned it when we first started dating. But we haven't been seeing each other as often lately. Am I to blame for this because I neglected to spend more time with her?

In an attempt to avoid keeping his family waiting for him to eat supper, Edwin cranked up his pace. He figured jogging part of the way would make up for the delay because he had spent some time up in the hayloft with Arie.

I might be getting bent out of shape for no reason at all, he told himself. *If she's really serious about joining the church and no longer dancing, then I ought to trust her. All I can hope is that everything will sort itself out and there will be no further surprises.*

As Edwin sprinted up the driveway, he managed to spook the red-winged blackbirds that had congregated at the feeders like church members, gathered around to chat after the noon meal. Edwin halted in his tracks, huffing in and out as he watched the birds flutter in the atmosphere. Their dark feathered bodies contrasted with the reddish-yellow hues of the day's end, but the males' shoulder patches matched the sky seamlessly.

Edwin's sight veered back to the feeder, swaying in accordance with the birds' flight. It was barren in the plexiglass enclosure, the sunflower seeds from the feeder strewn on the pavers below.

Edwin sauntered up to the yard and onto the concrete path that led to the front door, noting that the feeders needed to be replenished. When he turned the doorknob and stepped foot into the house, the rich aromatics of herbs, potatoes, and broth mingled through the entryway.

"I'm home!" Edwin shouted, hanging his straw hat on one of

the wall pegs. He untied his boots and set them in the customary location with the rest of the footwear lined up.

"Edwin, come in here!" Dad responded, his tone thunderous.

His father didn't sound too thrilled. Edwin figured Dad must be perturbed with him for arriving home so late. Edwin made his way down the hall and stood, peering into the dining room. On the table were a bowl of cooked vegetables and a loaf of onion cake, as well as dishware and a covered cast-iron saucepan. However, nobody occupied the chairs at the oval table, which seemed a bit odd.

"In here, Edwin!" his mother's voice called out.

Rolling his neck, he meandered into the living room. Edwin's family had formed a semicircle in the space, taking refuge on the couch and rocking chairs situated beside one another.

Edwin swallowed hard. "What's going on?"

"Have a seat, Son." His father pointed to the vacant wooden rocker next to Markel, who sat on the couch with Mom. Edwin was a little miffed that he had to sit there when everyone else had comfy chairs, but not enough for him to protest. Either the floor or the rocking chair felt about the same, with the exception that one had back support.

This has to be about Mom. He winced, revolving around the coffee table and easing himself onto the chair. *This can't be good news if it involves a family meeting.*

"Now, our supper is ready, and we don't want to be eating cold stew, so I'll get right to the point instead of dragging this out." Mom mashed her lips together before continuing her proclamation. "To put it simply, I'm in a family way."

Edwin's back stiffened. He sat there in absolute shock at what his mother had just revealed. Had he heard her correctly? There was no way his mom had actually said that. How his older brother reacted, however, reinforced Mom's words.

"You're what?" Markel's voice raised an octave. "But Mom, you're so old."

"Markel," Edwin hissed. "Our mamm is not old."

"Your brother's right, though blunt in his choice of words." Mom steepled her hands in front of her mouth. "I suspected pregnancy a month ago, but since my body is changing, and I'm not getting any younger, I didn't think much about it. After the first week of feeling unwell and sensing how it was all too familiar, I was almost sure that I was pregnant. I informed your father, and the results of the few tests I took were all positive."

"How do you feel about this?" Edwin questioned. "You've both expressed how content you will be once Markel and I are out of the house and on our own. You and Dad were no doubt looking forward to spending the rest of your lives together, without having to raise any more children."

It seemed as though Mom had been waiting for Dad to interject or take over the conversation when she glanced over at him. But Dad remained silent.

"I know what we've said, but we are coming to terms with this. Nothing is more precious than bringing life into this world, and I have no regrets about having cared for my two amazing boys. I mean men." His mother sighed, rubbing a knuckle across the creases on the outer edge of one eye. "Your sibling will be roughly the same age as their niece or nephew when you both become parents. Life's sure funny like that."

"Jah, that's true. Life can be funny at times." Edwin rose from the rocker and went over to wrap his arms around his mother's shoulders. "Congratulations, Mamm."

Markel followed suit, layering the embrace on top of Edwin like he'd donned a winter's jacket.

"I'm thankful for all of your kindness." Mom choked up as she spoke. "Your sibling will be fortunate to have two thoughtful brothers."

"All right then, enough harping on this for now." Dad clicked his fingernails against the surface of the small table next to his chair. "Supper's waiting to be eaten, and I don't know about you boys, but I'm starving."

When Dad got up from his chair and vacated the room, so did everyone else. As though it were any other typical evening, they all gathered in the dining room, prayed, and began serving their meals onto their empty plates. But it was far from normal. A pit formed at the bottom of Edwin's stomach, and his hunger vanished. Shouldn't an addition to the family be a joyous occasion? It would be, if not for the solemn demeanor of his parents.

Mom says she's fine, but she's not very adept at hiding how she really feels. She always tries to see the bright side of things, but I can tell that she was hoping not to have any more children. Edwin lifted up a small piece of potato and flipped the spoon about in his stew. His eyes darted to his father. *Dad doesn't seem excited either, barely uttering a word about it. It's all a bit too much to take in. First finding out that Arie has been dancing in her barn, and now this. Living in ignorance and assuming everything was going well made me considerably happier than I'm feeling right now.*

At last, the daylight was gone, and Arie had finished changing into her nightgown after waiting for her damp hair to dry. Although all was calm in her surroundings, it sounded like an assortment of instruments were blaring in her head, along with all the thoughts racing through her mind. She couldn't concentrate on one thing, and all Arie wanted was for her mind to be as quiet as her bedroom.

In the kitchen, before coming upstairs, Arie had prepared a cacao drink mix that she'd stumbled upon in the clearance section of the grocery store on her way home from the gift shop a few days before. Arie had carried the warm beverage into her room, and soon noticed the blurb written on the package claimed that it contained Reishi mushrooms, which sounded interesting. Arie sipped out of the mug while perched on the edge of her bed. The taste was mild and earthy, like a steeping cup of tea. A sliver of the moon's ivory light crept through the window where the drapes parted, accentuating the steam from the drink in her grasp.

It amazes me what transpired today, Arie pondered. *I'm not sure if Edwin finding out about my desire to dance was a good thing. No matter what excuses I had, I should have told him the truth previously. All I am is a liar, and a terrible one at that. If I'd stopped dancing in the barn, none of this would've ever happened.*

Finishing the contents in her mug, Arie set it down on the nightstand beside her bed. Usually, she'd take the cup back to the kitchen and rinse it out, but Arie lacked an incentive to do so right now. *I'd rather not dwell on this anymore. Maybe I'll wake up refreshed in the morning and feel a whole lot better about everything.*

Arie dimmed the battery-operated lamp near her bed, and the moonlight from the window guided her to the headboard. Her eyes welled with tears as she released a yawn. Though exhausted, Arie's concerns kept her brain active. She wondered if she'd get a wink of sleep tonight.

She slid beneath the lightweight sheet and hoped the sounds of vehicles passing by or the crickets chirping would drift through her partly open window and take her mind off her situation. But all she could think about was the incident in the hayloft, as well as what tomorrow and the following days would bring.

"Is Edwin going to uphold his promise and not tell my parents?" Arie mumbled, snuggling into the blanket she'd drawn up to her nose. "Will I even be able to keep my promise to him?"

As she lay on the mattress, readjusting her arms and twisting her body for more comfort, her eyelids began to droop, and the weariness of the day eventually took over.

Chapter 7

ARIE'S FATHER HAD GONE OUTSIDE an hour before time to leave for their church service, in order to fetch the family carriage and his horse, Gideon. He'd hitched his steed to the buggy and secured it to the rail while Mom began preparing breakfast. Dad carried out this ritual every Sunday when church was held in their district, and today the home hosting the service was about a fifteen-minute buggy ride from where Arie's family resided.

After Arie had arranged the breakfast dishes and utensils on the kitchen table, Mom asked her to get out a basket of cookies for the fellowship lunch that would take place following church. When that chore was done, Arie ventured out to the hitching post and reached into the family buggy to stow the basket on the floorboard in the back seat.

Her apprehensions were stacked up high this morning. Even though Arie had been looking forward to seeing Edwin today at church, their circumstances had been altered now that he was aware of what she'd been doing all along without him knowing. No doubt, Edwin perceived her as being deceitful, which admittedly, she was. For many years, Arie had played the role of a dutiful Amish daughter and always tried to do an excellent job falling in line. But all that had changed. It was difficult not to replay what had happened in the barn and more of a challenge to think about giving up her desire to dance.

After stepping away from the buggy, she glanced down at the phone shed. Unless it was an emergency, it was not customary for anyone in their family to make phone calls on Sunday. Even so, Arie felt compelled to give Lorrina a call.

She looked around to make sure Dad had gone into the house and that no one else had stepped outside. Certain that she was not being watched, Arie hurried her footsteps and soon entered the small building where their phone and answering machine were housed. Arie seated herself on the folding chair and dialed Lorrina's number. *These are thoughts I can no longer hold in,* she told herself. *Lorrina is the only person who knows I've been dancing. I should tell her what took place with Edwin.*

The phone rang a few times, and then someone picked up. "Arie?" Lorrina answered, following suit with a noisy yawn.

"Did I wake you? I'm sorry for calling so early."

"No biggie. I have to get up for church myself, and I think I forgot to set my alarm last night." Lorrina's voice sounded like the propeller blades of a boat scuffing up against rocks in shallow water. "You actually woke me up when I needed to get ready, so thank you."

"You're welcome, I guess." Arie drummed her feet against the floor. "By the way, how did your date go?"

"The sushi was outstanding, but the date itself. . .well, let's say that it wasn't the worst experience I've ever had, but he did take advantage of the fact that I offered to pay. And in addition to that, the entire evening, all he talked about was himself."

"You're kidding."

"Wish I was. He even ordered dessert to boot. I'll be starting my new job soon, so at least I'll be able to replenish the hole that burned in my wallet." Lorrina grunted. "There's no way that Casey and I are going on a second date, but I guess it was my fault for being so generous in the first place."

"That's unfortunate. I'm sorry things didn't go well."

"Yeah, it is what it is, though. I've come to realize that you can tell who someone is by their actions. Cutting it off now is preferable than carrying on with a relationship when you know it won't work out."

"Maybe you'll find someone who attends your church," Arie suggested.

"Eh, if only. We have mostly church members that are roughly a decade older than me and are married and already have children. The rest are either folks my parents' or grandparents' age. I haven't made a connection with any of the guys from my school either. To put it simply, it just hasn't panned out for me to meet that one special person yet."

"I'm sure you will when the time is right."

"I could hardly believe it, but my mom actually suggested I might want to try online dating, which is how my cousin found the man of her dreams. But I've heard some devastating stories about that type of dating, so I stood firm and said I wasn't about to meet a guy over the internet. I hope I never get to the point that I change my mind and end up turning to it as a last resort."

Arie tried to stay focused as her friend continued to speak, but her mind kept wandering as she pondered her own situation, which seemed to have taken precedence over Lorrina's words. As Arie attempted to sort through her thoughts, all she could hear was the ebb and flow of guilt versus her own desires, until

Lorrina's voice cut through the barricade.

"Is something wrong, Arie? You're awfully quiet."

Arie pressed the tips of her fingers against her throat. "Edwin and I have a date this afternoon."

"You don't sound too enthused about it."

"I always look forward to spending time with him, but I fear our relationship won't be the same going forward."

"Why's that?"

"Edwin saw me, Lorrina. He caught me dancing up in the hayloft."

"Goodness, Arie. How'd he take it?"

"Better than I thought he would. He didn't leave or yell at me. Edwin even said he understood why I didn't say anything about it, but I don't know. I feel that he's offering me too much grace."

"I warned that you should have been up-front with him."

"I know you did, and you were right. It wasn't good for Edwin to learn about it by catching me in the act. I promised to be truthful with him from now on, and that is all I can do, right?" With her words unspooling like threads, Arie scrubbed a hand over her face. "I didn't want to lie to Edwin, and I don't want to continue lying to my parents either. That was all a big mistake. I shouldn't have been dancing in the first place. I'm such a terrible person."

"Cut that out, Arie. Your desire to learn ballet does not make you a terrible person. However, masking your passions compromises your honesty. So, what are you going to do about it?"

"Well, I—"

"What are you doing here in the phone shed, Daughter?"

Click!

Arie stiffened. She had no idea if Mom, who'd opened the door to the phone shed, had overheard anything being said. She flexed her quivering fingers around the phone's base before mustering the courage to pivot in her chair and face her mother, who stood right at the door.

"I was wondering why it was taking you so long. Have you taken care of the basket?"

"Jah, Mamm," Arie breathlessly responded. "It's on the floor in the back of the buggy."

"What are you doing in the phone shack on a Sunday? And so early in the morning, no less?"

She held up the phone for her mother to see and pointed to it. "Our date. Edwin invited me to go somewhere with him after church."

Arie had doubts about whether her mom was going to buy that one. It was uncharacteristic for Arie to be out in the phone shack conversing with Edwin or anybody else, or for that matter on a Sunday. It would have been more credible if she had merely stated that she was checking phone messages. And yet, here she was, being untruthful again, and for no good reason at all.

Mom planted her hands against her hips. "Well, don't schedule it on a church morning. You should have made your call last night."

"You're right. I'm sorry, Mamm."

"Come back inside now, Arie. We haven't had breakfast yet, and there's not much time left before we'll have to leave for church."

Arie hunched over, expelling a pent-up breath as her mother departed the phone shack. *Mom certainly has impeccable timing*, she thought. Then, Arie sat upright, grasping the sides of her temples. *I hung up on my friend. I finally had a chance to call her, and then I hang up. I can only imagine what Lorrina thought. I really am a terrible person. What in the world is wrong with me? Why can't I just be honest with people and face the consequences if there are any?*

After folding her arms on the desk, Arie eyed the phone for a moment, hoping it would ring so she could answer, but it never rang. She considered phoning Lorrina back to explain what had happened, but assumed that her friend was probably getting ready for church. Besides, Arie knew she needed to return to the house and do the same.

In a section where most of the girls and young women sat, inside the spacious buggy shop where services were being held at a church member's home, Arie adjusted her body on the wooden backless bench. After an hour of singing from the *Ausbund* hymn book, it was time to focus on the sermon being preached.

Arie glanced up and spotted her boyfriend on the other side of the building. She knew it would be wrong to keep her focus on Edwin or anyone else in the men's section, so she quickly diverted her gaze and checked to see if her sister was behaving herself.

Maggie had insisted on sitting beside Arie today, and she noticed right away that her little sister had swept the cracker remnants from her lap onto the bench and then the floor. The crackers were among the snacks that had been passed out for the youngsters. Arie was unable to resist a grin at her sister's adorable, crumb-covered face as Maggie's eyes darted upward. Arie used her thumb to swipe at a few of them.

"Luke 12:2 reads, 'For there is nothing covered, that shall not be revealed; neither hid, that shall not be known,'" the preacher declared as he stood between the men and women's sides of the room, delivering his message in German. "Many people seem sincere and morally sound on the outside, but their hearts may reveal something entirely different. It's as clear as day that in scripture, all of what we do isn't veiled from God. Even the things we do behind closed doors that we shield from others will eventually come to light in due season. It is required of a Christian brother or sister to live a life of integrity and strive to be truthful in everything they do."

A pang of regret lurched in Arie's heart when she heard those words. If Edwin had unearthed her secret, her parents were bound to find out as well. It wasn't like she had a forbidden feeling rooted in deception. Arie wished her parents had given her permission to try ballet so she could be up-front and honest about how much she loved it. None of this was fair to Edwin, her parents, or Lorrina.

"Happiness is the fine art of making a beautiful bouquet from only those flowers in reach," Arie mused, clenching her bottom lip with her front teeth. *I lack gratitude for what I have around me.*

"There's a parable that Jesus shared," the minister continued. "Luke 8:16 reads, 'No man, when he hath lighted a candle, covereth it with a vessel, or putteth it under a bed; but setteth it on a candlestick, that they which enter in may see the light.' One does not light a candle to hide it." He feigned holding a candle and igniting it, mimicking the sound by creating a sizzle through his teeth. "It is aflame so it can shine, and what's true must be spoken without restriction, much like a burning wick that brightens a room. This also holds true for the talents we possess. Each of us has been bestowed with gracious gifts. It's unwise to disregard our abilities out of a sense of not serving or to hide them out of fear of judgment. First Peter 4:10 says, 'As every man hath received the gift, even so minister the same one to another, as good stewards of the manifold grace of God.'"

Arie recalled what Lorrina had said before—how it was a shame that her talents would go to waste. Was there a purpose for her infatuation with ballet? Was dancing the gift she'd been granted in her life? Could it be that she was snuffing a candle's ignited wick? Was giving it up a huge mistake on her part?

Elkhart, Indiana

Edwin glanced at Arie as they strolled along, enjoying the beauty at Krider World's Fair Gardens where he'd brought her for their after-church date. They had stumbled upon this botanical garden while cycling the Pumpkinvine Nature Trail on one of their previous dates. Today, they had brought a picnic basket so they could roll out a blanket amidst the canopy of trees.

They settled down near a pergola, where the placement of two benches mimicked one another. Edwin rummaged in the basket, plucking out sandwiches for the two of them, as well as some sliced apples and carrots. Since the weather had heated up as summer progressed, he had also brought along a few extra bottles of water.

"Wow, Edwin. You really went all out," Arie commented as she rested on the gingham blanket. "I feel like you're trying to impress me."

"All I'm doing is attempting to catch up on lost time. And yeah, I am trying to impress you, and it sounds like I've succeeded." Edwin gave her a wink and held out a bottle of water. "Moreover, making sandwiches is simple. It's not as though I cooked a gourmet meal."

"Still, you didn't have to go through all of this trouble. Supper at your house would have sufficed for me." The water bottle crackled as she gripped it. "How's your mom feeling, by the way? She wasn't there at church today."

"My mother's in a family way."

Arie's lips parted, but no words formed. Her mouth's motion lifted the little mole along her Cupid's bow.

"I was at a loss for words too when I heard the news."

"She's around my mom's age. So, she's having another child—"

"In her forties, yes," Edwin interjected.

"Your mother had to have been taken by surprise."

"Mom's coming to terms with it, as she says." Edwin didn't want to dwell on the matter, so he recommended that they pray silently before digging into their food. Afterward, he unraveled the plastic wrap from his sandwich and munched on a mouthful. There had been something on his mind, which he was curious about. His fascination influenced him to ask, even though he wasn't sure if it was proper to pose the question.

"Arie, can I ask you something?"

"Of course."

"What were those leaps called that you did up in the hayloft?"

With a downward motion of Arie's hand, a snap of the carrot between her teeth resounded. Her hazel irises complemented the vibrancy of their verdant surroundings. "They're called jetés. It's a jumping motion where you transfer weight from one leg to the other. There are other types, including grande jetés, petit jetés, and jeté battu, which involves beating your legs in the air before landing. That one's a bit trickier, though."

"Those are some big words I've never heard before, Arie. Is ballet all about jumping?"

"A lot of it is jumping, in a way. However, there's also some twirling and bending involved. Do you want me to show you?"

"Now?" Edwin gaped at her, taken aback by Arie's unreserved and frank offer. All he could hear was the breeze whistling through the canopy overhead as he fixed his gaze on her.

Arie's eyebrows gathered in. "I'm sorry. Forget I said anything. I shouldn't have asked—"

"Sure."

"W–what? What'd you say, Edwin?"

"I said sure. You can show me."

In all honesty, he was as flabbergasted as Arie that he'd blurted out the question. Edwin sought for more, so how could he pass up the opportunity to observe if Arie was willing to demonstrate her dance moves?

She lifted her chin and swiveled her head to the right. Subsequently, Arie slipped off her kapp and tossed it on the blanket. She then sprung up, writhing her limbs and arching her back before making a rapid motion with her feet. Arie rendered a succession of short steps throughout the blades of grass, her legs drawing together before extending in repetition. With her knees bent, she launched herself into a *jeté*.

To his amazement, Arie attempted to whirl against the turf's resistance. Ballet was unlike any other dancing style he'd seen, which entailed swaying the hips or tapping one's heel. These movements were flexible, like heated metal, but they also had framework and precision. His breaths swelled at the sight, and Edwin trailed his fingers along his jaw as Arie concluded, her rear leg elevated and arms raised high.

Edwin crossed his legs and leaned on his elbows to support his head. "I can't get over how good you are at that, Arie. That was amazing!"

"Danki, Edwin," Arie panted. Her face had reddened, and her hairline was dotted with beads of sweat, resulting in some thin strands of hair adhering to her forehead. Despite her apparent lack of energy, Arie had a wide grin plastered on her face. She grabbed her water bottle, unscrewed the cap, and took a swig. Her welcoming smile withered as she sank back down on the blanket.

"About what happened in the hayloft—"

Edwin grasped her hand. "Don't worry about it. You've already apologized."

"I understand, but—I'm sure it's complicated for you too—all of this. I assumed I would've driven you away, and I wouldn't blame you if you left. Even though I'm not the best at words, Edwin, I wanted to thank you for your trust."

Edwin nodded, tracing a thumb over the back of his girlfriend's hand. "Are you certain that you can let go of this? I can tell it makes you happy."

She tucked a strand of hair behind her ear. "It does, but it would also perturb my parents, and that would not make me happy."

"Right." He quirked an eyebrow. "Does my horseback riding make your folks happy?"

"They admit that the community benefits from the drill team, but as for the riding itself, they've often said it's too reckless."

"Arie, do your parents let you do anything fun?"

"Despite your recklessness, they allowed me to date you," she countered, puffing up her cheeks like a bird keeping warm in the winter.

"Yes, indeed, I'm such a rebellious boy, speeding through the countryside on my single horsepower." Edwin wiggled his brows.

Arie snickered. "What about your parents? Isn't your dad kind of difficult to deal with?"

"He has his moments, notably when he excuses Markel's behavior. The thing is, my brother is good at his job and has potential, but he gets distracted. Mostly from that phone of his. I only use mine when absolutely necessary. But Markel shares a name with my father, so maybe that's why Dad overlooks Markel's antics and doesn't appreciate my efforts the way I would like. With as much time and energy as I've invested in my father's company, I feel that I should be paid more than Markel."

"That isn't how he should be treating you. Your father ought to acknowledge the remarkable dedication you have toward your work ethic. I'm sorry, Edwin." Arie sighed. "Parents aren't always fair, are they?"

"No, but I guess they're doing their best. It's the same way that we carefully consider our options and do our best to fulfill our obligations, even though sometimes we fail."

Arie's lips pursed as her eyes strayed to the sky peeking through the treetops. "Do you think we'll be good parents someday?"

Her question seemed to Edwin as though she wasn't asking him, but rather seeking that answer heavenward.

"Already thinking about that, are we?" Edwin questioned.

"Yes, of course." She winced. "I mean, it's obviously too soon for that, but my mind tends to wander way too far."

"In my opinion, you'd make an excellent mother, based on how you've treated your siblings. For Maggie and Rudy, you're almost like a mother."

Arie shook her head. "I shouldn't be. My parents are preoccupied with the store, though, so I'm sure they appreciate my help. At least, I hope so. And since you'll have a younger sibling in the picture soon, you'll know what that's like."

"Maybe." He reached for her hand. "And someday we'll have our own *kinner* to worry about." Edwin shuddered, realizing what he'd let slip past his lips.

Arie wagged her finger at him. "We aren't even married yet, Edwin. It's too soon to be talking about children."

"Jah, way too soon," he concurred.

As Edwin gripped Arie's hand, he realized how clammy it

was. He had half a mind to wipe away the perspiration on his trousers, but instead, Edwin kept it there, intertwining his fingers with hers. Was it too soon for them to be considering a future together? After all, they were both barely grownups. Edwin's aim had been to settle down with someone from his community, and when he started dating Arie, he'd begun to envision her as the one with whom he would spend the rest of his life. But now he had some doubts. What if she changed her mind and didn't give up ballet? What if Arie decided not to join the church?

Arie leaned up against him. "Edwin?"

Blinking, he looked directly at her beautiful face. "What is it, Arie?"

"Thank you for arranging this picnic and bringing me here today." She tilted her head up at him, her eyes full of mirth. "Sharing my appreciation for dance with you meant a lot to me. I'm glad I can finally be honest with you."

A mellow golden tint appeared in patches above them, and he noticed that the temperature had dropped a little. It should've been an ideal means to finish a date, though a flicker of a thought lingered in the recesses of Edwin's mind.

Would I even matter to Arie if her parents weren't against her dancing? Would she leave her Amish heritage behind for ballet?

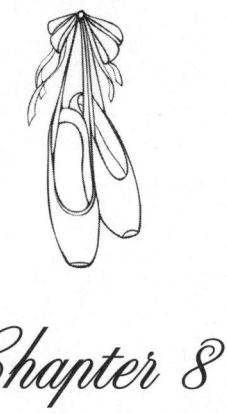

Chapter 8

Shipshewana

THE FIRST WEEKS OF A hot, humid summer had flown by, and early August continued the trend, with the warmer weather not letting up. Arie found it hard to believe, especially since it seemed as though her and Edwin's date at the park hadn't been so long ago.

Since then, Edwin had made an effort to visit her in the evening at least a couple of times per week, as well as arranging a date for Sundays whenever he could. However, many times he was away from Shipshewana, putting in additional hours at various existing homes and construction sites in one of the nearby towns. Arie had been compelled to return the favor by visiting Edwin's home a few times.

Aside from that, everything had fallen back into place. Although they both continued to be involved with their obligations at work and home, when they took the time to be together, Arie was convinced that Edwin loved her. He was always attentive, and in the grand scheme of things, Arie felt that there had been a wonderful shift in their relationship, because their time together seemed even more precious than before.

This Saturday morning, Arie was out running errands for her mother. An Amish woman, Miriam Bontrager from Grabill, was so adept at layering and batting potholders that Arie's mother had chosen to carry a variety of them for their customers and had put them on display in the housewares section of their store. It had been a wise decision, because they'd sold like hotcakes, and now they were out of stock. Arie had volunteered to go to the Shipshewana Flea Market today, knowing Miriam had a booth there and would hopefully have enough potholders to sell her the amount Mom needed. This would not be a difficult task in and of itself, with one exception: At their mother's request, Arie's two siblings had come along for the ride. In addition to the responsibility of keeping an eye on her brother and sister while they were at the flea market, Arie was concerned about how Rudy and Maggie had fussed at each other nearly the whole trip. Arie thought the ride would have been a lot easier if she could have come alone. But she had decided to make the best of it and hoped that everything would go smoothly as they sought out Miriam's booth.

Normally, market days were on Tuesdays and Wednesdays, but they held the August Weekend Market Saturdays from morning until midafternoon. The sellers offered a wide range of trinkets and oddities, including jewelry, furniture, antiques, books, homegrown produce, and various handcrafted items. It was understandable why an abundance of locals and visitors gathered for this special function.

For convenience, and to avoid the trouble of hitching a horse to the buggy, Arie had hired a driver. As they'd come into town and passed the Farmstead Inn, she'd noticed that the parking lot was full of vehicles. This hotel, as well as the Blue Gate Garden Inn and a few others on the main stretch of road, always did good business, since so many tourists needed a place to stay while visiting Shipshewana. The hotels were also in close proximity to the market. Their driver dropped them off near an entrance that was feasible to pull into, since the parking lot had become overrun with vehicles. The temperature steadily rose, and it was supposed to reach 80 degrees later in the afternoon. Above them, the sunlight triumphed through the clouds, and the humid air coated Arie's frame in cloying moisture.

Arie cocked her head, and with as much assurance as she could muster, she addressed her siblings, "The market's quite packed with people today, so it's best for you both to keep close to me. No wandering off or causing any trouble. Understand?"

Maggie didn't need to be told twice, as she had already extended her hand toward Arie. Her brother, however, stood there with his hands buried under his arms as Arie flitted her gaze at him.

"I'm not holding your hand," he huffed. "No way, Arie."

"That's fine, Rudy. You don't have to. But please stay by my side. I don't want anything to happen to you."

Rudy didn't protest any further, so after pinching the strap of her tote and adjusting it on her shoulder, Arie led the way toward the main entrance of the venue.

They reached the flea market, which was, as expected, brimming with people of all kinds. Spanning around forty acres, it was the largest flea market in the Midwest. Arie's gaze took in the many vendors' tents and booths, doing her best to soak in every detail of her surroundings. Despite having broad pathways throughout the market, the aisles were congested. She hadn't been to the flea market in a long time, and while her mother would have liked to have accompanied her today, business was booming at the general store. Hopefully, Mom would be able to make time to visit the flea market before it was over in September.

Among the items Mom had in mind for Arie to bring home were the potholders, of course, as well as some produce and table coverings. Arie deliberated on browsing the antiques at her leisure, and she would have if her younger siblings weren't present. Perhaps at a later day she might be able to come here by herself and spend a good deal of time simply browsing without interruption. For now, though, Arie strived to get out of the market as soon as possible.

After purchasing the table runners from one of the sellers, Arie ambled over to the produce stand located next door. The Amish vendor had sorted some of the fruit in bushel baskets arranged on tables. The laminated sign read, MICHIGAN STANLEY PLUMS, inscribed in black ink.

Arie's nose scrunched up. *We certainly don't need more plums*, she thought. *This summer has been a fruitful one for our Italian plum tree.*

"Eww, prunes," Maggie groused.

"Maggie, unless they're dehydrated, they're not prunes."

Rudy dabbed at flecks of perspiration along his upper lip. "Can we take a break now? I'm cravin' some real food."

Arie scratched an itchy spot on her earlobe. "I'm sorry, Rudy. We're not here for that. Mom requested that I get everything on her list, so that's what we'll do."

Her little sister had edged nearer, still clinging to Arie's free hand. Typically, Maggie would be quite chatty, but she seemed to be overwhelmed by the hectic environment surrounding them. Arie knelt to her sister's level, because she was all too familiar with the feeling and wanted to offer Maggie some reassurance. "Are you doing okay?"

Maggie gave a deliberate nod but didn't speak. The diminutive child was evidently intrigued by the developments unfolding around them, as her eyes darted around.

As Arie navigated the bustling traffic, she couldn't help smelling the tantalizing aromas of several food court meals and kettle corn wafting throughout the throng of people. Her brother's interest in eating here was reasonable. Arie was on the verge of ordering a crispy, luscious pretzel, but she stumbled upon the tent she'd been searching for. Skirting past an elderly couple who had wandered out, Arie went in, squeezing her sister's hand.

The underside of the canopy was alive with color, showcasing an array of quilted patchwork items displayed on hangers overhead, on clothes racks, and arranged on various tables. Miriam sat nearby with a cashbox in front of her. Even the apron she wore had a quilted bodice in the pinwheel pattern.

"Hey, it's the Kauffman children." Her smile crinkled, along with the skin around her eyes. "What can I do for you, dear?" she asked, focusing on Arie.

"My mother sent me to get more of your potholders for the store. Do you have any to spare?" Arie questioned.

"Well, now. Let's see if I have enough for you." Rising from her folding chair, Miriam went over to a tote bag tucked away in the corner. "I'm surprised that your mother didn't come here to see me."

"Mom wanted to, but she's working at our family store today," Arie replied.

"She must really have her hands full there," Miriam commented as she opened the bag and laid out several lovely potholders.

"Very much so, especially today with the flea market open. A lot of folks come out to our store after they are finished shopping here, or the other way around." Arie smiled. "But I'm here on her behalf."

"I see that, and on a Saturday too, when you could be hanging out with friends or even your boyfriend. Do you ever have time to do anything just for fun?"

Miriam's words cut Arie deep, even though she most likely meant for her remark to be a lighthearted jab. Arie's shoulders lifted almost to her ears, and she relinquished Maggie's hand long enough to massage her face, stretching her forced smile. "How much will these potholders cost?" she asked, changing the subject as she gestured to the objects in question.

After Miriam quoted the amount, Arie delved into her purse for her wallet. While Miriam fussed with some of the potholders in front of her, as if to showcase their quality, Arie peered down at them as she took money out of her wallet. Arie grazed her hand on the interwoven layers of the potholder resting atop the pile. *This woman must have spent many hours stitching all of these, not only binding them but also devising their patterns*, she thought. *Even something as simple as a potholder to use every day had been intricately stitched into an eye-catching and beloved piece, worthy of any woman's kitchen.*

More potholders were presented until there were enough for Arie's mother to be satisfied. After thumbing through the bills, Arie handed Miriam the amount owed.

"Here you go. You put a lot of effort into your quilting, so I gave you a little extra."

"How very kind of you, dear. Many thanks." Miriam glanced past Arie and her brows furrowed. "Wasn't there a young boy wearing a straw hat standing here beside you not too long ago?"

"Rudy?"

"Rudy went that way." Maggie gestured toward the tent's entrance.

Arie hurriedly shoved the potholders into the tote on her shoulder and whirled around, craning her neck to see over a mass of bodies. Across the way, at the tent of another vendor, Arie spotted her brother. From a distance, she had limited visibility, but based on what she'd seen, Rudy was at one of the display racks near the entrance of the white canopy. Then, Arie watched in horror as the display rack came toppling down. Her brother didn't appear to sense the impending catastrophe that loomed over him.

"Rudy," she bellowed. "Watch out!"

Thankfully, he hopped out of the way before it struck him. Arie grabbed Maggie's hand and ran to her brother, knowing she had to move quickly. The seller emerged from the tent, flinching at the sight, and her urgency amplified.

"I am so sorry, Miss," Arie remarked between gasps, while letting go of Maggie's hand long enough to reposition the strap on her shoulder that was close to falling off.

"You need to have a better eye on your kid." The vendor swatted the side of the canopy.

"He's not my kid. He's my brother."

"So where is your mother? Older sister doesn't seem to have the expertise she needs to handle this." With hands on her hips, the woman frowned.

Several folks stopped in their tracks and gawked at the scene before them. Embarrassment poured over Arie as a result of the attention this had garnered. She did her best to keep her eyes off of them and concentrate on the matter at hand. After inhaling and quelling her nerves, she turned to face the vendor.

"Excuse me, Miss," Arie said as she nudged her brother, herding him farther into the canopy and away from prying eyes and out of sight of onlookers. She took her sister's hand again and focused on her brother. "Rudy, this isn't an okay thing to do. You caused this mess, so the correct thing to do is rectify it."

Rudy's lips pressed into a thin line. "What's rectify?"

"Fix it," Arie stated firmly.

"Why should I? I didn't mean to knock it over."

"Even mistakes have consequences." The wind had picked up slightly, and Arie held tight to the ties of her kapp. "Whether it was an accident or not, you are responsible for the rack falling down. If someone accidentally knocked over something of yours, how would you like them to respond?"

Arie realized that asking her brother to apologize when he didn't feel sorry would only make him be untruthful about his emotions, so she hadn't urged him to apologize as she had in previous instances. Though she wasn't sure what he would do, Arie hoped he would take that step without her influence or insistence.

Rudy's arms were slack at his sides as he scuffed the ground with his shoe. He staggered over to the seller and muttered, "I'm sorry for knocking it over."

Arie flattened her dominant hand on the exposed portion of her neck. *I can't believe it. My brother actually said he was sorry, and without being told what he should do.*

The vendor inclined her head, as if weighing Rudy's apology. Soon after, she sighed. "Nothing expensive was on the rack—just the towels and aprons. I forgive you, but I must say, if something fragile had broken here, it would have been far more difficult for me to pardon."

"We understand," Arie chimed in. "We're willing to clean up the mess. Right, Rudy?"

"Sure," he agreed.

Arie hoisted the rack and set it upright while Rudy gathered the aprons and towels that had scattered on the gravel. It looked as if it had never fallen after they finished tidying up the disarray. Arie grasped her brother's shoulder to draw his attention. Rudy glanced up at her, his bobbed hair swishing like the hem of a dress.

"That was very mature, Rudy. I'm proud of you."

Rudy shuffled his feet. "You thought that was mature of me?"

"Of course. You did the right thing, even when it was hard. It takes courage to admit you've done something wrong, especially when many people go to great lengths to justify the way they act."

And I would be far too familiar with that, Arie thought with self-scrutiny. "So, before we head out, how about we grab something to eat? My treat," she added with a grin.

Edwin's mother handed him another clothespin, and he gingerly suspended the final pair of wet trousers on the line. The mellow odor of detergent from the clothing, along with the remnants of the morning rain, relaxed him and made him smile.

"I think this effort of hanging clothes calls for some downtime, don't you?" Mom chuckled, picking up the empty basket in her arms. "I made some iced tea earlier, unsweetened, of course."

"Is that okay for you, Mamm? I thought caffeine was off limits to expectant mothers."

She shook her head. "That's a common misconception. Yes, there's a limit on how much I can enjoy, but the kind of iced tea I made is low in caffeine. I'll be right back with a glass for each of us."

As Mom went back into the house, Edwin eased onto the Adirondack glider on the porch. He could see the bird feeders from here, and the largest one trembled on the shepherd's hook due to the charm of finches. The way it whirled gave the impression that the birds were riding on a frantic, fast-moving carousel.

"Here you go, Son. Nice and cold." Edwin's mother handed

him a glass of tea with a lemon wedge perched on the rim.

"Danki, Mamm." He squeezed the juice from the citrus slice into his tea. "Have any idea what it might be?"

"The baby you mean? Nope, and I don't wanna know till it happens. I'm keeping all of that a surprise."

"Really? Is that what you did for me and Markel?"

"Absolutely. I think it's kind of fun to wait." Mom sat next to him in the other glider.

Edwin shielded his eyes from the glare of the sun. "What did you think I was going to be?"

"I expected you to be a dedicated and compassionate person with a heart of gold."

"I meant the gender, Mom."

"I never gave any thought to that," she insisted. "I knew that whatever I was given, my child would be the best they could be, and you are, which is all I've ever wanted."

He arched his neck and took in a sharp sniff. "You wanted a girl, didn't you?"

"Well, having clothing sewn for a girl or sharing some of my passions with her would have been lovely." She gently struck the underside of her glass against the arm of the glider. "My midwife got my hopes up and told me that she had a gut feeling it would be a girl. She must've eaten something that bothered her stomach that day, because her gut was wrong." Mom snickered behind one hand.

"The things you mentioned, you could still do. This time, it might be a girl."

"I know my body, Son. This pregnancy feels exactly like it did when I was carrying you and Markel. I ended up with the two of you, and you're more than I could have asked for." His mother's cheekbones were prominent, and her overall countenance exuded radiance. "Edwin, thank you for helping me hang up the laundry, and I appreciate your ongoing support."

Edwin hummed a few seconds before sipping the tea. "I'm more than happy to help whenever I'm available, Mamm."

He felt grateful that Saturday had been kind to them as they sat comfortably on the porch. However, Edwin was concerned about Arie because she'd indicated that she would be too busy assisting her parents today at the store to make it over to see him as she'd originally promised. Although Edwin felt disappointed about not seeing his girlfriend today, he looked forward to seeing Arie tomorrow at church and hopefully getting together with her after the noon meal that would follow the service.

It had been an eventful afternoon for Arie and her siblings, and by the time they'd made it home from the flea market, it was around two o'clock, according to the grandfather clock in the living room. Maggie trailed Arie around the house while she unloaded the tote she had strapped on her shoulder, recalling that Rudy had muttered something about walking over to the store to see their father. As her mother had instructed, Arie set the potholders and table covers on their parents' bed.

While Arie stowed the last of the produce in the refrigerator, Mom showed up in the kitchen, flushed and out of breath. No doubt, she'd been in a hurry and had run instead of walked to the house from the store.

"How'd you fare at the flea market, Arie? Did you get everything I had asked for?"

"Yep, and I stored the produce." To emphasize her point, she shut the refrigerator door. "The other stuff is on the bed already, so that's done."

Maggie rushed up to greet Mom, hugging her knees. Then she declared, "Guess what Rudy did at the market today, Mamm?"

Arie's breath caught in her throat like a wad of lint. *Maggie just had to blurt that out, didn't she? Sure hope it doesn't upset Mom.*

"Maggie, what did I say about not being a tattletale?" Mom gave Arie a harsh squint. "What transpired at the market, Daughter?"

"Rudy knocked over one of the seller's display racks," Arie admitted.

"He did what? Arie, did you intend to tell me this?"

"I'm sorry. I would have if it hadn't been resolved, but nothing broke, and I handled the situation. We put things back together after Rudy apologized. No harm was done, Mom."

"Maggie, give me and your sister some privacy, please."

Despite giving their mother a sheepish look, Maggie followed her instructions and skirted out of the room. If Mom's query hadn't been point-blank, with Maggie stating that Rudy had done something, Arie could have avoided what was about to transpire. She should've asked Maggie and Rudy to keep quiet, but it would have forced them to be dishonest. Arie could never expect her siblings to do that.

"Arie, you need to watch your siblings more closely," her mother scolded. "Especially in a crowded environment like the market. Knocking over someone else's property can land us in a lot of trouble. Do you know what the damages may have resulted in? Money out of our pockets."

Arie's subconscious raced with everything she refused to say and was often encumbered with, and all of a sudden, part of it slipped out of Arie's mind and onto the tip of her tongue.

"I'm sorry for not properly watching him. I can own up to that. But Rudy knocked it over, not me. Shouldn't you be telling your son this?" Arie folded her arms. "I told him to stay with me, and he's old enough to know better. He chose to leave. I did what you directed me to do, which was to get what you wanted from the market."

Mom's eyes grew wide, yet she kept that fevered stare. "Do not correct me on my parenting. You're their older sibling, and you know better. It's your responsibility to watch over your sister and brother and to make sure that they both stay out of trouble. You were not watching Rudy, so it's your fault that he knocked over anything. End of discussion."

"But Mom, I was just—"

"End of discussion. This isn't like you to talk back to me, Arie, and if you say another word, you'll regret it."

Oh, believe me, I've already regretted being obedient to you. Arie gritted her teeth as she fought to stay quiet.

Mom stormed out of the kitchen, leaving Arie fuming over her mother's tongue-lashing. Here she was being blamed for what Rudy had done, and she didn't even get a thank-you for purchasing what her mother had asked her to get at the flea market. Arie's stomach roiled, but it hadn't stemmed from dread or panic. It was sheer pent-up resentment.

Every time Arie found herself in a predicament like this with her mother, she tended to make amends and promised to do better. But hadn't she already done enough? *If my mother will misconstrue everything I do, I'm only wasting my time and energy attempting to do what my parents expect of me.* Arie was unaware until now that her body had begun to tremble. She winced, then scooted out a bar stool and promptly sat down. Arie rested her head on the surface of the kitchen island. *No, I cannot be thinking like that. Like Edwin said, our parents are stressed out and they're trying their hardest. But I'm under stress too, and they don't seem to even notice or care.*

Chapter 9

THE BRILLIANCE OF THE GOLDEN hour radiated as Arie gazed out at the horses' pasture on the left side of her parents' property. Strangely enough, Arie's eyes did not moisten from the intensity of the sunlight. The clover and shrubs in the fenced-in area drifted by, and Arie figured out she wasn't standing in the pasture but rather moving at a quickened pace outside of it.

Arie turned her attention to her hands, which were resting on what she recognized as a horse's torso. But when she glanced directly in front of her, an ivory tail flicked up and down with the horse's rushing momentum instead of the mane that extended from the withers to the poll. She was balancing rearward on the horse.

Alongside her, an entourage of horses galloped, their bodies stark white. A woman's voice called out to her, but it reverberated, like bellowing in a cavern. Slowly Arie recognized the voice as belonging to her mother.

Standing on the northern border of the pasture, Mom held a note and was waving it in her hands. "These horses belong to the neighbors, and they must enter the pasture every day at this designated time," she hollered.

Arie had reservations since she was riding backward on a

horse, while Mom stood there reading a note from the presumed neighbor.

"Life is too short, Arie. Perhaps we were given those resources for that reason, to allow you to ride as you used to. Daughter, I don't have many years left. Make use of yours wisely." Those were Mom's final words.

The glimpses before Arie's vision faded, and the dim interior of her room swam into view. At first, it was hard to distinguish between the ceiling above and her eyelids as she blinked in succession. She felt jittery, all the way to the depths of her being, as if it had been ruffled and was now lodged in some strange, improper way. Arie had never been fond of waking in the wee hours of the morning. When Lorrina had told her that she got to sleep in until ten on most summer days, Arie found herself feeling envious.

That was the benefit of not being Amish: fewer chores to worry about. Arie didn't mind carrying out the tasks themselves, but having to get up early to do them wasn't ideal. The sudden cold front that had swept through the region had brought the brisk morning air into the house. She simply didn't have the will to do anything because it was so frigid inside.

Arie fought to squelch a yawn, but a deep ache erupted from the slight movement of her jawbone.

I must've spent the entire night grinding my teeth. She stroked her jaw with her fingers. *That was a bizarre dream I had, but I just have vague recollections of it now. It's remarkable how real it feels in the moment when a person is dreaming, and even afterward, some of the details linger. But now, I can't remember exactly what stirred up my emotions. When I come fully awake, I can't help but wonder where the dreams go. Do they dwell in the mind and resurface later in the same way as a memory? Could that be why I have sometimes experienced recurring dreams?*

Arie turned her head to the right and glanced at the alarm clock on her nightstand. It was time for her to wake up anyway, though she was certain that sleeping for an extra half hour would have done her some good. She nestled onto her pillow and burrowed under the covers, seeking the comfort and warmth. If she were to succumb to her desire to close her eyes, she would fall right back to sleep.

Would sleeping be so awful? she asked herself. With the thickness of her lovely quilt, in addition to the warmth of the blanket atop her soft sheets, Arie's mattress was so inviting, but she was obligated to get up. Soon she'd be hearing her family stirring in the hallways anyway, so there was no point in prolonging the inevitable.

She forced herself to sit up, reached toward her nightstand, and fumbled to turn on the battery-operated lamp. When Arie finally identified and clicked the switch, the bulb supplied enough light in the bedroom to discern her surroundings. She turned off her alarm and reluctantly slid out of bed, recoiling a bit when her feet met the cold wooden floor.

After searching her closet for the dress she would wear, Arie shifted it over her shoulders and smoothed the fabric before padding across the room to the full-length mirror beside her dresser. The hem swirled as she twisted her body, revolving into a single pirouette. The mirror's reflection revealed an expression of delight on her face as the faint light from the bulb bounced off her cheekbones.

Just a girl in an Amish dress. Her smile faltered. *That's all I see in the mirror.*

Once again, it was time to take care of the plums that had fallen to the ground in their yard. With all of its might, the grapevine that had scaled the fence latched onto the garden gate. Arie swung the gate back and forth, but the grip remained firm. She stretched out and pried the vine off and took the bucket and rake over to the tree. Much of the burgundy-tinted fruit had descended into the yard where the Italian plum tree's limbs fanned out. Arie outstretched the rake and skimmed the tines through the grass, capturing the plums in her general vicinity.

She snatched up a plum that had missed the bucket's opening, and upon closer inspection revealed some slugs, scarcely larger than a grain of rice, crawling over the rind, leaving a trail of slime behind them. With a groan, Arie ambled toward the garden plots, setting the plum right at the base of one of the blueberry bushes.

After filling the bucket with healthy plums, Arie hauled it up to the house with the intention of extracting the pits and feeding the fruit to the hens. Although she hadn't seen her sister for a while, Maggie had informed Arie earlier that she wanted to visit their mother at the store. More to the point, Arie was quite certain that her little sister had no desire to assist in removing the "prunes" from the garden. There was a good chance that Maggie could be in the house right now, since Arie had requested that she meet her there to help take care of today's laundry. But all her plans stalled when she rounded the corner near the front of the house.

The hummingbird feeder was overrun with wasps, and her brother was on the porch batting at them barehanded. Her body seemed to freeze in place as she stared at Rudy attempting to swat the insects out of the air. The nape of Arie's neck tingled, and she heard herself yelling from within, calling out to her brother, but no words formed.

Rudy kept raising his hands to the buzzing insects, and Arie was well aware that the wasps were growing more agitated as her brother encroached on their nectar haven. She had to do something, so Arie relinquished the breath she'd been holding and dropped the bucket of plums. She pushed off the balls of her feet and rushed to the porch, and as Arie enveloped her brother in her arms, she heard him holler along with an incessant humming passing her ears. Everything in that dire moment was a blur, and when the world around Arie finally caught up with her, she realized that they were in the house and her brother was saying something she couldn't make out at first.

"It got me! Dumm bug!"

"I'm sorry, Rudy. May I please see it?"

He leaned away from Arie, his eyes darting to the ceiling. After asking again, her brother hesitated at first but then stepped forward and stuck out his arm. She inspected the spot where he'd been stung. It was fortunate that the stinger didn't seem to be lodged in the skin. However, the redness and swelling made it quite apparent that the wasp had pierced her brother's forearm beneath his elbow.

"All right now, you'll need to wash that wound with soap and water, so it doesn't get infected." Arie gave him a pat on the back and pointed in the direction of the bathroom.

Rudy let out a theatrical sigh. "Got it. Mom has gotten upset with me even when I don't wash my hands. So for cuts and scrapes she really insists that I get the wound good and clean. I know the drill, Arie."

He sauntered down the hallway, giving her ample opportunity to come to terms with what had transpired. She hadn't been stung in a few years, but seeing her brother near the wasps caused Arie to freeze. Arie couldn't believe she'd almost watched the whole scene without running right away to Rudy to offer him the help he needed.

Whenever wasps are around, it puts me in a panic. Arie shook her head. *There's nothing to worry about, though. All I have to do is check on Rudy and then go back to what I was doing outside.*

She proceeded down the hall and circled the bend into the restroom's open doorway. Rudy had turned off the water at the sink and dried his arm with a hand towel. Another addition to today's laundry pile. Arie knocked on the doorframe then entered the bathroom. When she realized from her brother's expression that she was in his personal space, Arie backed up a few steps, and with his permission, she hunkered down to her brother's height.

"Got it all cleaned up?" she questioned.

"Jah, all done. You were stung too, Arie." Rudy motioned to her with his bent, wounded elbow.

"I was?" Arie tilted her hand, and there it was, a welt that had swelled a bit on her wrist. "Guess I did get stung."

"I thought you were scared of wasps."

"I am terrified of them, Rudy. But I was more worried about you getting hurt than myself. That's why I wanted to keep you safe from them." She narrowed her eyes. "Why did you mess with the wasps earlier?"

"I wasn't. They went after me first as I tried to get back inside the house."

Arie nodded. "How are you feeling now?"

Rudy pinched at the tip of his snub nose. "I've been stung by honeybees before when running in the grass barefoot. When it happens, it's not that bad. This was much more painful, though. More angry and nasty."

"Only in exceptional circumstances, when they feel they have no other choice, do honeybees sting," Arie explained. "Wasps, on the other hand, will attack when they feel threatened, even if you don't mean to cause harm." She raised her hands as she sprang from the floor. "Hold on, you'll need some ice to lessen the swelling. I'll get it for you."

After assisting with Rudy's wound, Arie intended to care for her own, but it didn't hurt, and for the moment she was focused on making her brother comfortable. She left him in the bathroom and went to the kitchen to retrieve an ice pack from the freezer. She grabbed a hand towel from the drawer and made a beeline back to where he waited. She wrapped the ice pack with the towel around her brother's arm, and he flinched as it made contact with the welt. Arie tied the towel's ends together and smiled reassuringly at Rudy. "That should feel better."

"Where are you, Arie? There's a bucket of spoiled plums in front of our house!"

Hearing her father's familiar voice behind her, she whirled around. Dad was positioned at the door's threshold, his boots making contact with the tile floor.

Dad scratched at his sunken temples and cocked an eyebrow at Arie. "What's going on in here?"

"Rudy and I got stung by a wasp. I'm handling it, though."

"Oh, that's not a big deal. Just walk it off, Son. You'll be fine after a while."

And just like that, Dad took his leave. She heard the wall hanging near the front door jostle enough for it to scrape as he slammed the door. Arie questioned why he had come into the house at all. Water perhaps? Did he notice the wasps feasting at the hummingbird feeder when he walked in?

"Don't pay attention to Dad's comment. If you're still hurting, it's best to speak up." When Arie looked back at her brother, her eyes expanded. "Rudy?"

"I don't..." he trailed off. "I don't feel so good."

Arie hoisted her brother up and helped him walk to the living room, seating him on the couch. Rudy groaned as he scooted up against the cushion and reclined. She unwrapped the ice pack from his arm, and Arie's heart leapt at the sight. Her brother's skin had mushroomed where the wasp had embedded its stinger into him.

He's having a reaction to the sting. I have to do something quickly, but I can't leave Rudy alone in the house. Dad just went out the door. Hopefully, he didn't get very far.

After telling her brother that she'd be right back, Arie hustled out of the living room. She flung the front door open without bothering to check if there were any wasps on the feeder. Arie wasn't concerned with being stung again at this point because she wasn't sensitive to the venom, whereas her brother's reaction could be fatal. When she spotted her father heading up the gravel path back to the store, Arie yelled at the top of her lungs. Thankfully, she caught his attention, and he spun around, trotting back up to the porch.

"What's up, Arie?"

"Rudy's reacting negatively to the wasp sting." She clutched the porch railing, striking the pad of her thumb on the post cap like a match.

Her father's mouth slackened. "Hasn't Rudy been stung before? He never had a reaction in the past."

"Rudy had been stung by honeybees, not wasps," Arie protested.

"Please, it's not looking good."

"Okay, now relax, Arie. I'm sure he'll be all right, and there's nothing to worry about."

"How do you know that?" Arie leaned over the railing, feeling the thrum of her own pulse. "You didn't even check for yourself to be sure. I'm telling you how serious this is. Why can't you simply take my word for it?"

Arie shuddered, peering down at her wrist. The discomfort from her sting had finally set in. Although the skin burned and itched profusely, it didn't appear that a stinger had become entrenched. However, she hadn't taken the time to clean the wound. At the moment, however, that was irrelevant.

Dad closed in, muttering angrily, and tromped to the porch's edge. She was ahead of her father, bounding to the door, swinging it open, and rushing up to her brother, panic evident in the poor boy's eyes.

Arie knelt before her brother and blurted out, "Hang in there, Rudy. Dad's coming."

"Where are you two?" he called.

"We're in the living room!"

Dad nearly stumbled on the braided throw rug upon entering the space. Her father's strained neck muscles and intake of deep breaths gave indication of the concern he felt as he neared the couch. Rudy scraped trails on his skin as he clawed at his throat. His scarlet lips stood out against his pale complexion.

"See, Dad? It's getting worse." Suppressing the violent tremors that swept through her body, Arie clenched her arm as though her life depended on it.

"Jah, that's an allergic reaction." Like an arrow from a bow, his gaze sprang at her. "Stay here, Arie. I'm calling 911!"

Dad raced out of the living room and as the front door flew open, Arie pushed herself upright and looked toward her brother. After her adrenaline rush waned, she settled on the couch next to him, her arm looping around his shoulders.

"Just hold on a moment, Rudy. You need some extra support to get through this, but I'm here for you and Dad's gone to call for help."

"I'm...sorry." Rudy spoke hoarsely, a couple of tears trickling down his pale cheeks.

Arie tried her hardest to keep up a brave front for her brother, even though all she longed for was to shed tears with him. "It's not your fault," she consoled. "It's not your fault at all."

Upon entering the living room a few minutes later, Mom's hands hovered over the bridge of her mouth. Right behind her was Maggie, who was backing away and shielding her eyes after catching sight of Rudy.

Mom squatted in front of Rudy, her hands fluttering as she stretched out to brush away his hair. "Why'd you let your brother get stung by wasps?" Her question was directed at Arie.

Arie's throat grew rigid as she struggled to express her feelings in words. "I was stung too, Mamm, but I got Rudy off the porch before more wasps could sting him."

"Well, that didn't do much good, now did it?" Mom's extended breath rattled her slim lips. "You weren't keeping a close eye on Rudy."

If the feeder hadn't been hung by the door, this wouldn't have happened. It wouldn't have done any good to voice the thought, so Arie pushed it aside. Her mother would have become more frustrated, and her poor brother would be subjected to their anger while already feeling miserable. Tears welled in Arie's eyes as pressure accumulated in her forehead. *I just can't seem to* do anything right. I always try my best to do what I can, but it never feels like what I say or do is good enough.

"*Ich will mit geh.*" Maggie blubbered, permeating through the sense of panic and disorientation that flooded Arie's consciousness.

"No, Maggie, you can't come along. You need to stay here with your sister."

Mom glanced over her shoulder at Arie, the veins on her neck clearly visible. "What are you standing around for, Arie? You need to let your daed know if you're willing to take over the store while we take Rudy to Parkview."

"R–right, Mamm. I'm sorry." Arie choked the words out. "I need to use the restroom first."

Arie scrambled down the hall to the bathroom, despite the fact that the world seemed to be whirling around her. She noticed splotches of darkness in her vision and staggered slightly as she shut the door behind her. Due to her visual impairment, Arie ended up bumping into the wall and sinking all the way down to the floor.

Isn't that selfish of me? Having such thoughts in this crucial moment, when Rudy was relying on me. I was too caught up with my own foolish thoughts. In an effort to retake control, she blew out several puffs of quick breaths and hugged her shoulders. Inevitably, Arie was unsuccessful, heaving a few sobs till tears streamed down her face. The dark spots gradually receded from her view. *Mom is perfectly entitled to be disappointed with me. I should have been watching Rudy, but I failed him. My only hope at the moment is that he'll be okay. But what if it's too late already? What if I hindered Rudy from arriving at Parkview sooner and getting him help in time?*

Chapter 10

Arie was left to handle the store while her parents went with her brother to the hospital in the ambulance. Maggie was there with her, but fortunately, she kept to herself for the most part in their father's office. Before they'd left, Mom had told Arie that she didn't want Maggie to witness anything else and that it was too much for a child of her age. Maggie had been wailing when the ambulance drove away, but she had gradually quieted down. Arie's mother had also advised her that she could close the store early if things became excessively difficult for her to deal with. Thankfully, Arie would be flipping the OPEN sign to CLOSED soon, and only a couple of people had wandered in since she'd been managing the checkout counter.

Arie struggled to put into words how she'd been feeling about her brother's predicament. All her thoughts were sporadic, filled with too many questions. How could a typical day transpire into life-threatening circumstances so quickly and in such an abrupt manner? Her parents and brother had been gone for a few hours, and now it was a waiting game. Her mind's eye flicked back and forth between images from earlier—the intense redness of Rudy's lips and how Mom's face had been engraved with sheer horror as she hurried over to the once-exuberant youngster.

At the hourly interval, Arie turned her head toward the wall-mounted rhythm clocks they sold in the store. Their resounding, uplifting melodies detracted Arie from her own thoughts momentarily. Since there was a lull in shoppers entering the store, Arie went into the back room and dragged out a box to restock some of the products that were absent from the shelves, particularly down the aisle where the kitchen supplies were located. Finding things to do diverted her attention from the concern she felt for Rudy. And if she did a few extra things in the store, her parents would have less to worry about when they returned to work tomorrow morning.

The corded telephone on the counter caught Arie's eye. It was a business phone, used strictly for business purposes. She was dismayed that her parents hadn't called from the hospital to give an update on Rudy's condition, which would have eased her mind. If she owned a cell phone like some Amish young people, Arie could have contacted 911 right away when she'd seen how swollen Rudy's arm had become from the wasp sting. Arie wished she had a way to contact her parents, even if for a moment, so she'd know if her brother was okay and would be coming home soon.

Arie was in the middle of arranging jars of fruit spread on the shelf. She picked up one of the glass jars too abruptly, and because she wasn't holding it tightly enough, it toppled out of her fingers and shattered on the newly installed flooring. Rigid shards of glass and strawberry glops surrounded her feet.

"That's just great," Arie groaned. "Of course, I'd have to go and do something so stupid. Dad's going to rightfully blow a gasket if the new flooring is ruined."

"Arie?" Maggie neared Arie, passing between the shelves'

columns, before coming to a standstill. She pointed. "Is that—"

"Yes, Maggie, it's jam, and don't come any closer because there's glass all over the place here. Would you please bring me a broom and dustpan and some paper towels? You know where those are, right?"

Maggie bobbed her head and swerved out of sight past the aisle. Since Maggie knew where the supplies were kept, it took her no time to bring over what Arie required to clean up the strawberry mess. Arie promptly thanked her sister before stooping down to the floor and ripping the paper towels from the roll.

Mindful of the fragments of glass wedged in the fruit preserve, Arie wiped as much of the mess up as she could and then inspected the glossy surface of the floor for chipping. Thankfully, there wasn't any, proving the epoxy's resilience was a plus. *What would've happened if it had been any other type of flooring, such as tile, with all that sticky gunk seeping into the grout?*

"Arie, why haven't Mamm and Daed come home with Rudy yet?"

Arie arched her back while taking the broom and dustpan from Maggie. "I'm wondering the same thing. But I've never experienced an allergic reaction before, so I'm not sure what goes into treating it. I'm sure that from now on, our brother will need to have an EpiPen with him at all times, in case he comes up against something he's allergic to and has a severe reaction."

"What's an EpiPen?" Maggie asked.

"It's a medical device that helps with allergies. Rudy may need to carry one with him in case he ends up getting stung again." Arie swept the remaining shards of glass into the dustpan in a continuous motion.

"Am I allergic to wasps too?"

"You might be, but some allergies arise over time." Setting the dustpan and broom aside, Arie knelt and cupped her sister's shoulder. "You may not be allergic right now, but as you grow older, your body might reject some things."

"That's so scary. Rudy looked like he was in a lot of pain."

"He was. That's why our brother needed to go to the hospital, so the doctors could properly treat him and prevent his condition from worsening."

"What if it does get worse, Arie? What if Rudy doesn't come home?"

"Maggie, we have to hope and pray that he will." Arie brushed away the tears that streamed down her sister's cheeks, right along her chin. "It's okay to cry. It shows how deeply you care for our brother."

Arie's sister crumbled into her arms. "Why aren't you crying, Arie? Don't you care?"

Arie hitched a breath through gritted teeth. Whenever Arie began to cry, her parents always warned that it was improper and would make her siblings feel even more frightened, so she should put on a brave face for them. Maggie and Rudy were already dealing with their own personal burdens, so it wasn't fair for her to heap more on them by allowing her pent-up emotions to show.

"Like you, I'm concerned about Rudy." In order to stop the tears seeking to escape her eyes, she squinted and blotted at the moisture with her finger. "However, it's out of our hands right now, so I'm going to do what I can around here for our parents until I'm certain that Rudy is okay."

"I'd feel better if you cried with me." Maggie sniffled. "You said it's okay to cry, so you shouldn't hide behind your smile."

Arie thought long and hard about how much of a hypocrite

she was. Arie couldn't expect her sister to express her emotions when she constantly suppressed her own. Here, she attempted to set an example for her siblings, but Maggie saw right through her ruse. Arie's lips quivered uncontrollably, and tears spilled over as she brought her sister into a tight embrace.

Maggie had fallen asleep on Dad's office chair, lolling up against the back cushion, by the time Arie flipped the sign around, wrapped up inventory management, and cleaned up for the doors to open the next day. Arie couldn't get over the fact that, like their father, her little sister would settle into a chair and sleep without any issue. Drool had leaked from the sides of Maggie's mouth in place of the tears that had previously fallen. The likeness between parent and child was remarkable at times, and it didn't help that Arie's sister had inherited her father's hair color and smile.

Arie scooped Maggie up and carried her over to the entrance of the building, officially locking up and heading out in the mild summer weather. The howling of the neighbors' dogs rang true throughout the neighborhood as she proceeded toward the house.

Maggie weighed less than a small bale of hay, so holding her sister in her arms and laying the young girl on her bed was almost effortless. Given what had transpired earlier today, she had every right to be tuckered out. Despite her longing to get some rest, Arie thought about all the things she could and should be doing right now.

Arie decided it would be prudent to begin preparing supper since it was almost six o'clock. Even though Arie wasn't much of a cook—at least not as enthusiastic about it as her mother—she had undoubtedly picked up some tips from watching her over the years. Keeping it relatively simple, she opted to make some scalloped potatoes.

Arie got out a baking dish, Yukon Gold potatoes, onions, garlic, and the rest of the ingredients, which she planned to dice on the cutting board.

She whisked the contents inside the skillet for a few minutes before lifting the spoon and moving the pan from the stove. Peeling and finely slicing the potatoes, she stacked them on the bottom of the dish and then layered everything else, including additional potato slices, atop of them. Arie paused to admire her work before opening the oven door. An influx of radiant warmth swept across her face, and she glided the ceramic platter carefully inside. The scallops would be ready to eat in an hour or so, and hopefully, she and Maggie wouldn't be the only ones enjoying them this evening.

Arie took a moment to head over to the bathroom, squirming a little as she recalled her time spent lamenting there. Was it normal to experience such foreboding? Although Arie was unable to determine the exact moment she'd first started having the foregoing issues, they tended to be exacerbated by heightened feelings. Arie slumped against the sink and gazed at her reflection in the mirror. The only obvious sign of Arie's exhaustion was her slightly sunken eyes, but she felt as though her energy had been physically siphoned. Sometimes she wondered whether everything was in her head. Her parents were right: Arie had a tendency to exaggerate at times. It was merely a falsehood of her own devising. It made sense that when Arie was younger, everyone thought she was overly sensitive.

After scrubbing her hands in the sink and drying them on the towel, Arie clicked the door open and set foot in the hallway. When she wandered back to the kitchen to check on the scalloped potatoes, she heard the sound of her mother humming her usual tunes. The dishes clanged as Mom lined up a plate in between the steel ribs of the drying rack. Arie chastised herself for neglecting to drain the soaked dishes in a timely manner before Mom got to them.

"Hi, Mamm," Arie greeted, hoping her mother wasn't too engrossed in humming while drying the dishes to hear what she'd said. "Where's Rudy? Is he doing okay?"

Mom tilted her head to see Arie. "Your father carried him to his bed, and he's resting now."

Arie lifted her head and whispered, "Thank the Lord." But her abdomen constricted. It was clear by the seriousness of her mother's answer and the way her shoulders were bowed that she wasn't entirely relieved. "How about you, Mom? Are you doing okay?"

"Could be better." Mom flopped the dishrag on the granite countertop. "Let's have this conversation in the living room. I need to rest my legs."

Nodding without words, Arie stood by in silence until Mom left the kitchen, at which point she trailed behind her like a chick being led by a mother hen. Arie took a seat next to Mom as she settled on the couch.

With an extended, uneven sigh, Mom crossed her ankles and pointed her knees toward Arie, saying, "We need to monitor Rudy for the rest of the night. It was a pretty severe reaction to the hymenoptera venom, but as it turns out, wasp allergies are distinct from honeybee allergies. So, it's possible to be allergic to wasps and not honeybees. Rudy has to have epinephrine on him, and I'll be telling him he can't wander around barefoot anymore. But knowing your brother, he'll probably do it anyway."

"I don't know. He may be more cautious from now on. After being stung by them as a child, I can say that I certainly was."

"Except you did not have a life-threatening reaction, like your brother did." Mom frowned. "He should be terrified of wasps, not you. Before this, I believed that none of my children had problems at all. On top of everything else, this is just one more thing for me to worry about."

"I wish I could've been with you and Daed at Parkview to be supportive," Arie murmured, interlocking her numb fingers. "I'm sorry I wasn't much help."

Mom's eyes expanded a margin. "What are you talking about, Arie? You watched the store for us and kept Maggie busy. Not only that, but you treated Rudy's injury. He told me what you did for him. Your haste saved your brother's life. Rudy's very grateful, and so are your father and I."

"But what happened was my fault. I let him get stung since I wasn't watching him."

"Is this because of what I said earlier? Arie, you should stop harping on that. I was upset at the time, and it was wrong of me to blame you for Rudy getting stung. We didn't know he had an allergy, and you can't watch your brother every minute." With a smack of her lips, she patted Arie's upper arm. "To be honest, I don't know what I would do without your help with the children. I'm under a lot of pressure to help your daed keep a roof over our heads through the work we do at the store. You're a good daughter, Arie. I don't tell you enough about how respectful and responsible you are. I sincerely hope you have the heart to forgive me for what I said earlier today."

Is Mom saying that because she truly appreciates what I do, or because she wants me to quit harping on it? Arie wondered as she peered at her lap, reluctant to meet her mother's deep ebony eyes. She observed a little clump of strawberry preserve that blended into the burgundy fabric of her dress. Arie questioned how long it would be until Maggie mentioned the broken jar and how quickly Mom would change her mind about what a good daughter she was. *If she were aware that I've been keeping secrets this entire time, would she still hold that opinion? Mom has always lived the right way, and what am I doing? All I'm doing is pretending.* Her eyelashes clung together as she fended off her tears. *Calm yourself, Arie. Be the mature person you should be. There's no need to let yourself get overwhelmed, since that only serves to make matters worse.*

Arie's arm grew taut, so she kneaded the couch arm to relieve the strain. "Mom, it's all right. I'm just glad to hear that Rudy is doing better."

"Well, aside from that, I've sure had a long day. I need your help fixing supper before the night is over."

"Scalloped potatoes are already in the oven."

"I appreciate that, but surely we'll need something to go with those scallops, Arie. You can set the table while I steam some asparagus and brussels sprouts."

Together with her mother, Arie footslogged out of the living room like a wound-up toy. Despite Mom's assurances, a peculiar sensation resided in her chest. She thought back to what Lorrina had said—that masking her passions compromised her honesty. Arie had grown weary of pretending, but if it meant causing a rift between her and her family, was it really worth it?

I wish there could be less expected of me when it comes to watching out for my siblings when I'm at home and not working. My parents should hire someone to watch the kids, but I highly doubt that's ever going to happen.

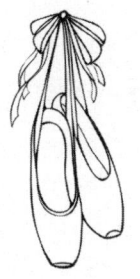

Chapter 11

"All right, I'm back. I got what I needed over at Yoders'." Edwin took a seat across from Markel in the restaurant where they had gone for lunch.

"What exactly did you get over there at the popcorn store?" Markel questioned as he bit into a slice of his single-serve cheese pizza. "You don't even like popcorn."

"Markel, it's not for me. I bought something for my girlfriend."

"Why? Is her *gebottsdaag* coming up?"

Edwin rolled his eyes in frustration. "Arie was over at our house for her birthday months ago. When there was snow on the ground."

"I'm pretty sure that was Christmas last year."

"Yes, that's why Arie was the only one who received something." Edwin swept a finger over the Corn Crib Cafe's menu. "You know, you can give someone a gift, even when it isn't their birthday or some special holiday."

Markel scowled. "You can, but it's totally unneeded and a waste of money."

"The brief lifespan of your relationships is a wonder."

"Is that how you keep them? Through bribery?"

"It's not bribing, Markel. My girlfriend has plenty to contend with at home, being the oldest child and shouldered with too many responsibilities. Arie's always thinking of others and tends to neglect her own needs. So, I do all I can to assure her that she matters as much as everyone else. It's about showing you care, even if it's in small ways."

"Jah, except a bag of popcorn won't make her life easier."

"How come you're so fixated on how I go about my business? I can't expect you to get it since you've only dated for a gnat's lifespan," Edwin quipped.

"You know, I can see where your girlfriend's coming from." Markel smirked. "Being the firstborn and constantly being expected to look out for the snotty little babies in the family is not easy."

"Ah yes, a two-year age difference. That's exactly the same. You didn't have to wrangle two babies. Our mom did that."

"Hey, show some respect. I've taught you what to do on plenty of occasions, Edwin. Without me, you wouldn't know how to do much of anything."

"Yeah, right. And I'm sure you're going to impart wisdom to our new addition in the family. You taught me exactly what not to do, if anything."

"Enough of the brotherly bickering already," Keaton, who sat next to Markel, protested. Edwin had about overlooked the man, nibbling on his meal in silence the entire time. "Just because your dad isn't working with us today doesn't give you two leeway to argue, and I'm not gonna be your would-be father while he's not here. I'd like to have a leisurely lunch before we head back to work."

Edwin apologized to Keaton, while glaring at his brother, who chose to play around on his phone instead of offering an apology.

He wondered how much of a challenge that cage-shaped chandelier above them must have been to install. All Markel could say was that he was glad they were roofers rather than electricians, because being exposed to electrical currents and the danger of potentially being electrocuted did not appeal to him at all. The irony of his deliberations, given that his employment was fraught with potentially fatal hazards, was not lost on Edwin.

If our father were here right now, he'd probably side with Markel. Despite him being Dad's namesake, for some reason, Dad has much higher expectations of me than Markel.

Edwin looked at the menu again and figured he couldn't go wrong with a sweet potato quesadilla. *Here I am complaining, yet Arie has two younger siblings to look out for. At least my brother and I are on equal footing, despite his refusal to believe it. I truly hope Arie is holding out well. After drill practice tomorrow, I will definitely find time to visit her for a while.*

After finishing their lunch, disposing of the table scraps, and leaving the premises, Edwin couldn't help but notice his older brother had concealed the remainder of his food in a grease-splattered napkin.

"We gotta top off the gas before heading out to our next job," Keaton commented.

"All right." Edwin nodded. "Let's get the fuel and head on out."

They approached the cargo van in the parking lot, and while Keaton went to the driver's side to start it, Markel set his leftovers on the hood, unfolding the napkin to expose what was left of his meal to the humid August heat. Drawing his phone from the pocket of his trousers, Markel raised it almost to his nose and leaned against the front passenger's door.

Something gliding from above caught Edwin's attention. There before him was an onlooker perched on the van's hood. From the looks of the small bird, it was a house sparrow, no doubt in search of any morsel it could find. As it crept closer and closer, the sparrow's claws tapped on the coated steel surface, fanning out the distinctive markings on its wings.

Edwin gave his brother's arm a little shove. "Markel, hey! You've got a feathered companion there."

Markel whipped around, stowing the phone in his pocket. "Get away, you pesky bird!"

The sparrow landed right beside the pizza slice and nipped at the cheese several times, while revealing the black bib under its beak. His brother swept his hand, and with a small string of cheese attached to its beak, the hungry bird flew into the sky, leaving behind the now tainted food. The sheer chaos of it all overtook Edwin, and he couldn't help the boisterous laughter as he watched Markel floundering and yelling baseless threats of retaliation.

Still chortling, Edwin approached him and said, "See, Markel? That's why you shouldn't use your phone so much."

"Reveling in my misery?" Markel jabbed Edwin with his elbow. "You're a real jerk, you know that?"

"It's one of the many things you taught me." Edwin grinned. "Don't fret, Markel. I'll order some mozzarella sticks for you to take with you to the next job. My treat for giving me such riveting entertainment."

"You did all you could for your brother. You know that, right?" Lorrina asked, bending at the waist and setting her hedgehog on the freshly cut bed of grass beneath her feet.

Arie shrugged. "Soon after it happened, my mother scolded me for failing to stop him from being stung. She's not wrong. I froze, and if I hadn't been concerned about getting stung myself, maybe I could have prevented what happened to Rudy."

"If so, your dad is also at fault for downplaying what you had told him about everything that unfolded." Lorrina dropped down on the lawn and patted the space near her. "The problem is that you care too much about how your choices impact other people, which makes you unsure of your own judgment."

With a sigh, Arie stretched her legs and slumped to the earth, accepting her friend's invitation to sit with her. "I would much rather be uncertain in some respects. It's this feeling that nothing is ever enough. Though I always have hope for the future, I do wish I were more like you and knew for sure what I want out of life. I try to be grateful for what I have, but I feel like my efforts are in vain. Either I'm doing too much, or I can't take enough. It's hard to tell." With a laugh that sounded more strangled than she intended, Arie slipped off her kapp and tossed it on the grass. "I'm sorry. I know I'm not making much sense."

"It makes plenty of sense to me. You're plagued with trying to uphold unrealistic expectations. How can you be content with that? Being thoughtful is a very worthwhile trait, and you are a generous person, Arie. However, some people will regrettably overlook that or take it for granted. That's why you've gotta speak up for yourself and take action for a change." Lorrina bent her head toward the lush grass, her tight curls cascading over her sweatshirt-clad shoulder. "That little goober. Look at him go."

Quillace had the appearance of a cotton cloud with rows of toothpicks on top, but his elongated muzzle and drooping, beady eyes would cause even the most cynical person to be smitten. The way the prickly little darling scuttled about reminded Arie of the possum she had seen in the arborvitae from her bedroom window the previous evening.

Arie pinched her lips together. "Is it safe for hedgehogs to roam around a yard like this?"

"Actually, they're a common wild animal in the UK. They also help gardens thrive since hedgehogs eat many types of bugs. It's all right as long as I'm keeping an eye on him and there aren't any potential hazards, like a lawnmower. Quillace needs all the fresh air and freedom from his cage that he can get."

They sat in silence, looking down at the hedgehog as he surveyed his surroundings. He'd speed up, then slow down, pivoting his gaze every which way, then move around again. Arie's thoughts drifted straight into the trove that she had ventured into on multiple occasions while the quiet moment dragged on.

Wiping perspiration from her brow, Arie asked, "I take it that you'll be beginning ballet soon?"

"Yes, in a couple of weeks." Lorrina lifted her hand and gasped. "Goodness, Arie. Do you want to attend classes with me? Is that what you're hinting at?"

"Don't get too excited. If I went, all I would do is watch, and that's it."

"Is that what you want to do?"

"I think I might want to go."

"It's a yes or a no, Arie. Which one will it be?"

"Yes, I want to go watch."

"Even if it upsets your parents?"

"I'm just going to watch, Lorrina." Arie hesitated, then added, "Admittedly, I've been questioning things regarding dance again. And you know, I sometimes want to explore where my absurd ideas take me."

"There's nothing absurd about trying to figure out what you

want to do with your life. You're an adult after all."

"I don't plan on dancing, though. For a myriad of reasons, I can't. I'm aware of this, and all I want to do is witness it once more, like I did when I went with you and your mother many years ago."

"But Arie, you love to dance. From the time I first started teaching you ballet, that's what has brought you so much joy. You asked me with such enthusiasm, but now you're seeking to avoid it, and you aren't doing a very good job."

"Wouldn't I be wasting my time, though? It's not like I'll be able to apply ballet for anything in the future. All I'd be doing is fostering my parents' disappointment in me. They have other things to worry about, so I don't want to add this to their load."

"We've had this conversation many times throughout the years. To determine what's best for you, you must choose to embrace the discomforting parts of the uncertainty." Her friend lifted herself up on her knees and brought a hand to her mouth. "Oh, hang on. Looks like he's running out of energy."

When Lorrina rose from the ground and wandered over to her pet, Arie flinched as her friend laid a palm right on the quills and lifted him up.

"Doesn't it hurt to pick him up like that, Lorrina?"

"It does, but you become used to the pricks from the quills after a while. They're more of a line of defense than an instrument of warfare." Lorrina sauntered back over, seating herself in the imprint she'd made in the grass. "Hey Arie, I understand you may not want to do this, but I believe you should let your parents know first."

Arie narrowed her eyes. "Wouldn't asking for their permission make me less of an adult?"

"It's not about seeking permission. It's about being truthful with others while also being truthful with oneself. I get that it's a tough pill to swallow, because my own mom gets defensive about anything that goes against what she wants. But you need to push past what your parents may think and just do it. Living for their approval is not a fulfilling life, Arie, because you can never fully attain it."

"Alright, fine. I'll tell them. Who knows? Maybe they'll be okay with me going this time." She lowered her head a bit in Lorrina's direction, arching an eyebrow. "Wishful thinking."

"And if they're not pleased, remind them that you have every right to decide what you want out of life, and you're going to do it anyway." Lorrina rubbed her thumb under Quillace's mouth, and he seemed to melt right into her touch. "Do you want to pet him? Just be careful. Some of the quills are sharp, especially around the top of his head."

The hedgehog's cheek contoured to Lorrina's palm, and with a twitch of his snout, he licked her skin in a brief gesture. It reminded Arie of when her sister grew drowsy: full of energy one moment and sleeping the next. Arie chuckled as she extended her other hand to him and stroked behind his round ears. For a brief moment, she considered how similar hedgehogs were to a sea urchin with the quills, but her mind reverted back to what Lorrina had said to her.

Lorrina doesn't understand how much tougher it is to be in my position. Arie pulled her arm away, lightly clasping her hands in her lap. *She doesn't have as many responsibilities to uphold, and I'm not sure if I should even bother going to the dance studio. I feel so torn over this. Should I try bringing this up with my parents and risk upsetting them, or should I simply forget about it? Would I truly want to live my entire life wondering what could have been?*

Chapter 12

BRENDA MANEUVERED ABOUT IN THE store's home decor section, replenishing the shelf with small pillows suitable to put on one's couch or loveseat. She set the box down, wiping away the dust that had collected along her apron.

I need a break from work, she thought. *My back hurts, my legs hurt. Everything hurts.*

It didn't help that they'd been dealing with a dubious supplier over the phone. Brenda and Jerome had established a strong relationship with the company and had been doing business with them for a couple of years. But for whatever reason, their expectations were no longer being met. There was a fairly good chance that she and Jerome would have to consider another supplier, which was a nuisance she'd rather avoid.

"Look, Mamm. See what I made? Do you like it?"

Brenda regarded the sheet of paper Maggie held up before her. She'd noticed it was an upside-down heart-shaped doodle of some sort, but broke away from the sight of the paper in a manner of seconds. "Jah, Maggie. That's very nice."

"You didn't even look that long. It's not good, is it?"

"Maggie, can't you see that I'm busy right now? Why don't

you go show your father or find something else in the store to do right now, okay?"

"Like what?" Maggie held the piece of paper in one hand while her other hand was anchored to her small hip.

"You could get out the broom and sweep. The floors are always dirty."

Brenda heard a grunt from the youngster, followed by the pitter-patter of her daughter's feet trailing away. Brenda appreciated only having Maggie to care for today. Rudy had gone over to his friend Samuel's place and would not return home till later. Brenda had to go to their house across the road and give Samuel's mother Rudy's EpiPen because he'd left it at home earlier in the day. For whatever reason, her son did not seem to grasp the significance of having an EpiPen, even after experiencing such a severe reaction to the wasp sting. Brenda had to wonder whether it was deliberate rebellion on Rudy's part or just a case of forgetfulness.

Maggie will be going off to school with her brother in the mornings, and I still need to let his teacher know about the wasp sensitivity, Brenda reminded herself. Rudy had started school when Arie was about his age now, and he'd accompanied his elder sister to the schoolhouse in the morning not so long ago.

Brenda's thoughts continued. *It won't be long before Rudy will be in eighth grade. When that day comes, I hope he is as obedient as his big sister and does not act recklessly. Arie never sneaks out or participates in rumspringa like so many other teenagers do. Maybe there's hope for my other children since their sister isn't exposing them to that type of behavior.* She glanced toward the front of the store. *Speaking of Arie, she should have arrived home by now, and she'd better have a good explanation for leaving me to restock the shelves on my own.*

As soon as the front door cracked open, Brenda peered up from her task in anticipation of greeting whomever had come into the shop. She soon knew, however, that it was Arie who had finally trod on in when her white kapp and cornstalk stature came into view. Brenda's irritation increased when she looked at the wall where their battery-operated clocks all hung and was reminded of Arie's tardiness. She kept on with her task, until Arie approached.

Exasperated, Brenda picked up the emptied cardboard box and said in a firm tone: "You're late, Arie."

"Jah, I know, and I'm sorry, Mamm. I can see you're in the middle of something, so I won't bother you with what else I was going to say—"

"Of course I'm bothered. The cooler weather we had was brief, and now it's too hot in this building." She gestured to the box at her feet. "I'm also swamped with work." Brenda lifted her hands in defeat and released a huff. "Oh, never mind. Just tell me what you were going to say."

"Really, it's fine. Not anything important."

"Well, it was significant enough to disrupt what I was doing, so you may as well tell me."

"Okay, well, uh... I talked with Lorrina recently and—"

"Lorrina, the dancer girl? You're still friends with her?"

"We talk every now and then. I stopped by her place on the way back from work."

"That explains why you weren't home right away. What about Lorrina?" Brenda's irritation grew with each word she spoke.

Arie's hazel eyes flitted all over the store and then briefly back to Brenda, as she stuttered, "Sh–she asked me to go with her to observe one of her dance classes, and I think I might want to, Mamm."

Brenda stared at her daughter, entirely dumbfounded by what

she'd said. *Could I have misunderstood, or perhaps the fatigue I feel from the busyness of today has affected my hearing.*

"We're not discussing this here." Brenda motioned to Arie with the curl of her finger. "Please, come with me."

Brenda led the way to the office at the rear of the store. When she and Arie entered, Brenda's husband sprang out of the desk chair with furrowed brows.

"Jerome, I need to speak to our daughter alone." Brenda made every effort to remain calm, despite the cords in her neck throbbing from an attempt to keep her voice down.

"What's going on?" he asked. "Is it something I should be part of?"

"No, that's okay. I can deal with it on my own. This matter is between mother and daughter." Brenda glanced toward the office door. "Oh, Maggie is going about the store on her own, with a piece of paper and a box of crayons. Or maybe she set those aside and got out the broom to sweep the floors. Oh, and the front counter needs to be managed while I'm away."

It appeared from Jerome's quick nod that what she had said to him was sufficient, as he did not inquire further and headed out of the room, leaving only her and Arie.

Brenda struck her dominant hand against the desk like a gavel. "I can't believe you're asking for this again. The thought of you going to your friend's dance class is too much for me to take in."

"Lorrina only invited me to sit and watch, Mom. Where's the harm in that?"

"There's plenty of harm. It undermines all that we've taught you about avoiding temptations and worldly things." Brenda swiveled the office chair around and plopped down on the leather cushion. "All your friend is doing is trying to drag you down with her."

"Lorrina is not dragging me down." Arie tugged at the waistline of her dress. "I was barely a teenager when she invited me the last time, and I can see why you didn't want me going with her before. But I'm not a child anymore, and you've said yourself that I'm a responsible young woman."

"Well, you're not being responsible right now. If anything, you're demonstrating to me that I can't rely on you to make the right decisions."

Brenda's statements elicited an immediate reaction from her daughter, who yanked her kapp ties, nearly pulling the head covering off. "Mom, I'm really hurt that you don't trust me."

"You saying that hurts me. You think I know nothing? This is not about distrusting you, Arie. This is about you choosing something that will lead you down a path of destruction. All I'm doing is making it clear to you that it's a terrible idea."

She kept her gaze fixed on Arie, waiting for her to drop the whole thing and leave the office. When her daughter remained motionless, Brenda observed the mounds of paperwork on the desk. Jerome had assured Brenda that he would clear up the clutter, but he'd yet to do so.

"How about my part-time work?" Arie asked, pulling Brenda's thoughts back to the matter at hand.

Leaning forward, Brenda hooked her index finger on the hardware of the upper drawer. "What about it?"

"Before you changed your mind, you said I could only work in the store for you and Dad. But then you gave me permission to work part-time in the gift store in town."

"That's completely different." Brenda hunched in the chair, folding her arms. "Working at a gift shop doesn't conflict with the values of our church."

Arie emitted a groan. "You're saying this as if I've already become a church member."

"Aren't you planning to join? You're dating a fine young man who seems to be set on getting baptized and joining the church, yet it seems as though you don't want to walk the same path. That makes absolutely no sense, Arie. To me, it sounds like you aren't thinking things through, and all I'm doing is reminding you how ridiculous it is to disregard those in your life for selfish wants. Here I thought you were level-headed, Arie. I suppose I was mistaken."

Another lapse in conversation threw them into bothersome silence. Brenda wanted this to be over, so she shoved the papers on the desk aside and observed the handcrafted brown maple surface underneath. After a few seconds passed, Brenda scooped up some of the papers and stacked them, to give the impression that she'd moved on from the distasteful interaction with her daughter. With a cracked, wispy voice, she heard Arie murmur something. Through her sparse lashes, Brenda looked up at her.

"Huh? I didn't quite catch that, Arie."

"I said, 'What if I went to see Lorrina dance without your permission?'"

A sharp sensation, like an open flame spreading along Brenda's flesh, sent an abrupt surge up her wrist. Like fierce winter kindling, her inner temperature felt like it had been set ablaze, and those last layers fueled it like flaking bark.

"Arie, you are living under your father's and my roof, so you must do as we say. If you don't agree with our rules, then you know where the door is located." Brenda blinked at her daughter in a flurry of agitation, aiming her finger at the office door, as if to make her point. Then she lowered her hand and went back to fussing with the papers. "Now, you can either work here in the store or head over to the house with your sister. Just be sure you keep a close eye on her."

Brenda glanced up from the desk and saw the hem of Arie's dress as she breezed through the doorway and out of sight, leaving Brenda alone to deal with the adverse consequences from her daughter's display of defiance.

Unbelievable that Arie would choose to act in this way. Where did I go wrong? Giving a deep sigh, Brenda laid her head on the desk where it was devoid of paperwork. *Have I been doling out my teachings in the wrong way, causing my daughter to question her faith? Perhaps God has given me more than I can handle.*

Resting atop a heap of hay, Arie squinted up to where the weathered wood knots cracked open. The remnants of sunlight crept through, and Arie felt them glinting along her cheekbones.

"I don't have much time to think about this." Arie fussed, forming her sentences aloud. "Since they don't offer classes for adults over the twelfth grade, this is Lorrina's final year. It may be my only chance, but I'm not sure I should take it."

She stretched and pointed her toes, her legs dangling at the edge of the bale. Within the depths of herself, Arie's thoughts whirled like a raging storm as she reenacted the exchange she'd had with her mother. Mom was much shorter than Arie, yet she managed to seem taller than Arie in comparison. After their most recent interaction, Arie understood that she'd drooped like fresh-cut flowers when Mom's eyes burrowed into her.

"If I don't do what I want to do, I'm miserable. If I decide to do what I want, then I'll still be miserable. Why can't I just be happy with what I have? My mother's right when she says sometimes I'm not a level-headed person. I'm with Edwin, and my life is going well, so why am I struggling to accept it? What if Mom's right about my friendship with Lorrina too?"

Stilling her limbs, she hefted her legs onto the hay and turned over to Aster's deserted stable. Arie had planned to take her horse out and ride somewhere when she headed out to the barn. But instead, Arie had let Aster roam the pasture, well aware that in her present frame of mind, she couldn't ride her mare. As Edwin had often reminded Arie, horses were attuned to their rider's temperament, and her mare would surely sense her mood. Arie lay motionless, studying every aspect of her situation to the point where even dancing didn't appeal to her.

Arie scrubbed her face with frigid fingers against her scalding flesh. "I'm an awful person for ever considering this, aren't I? Mom made her feelings obvious, and I ignored them. I know what the proper decision is, so I need to quit toying around with my selfishness. I have to move on and not let my infatuation with ballet get in the way of what is important."

Drawing the fullest breaths she could muster, Arie tried to disregard the relentless discomfort in her throat and focus on the pleasant scent of the hay here in the barn. "My life is a gorgeous bouquet filled with beautiful flowers, except I'm not sure whether the flowers in the arrangement are mine."

"Jerome, have you taken care of the boxes of tax documents that are piled high in our dining room corner?" Brenda inquired, pressing the button of her battery-powered handheld mixer. She inhaled the delightful fragrance of her coffee frothing. "Tax season came and went months ago, and whoever we've had visit our home has eyed that mess every time."

"Can you give it a rest, Brenda? I'll get around to it when I find the time."

"Our house is beginning to look like it's been torn up by a tornado with all of this clutter, and I'm sick and tired of the disarray in here. Even our office in the store is still a mess. It's spreading everywhere."

"Why are you so riled up over it?" Jerome asked in a snarky tone. "No one but us sees our office anyway."

"But it would make our lives so much easier if we were organized. After we close for the day, can't you at least tidy up in here? I know you're annoyed with me bothering you about it, but think how you feel when you walk into someone's home and they haven't cleaned up after themselves."

"I don't really care that much, honestly."

"And yet, I've heard you gripe about it."

Jerome smacked his lips in a deliberate manner. "Brenda, changing the subject, I have to say that I'm a bit concerned about Arie."

"Why's that?" When her brain finally caught up to what he alluded to, Brenda set the mixer on the kitchen counter and looked toward Jerome, folding her arms. "Were you listening in on my conversation with Arie earlier, or did our daughter tell you what had been said?"

"She didn't say anything about it to me. Your voice tends to carry, and the office door was slightly open. At any rate, I know what was spoken between you two yesterday. You should really be concentrating more on that." Backhanding the page he'd been reading, Jerome fluttered the unfolded newspaper in his hand while squinting in the light from the gas lamp above. "Well, I'll be. According to this excerpt from *The Budget*, Pennsylvanian David Miller and his family finally welcomed their first grandchild into the world. Exciting news for the Millers, wouldn't you agree?"

Surprise, surprise, Brenda pondered, groaning and shaking her head. *The only reason my husband is bringing that up is to draw attention away from the fact that he hasn't cleaned up our workspace in months. I know very well that I'll have to circle back to it later.*

Carrying her coffee cup to join her husband at the kitchen island, Brenda slid out a seat and replied, "You have every right to be concerned about Arie, regardless of your pitiful attempt to change the subject. I can't believe after all this time, that she still wants to dance."

Jerome laid down the paper, clenching the curling strands of hair surrounding his chin. "Brenda, you were getting too heated with her, don't you think? Arie said that she just wanted to go watch. Our daughter never actually said she was gonna dance."

"What do you suppose watching would lead to? If our eldest daughter began dancing, is that something you would approve of?"

"No, of course not, but Arie should be making decisions based on her own views since she's mature enough to do so." The clatter of his multivitamins resounded as they tumbled out over his calloused palms. Among all the things Brenda struggled to persuade her husband to do, she offered an unspoken prayer, thankful that Jerome had finally begun taking the vitamins she'd advised for his health.

Like a pendulum, her leg swung back and forth underneath the island counter. "Making her own decision is not a good thing if she decides wrongfully. If Arie were to begin taking ballet lessons, there's a good likelihood that she would abandon the Amish faith. It'll trickle down to Rudy and Maggie as well. We don't want that for our family, and I've witnessed it happening many times with other Amish families."

"Brenda, you don't think there's more to it than that? Is your biggest concern that without our daughter's assistance, you can't manage the store with just my help?"

"What are you getting at, Jerome?"

"I'm saying that we depend on Arie for a lot, and I'm sure because of that, she doesn't have much breathing room to figure herself out."

"I am sure that Arie has figured herself out. I taught her to be a responsible woman in the areas where it counts."

"We could always hire a sitter to come and watch the kids or employ someone to help us out at the store," he suggested.

"Jerome, we don't have the funds to hire anyone to work for us. We're barely making ends meet, and Arie gets along well with her siblings and knows what they need, so there's no sense of having someone else watch them. Besides, she'll have more free time when they both set off for school in the mornings."

"Or I can manage the store by myself while you watch the youngsters when they get home from school."

"We committed to doing this alongside each other, and you can't do that solo." Brenda got up and flicked a hand in front of her nose. "I don't want to talk about this anymore. Just please clean up after yourself."

Brenda couldn't interpret her husband's expression, but he let out a modest cough. When she didn't get an answer, she abandoned her morning coffee and crouched down to fetch the stockpot in the lower cabinets. She wanted nothing more than to get started on supper preparations. She intended to prepare a lentil soup to serve with garlic bread made from scratch. The ingredients for the bread would be combined in a glass bowl and kept there while the dough gradually rose. For an idle moment, Brenda hummed, delighted in the task ahead of her.

"I get where you're coming from," Jerome affirmed. "But we both know how exacting our parents were. It's likely that we'll push Arie away if you keep being overly authoritative with her."

Brenda weighed her husband's comments while listening to the hailstorm ricocheting off the windowpane. They'd been subjected to a downpour that carried on throughout last night, and the inclement weather outside didn't appear to be waning anytime soon. She had been unyielding toward her children at times. Brenda's upbringing taught her how to distinguish order of precedence. For Arie's younger siblings to have guidance, it was essential for her daughter to lead by example. The oldest was supposed to protect and look out for the younger ones, and Arie had been vigilant ever since Rudy was born. She'd caught onto that from Brenda, and it wasn't straightforward since Brenda didn't have that kind of guidance growing up. She had to learn how to take charge and be dependable, yet every now and then, Brenda questioned whether she'd actually gotten the hang of it.

"All I know is that if we're lenient with the rules we have set, we cannot expect any of our kids to handle themselves well." Brenda placed the pot on the stove and stared up at the ceiling, beyond the layers of paint the color of corn silk that adorned the kitchen walls. "We're really spreading ourselves too thin, aren't we? Do you feel that our children will find out one day that we have little idea what we're doing, even after all these years?"

"Hard to say for sure. As quickly as we figured out our parents weren't sure of what they were doing with us, it's possible that they already knew about the areas they had failed." Jerome looked at Brenda with a steady gaze. "Although we will never be perfect parents, the important thing is for us to keep doing our best and put our faith and trust in the Lord."

Brenda gave a slow nod, knowing that her husband was right. The question was, could she remember to trust God and not try to solve every problem in her own strength?

Chapter 13

ALTHOUGH THE HAIL HAD STOPPED, the splendor of golden rays hadn't broken through the gray skies. Gusts intensified with the summer torrent, accentuated by an eerie dimness and enormous white and gray clouds covering the countryside with a steady downpour. No one had shown up today in their store, so Brenda was left to perform menial tasks, all the while watching Maggie. In practical terms, though, she was mostly mopping the diluted traces of soil that Rudy and Jerome had left behind on the floor. Her husband and son had gone out again to check on how their animals were faring in this afternoon storm, leaving Brenda and Maggie alone in the store.

As she sauntered across the room to the front windows to gaze out at the surroundings, Brenda spotted her husband approaching from the gravel walkway that led to the store. The pools of water beside the storefront no longer rippled, indicating that the rain had finally let up.

"That was some downpour we had for a while," Jerome commented, followed by a shrill whistle as he opened the front door and entered the store. When he stepped into the light provided by what little the overcast sky would allow in, Brenda noticed that her husband's face was quite wet and his beard held much of the residual rain, all except for the occasional droplets that escaped and landed on the floor.

"I just mopped the floors again, and now you're back in here sopping wet." Brenda's lips flattened as she pressed them together.

"Can't be helped. I have no control over the weather," Jerome countered. "At least you won't have to drag the hose across the lawn today. One thing is for sure—all of the plants have gotten their fill of *wasser*."

"That's true, and now Arie doesn't have to worry about watering when she gets home. And Jerome, after shaking off your jacket, please wipe your boots on the welcome mat outside the door. That is what it's there for, you know. You and our son have tracked in the mud, so you should both mop it up, not wait for me to do it for you."

"*Jah*, but you're so on top of things that you haven't even given me an opportunity to do so," he remarked with a wink.

Instead of going back and forth with her husband on the subject, Brenda glanced at Jerome's side as he swaggered past her wearing a grin. "Why isn't Rudy with you?"

"He found some frogs in the ditch and wanted to relocate them to the area near the garden, not far from the faucet."

"And you abandoned Rudy, leaving him out in this nasty weather by himself? What were you thinking?" She pointed a finger at him.

"Our boy wanted to have some fun, so I allowed him to do so." Jerome yawned, gesturing to the rear of the store. "Speaking of fun, I have hurdles of my own to jump over today, so I'd better get right on it."

Brenda stared at the mess on the floor. *So he's going to just leave it there? Completely unconcerned with it? This is why I need Arie here. Jerome should've brought our boy back to the store, not allowing him to handle creatures that could potentially give him salmonella. And Rudy could possibly wind up with a fever if he stays out there for too long. This makes me wonder sometimes if my husband lacks consideration for me or our kinner.*

"Jerome, the sky looks foreboding. Nobody has shown up here today. Perhaps they sense it too."

"People moan and groan over a little bit of rain, even though it does so much good for our farmlands. Guess a lot of people are just afraid of getting a bit soaked," he responded.

"And bombarded by pebble-sized hail." Brenda paused to glance out the front window again. "But doesn't it feel familiar?"

"In what way?"

"It reminds me of when we first had only Arie, and the impact on all the housing and families in the days following the catastrophe we all faced."

"You mean the Nappanee tornado, years back?"

She gave a deliberate nod. "Exactly."

"Brenda, it's normal for us to get storms in the summer. And even if, by some chance, a twister were to develop, it probably wouldn't make its way through here. Besides, the ones that have formed lately in this part of the state weren't anything serious."

Brenda gritted her teeth, dismayed at her husband's apparent refusal to grasp the potential danger of the weather. *Sure, most of the bad storms we've had around here haven't been fatal, but they were prone to causing significant damage.* Brenda remembered the ferocity of the tornado that took place in the beginning of autumn about eighteen years ago. It had blown through northern Indiana during the evening hours. Although their farmhouse was well off the tornado's path, they'd heard that many people had witnessed all types of wreckage the tornado had caused. The twenty-mile trajectory brought about tremendous damage, including deconstructed rooftops, bent power poles, knocked-down cinderblock walls, and uprooted trees.

The one saving grace, especially given that it was an EF3 at its height, was that no one had perished in the calamity. In any case, the families had to confront the natural disaster, both in the moment and in the days and weeks that followed. They could very well be grappling with it themselves in a matter of minutes.

"If a tornado should approach, what if it were to demolish our house, or even worse, our store?" Brenda moved away from the window to face Jerome directly. "How would we care for our children without a source of income and having to pay for losses that could add up to thousands of dollars? Have you considered any of this, Jerome?"

"So let that be the Lord's will. But like I said, it's doubtful to be any cause for concern."

Brenda was neither convinced nor reassured by her husband's words. She stepped up to the window again. All was quiet, but not in a manner that mirrored the disposition of serenity. The typical bird chattering had stopped. She whipped around, went out the door, and over to the edge of the storefront to take a gander at the sky. From the east, an audible wailing graced Brenda's ears, and she could visibly see a wall of gray in the foreground.

With tornadoes, there wasn't much forewarning about when and where they'd form. The storm and cloud patterns were the only indicators, but that didn't always guarantee a twister was about to touch down. But every fiber of her being knew to take those patterns as a warning for what might be heading their way. The creak of the door behind Brenda resembled a feline's trill, and she swiveled around to see her husband looming as he joined her in peering out at the ominous sight before them.

"Jerome, we need to close up the store and take cover."

His eyes widened at the sight. "I'll round up Rudy, and you take Maggie to the basement. We'll meet you there."

"Now hold on, Jerome." She gripped her husband's jacket as he lurched forward from the awning. "What about Arie? She'll be home from work soon."

"We don't have much time. All we can do is take care of what's in front of us, Brenda. I'm sure Arie's safe and far enough away from here. And if she's not, I'm certain that she's smart enough to seek out a place to take cover."

Brenda darted back inside, shouting Maggie's name as she scanned the row of aisles, hoping to locate her daughter somewhere in the building. She was thankful the business was not full of customers right now. Finding the child while maneuvering through a throng of people would have raised the stakes for getting her family to safety. No sign of Maggie in the central area of the building, so Brenda burst into the office. At first, her pulse throbbed at the sight of a vacant room, and Brenda wondered where the young girl had gone. But then she heard a soft whimper. She pushed the chair aside and crouched down. Maggie was beneath the desk, her face smeared with tears that gleamed from the hanging, battery-powered lamp..

"Maggie, sweetheart. Please come out of there," she entreated. "We need to leave. It isn't safe here in the store."

The youngster nodded, crawled out, and stretched out her arms. Brenda gathered Maggie up and held her close. She then reached up all the way on her toes and unhooked the lamp, recalling that the one in the basement had been damaged from when her husband had gone on the hunt for the stepladder. Still holding Maggie, Brenda fled to the house. She wished she had more time to properly secure everything. But there was nothing that could be done about it now.

Upon entering the basement, Brenda set Maggie down and instructed her to keep her head low. The howling gale from outdoors bore down upon them, and the pungent stench of mildew filled Brenda's nostrils as she inhaled. Mounting fear of the whirlwind forming just above the staircase caused her lips to tremble.

"Is what's out there gonna get us?" Maggie questioned as she drew her knees close to her chest.

"Of course not. We'll only be sheltering down here for a little while, until the storm passes."

"Where are Daed and Rudy?"

"Your father is getting him, so don't worry. They'll make it to the house and join us soon," Brenda assured, attempting to uphold a brave face as she glanced down at her daughter. Tears clouded Brenda's eyes, threatening to spill out like rain and land on Maggie's hair.

"But what if they don't make it back? What if the storm gets 'em?"

"Maggie, listen to me. I don't want you saying things like that. I promise you the storm isn't that bad. Your father and brother will be here soon, and the tornado won't be anywhere near us." It wasn't right to lie to her daughter, but Brenda didn't want to frighten the girl. Besides, maybe she hadn't told an untruth. It was possible that things weren't as bad as she now believed them to be.

"If it's not bad, why are we hiding?"

Brenda's tongue felt sore from being pressed against the roof of her mouth. "Maggie, we just need to remain here for a while. Trust me. It's much safer for us to be in the basement."

"Arie isn't with us either," Maggie cried as she clawed at the sides of her plump face. "That means Arie isn't safe, Mamm. What if something happens to her?"

"Crying won't help us, Maggie!" Brenda took hold of her daughter's hands. "By saying all of those things, you're only making yourself feel worse. Please calm down and try to stop crying."

Maggie covered her flushed, puffy face with both hands briefly before pulling them away. A deep ache swelled in Brenda's throat, seeing that her daughter's sobs came in brief bouts, yet her tears continued to flow.

I can't believe I made her cry more, but how else am I supposed to get her to stop? She exhaled sharply and smoothed her palms down the neckline of her dress to rid herself of the moisture. *Don't get angry, Brenda. Maggie is still a very young child, and she doesn't understand what's going on. I need to stop letting my kids agitate me and help my daughter calm down.*

Brenda drew Maggie into an embrace, massaging her fingers along the ridge of the child's scalp. "Listen, I'm having trouble with all of this too. We just need to pray, Maggie, and ask God to keep us safe. Now, I need you to be strong right now. Can you do that for me?"

"Jah." Maggie bowed into the nook of Brenda's shoulder and muttered, "I'm sorry, Mamm."

She kissed her daughter's forehead and whispered, "We're all right. We're going to be fine." Brenda's words were spoken more to soothe and convince herself that everything would work out, but she had no grasp of the outcome. Her son and husband were yet to tromp downstairs to huddle with them, and that was a concern.

Lord, please let this storm pass over without causing harm to anyone. Brenda's lower lip trembled as she held her daughter and prayed fervently. *Please guide my family and myself through this potentially dangerous situation and ensure our safety during this moment of unpredictability in our lives. All of this is up to You.*

The storm's winds were relentless, circling about Arie's body, with forthright wrath. It had begun with a slight drizzle the moment she'd set off early in the morning. While working in the gift shop, the gentle rain had given way to ice chunks that battered the sidewalks and automobiles passing through downtown Shipshewana. By the time Abigail entered the gift shop, Barbara had advised Arie to hold off on going home until the storm had passed. Arie had considered calling the phone in her parents' store to let them know, but once the pouring rain stopped, she figured it'd be better to just go on home. If Arie got home too late, her mother would likely suspect that she was at Lorrina's house again, and Arie was already in enough trouble with Mom.

When she arrived at the property's boundary, Arie stared out past the space beyond the store and her home. Debris fragments journeyed skyward in the swirling funnel cresting the expanse of terrain. The funnel was pure white and slender, but once it had swept up more of the prairie's landscape, what whirled along within it showed it had sucked up lush vegetation and the loamy soil beneath it. Arie then knew she was in dire peril.

This can't be real, Arie thought, trying to make sense of it all. The tornado appeared to be stationary, but according to what she'd heard from her parents and others in the community, if it seemed like it wasn't moving, it was heading straight for you.

Arie clamped a hand over her chin and lips before hoisting her purse strap farther up her arm and hastening toward the house. *Everything will be fine. Several times Mom has gone over what to do if something like this should happen. I just need to get into the house and downstairs to the basement. Everything is going to be okay.*

Things around her began to slow down. The sooty little spots that she was all too familiar with started to bulge up the corners of Arie's vision, and her legs felt as if they were bogged down. Pushing against the forces from the whirlwind took a lot out of her, and the adrenaline rush she'd been making use of faded, revealing to Arie that she was out of energy. She tried to make her way to the steps leading to the basement, but the low-lit luminaries within the house's threshold whirled about her, threatening to hit her. Arie had no other alternative but to stumble into the bathroom before she collapsed.

I'm nauseous, and I feel like I might faint. Struggling to breathe, and overcome by her weakness, Arie let out a ragged breath. *I should have fought against this. If I weren't such a bundle of nerves, I could have made it to the basement.*

She hunkered down in the bathtub, dragging the shower curtain over her, but she knew that these measures would do little to no good if the tornado ravaged their house. The inky specks took over her perception fully, as though her eyes were glued shut, yet they were very much open. She pushed both hands to her ears. Even though Arie's fingers were as cold as if she had been gripping a fistful of ice cubes, warmth permeated her extremities. The hurled fury of the storm pounded against the farmhouse's eaves, just as Arie imagined ocean water with crashing waves would sound. The only thing that drowned out the turmoil outdoors was the monotonous ringing in Arie's ears, which mingled with the frantic din of her thoughts rushing to the forefront of her mind.

I wasn't reliable enough, even when I tried to do my best. I can't even take care of myself, let alone my family. I have always tried to keep everyone else happy, but for what? I'm left all alone in the bathroom, and no one will come looking for me.

From within, the memory of her leaping in the hayloft filled her mind. Arie remembered how overwhelmed she'd felt when Edwin had stumbled upon her secret and seen her dancing. He had been able to coax her out of that panicked state by sitting beside her and encouraging her to breathe. But despite her best efforts to take deep breaths, it didn't subside right away. Arie yearned for Edwin's company and his help to weather the storm, regardless of the outcome. Any other person who might have been dating her would likely have been put off by learning about her dancing, but Edwin had been exceptionally compassionate. Arie had confided in him about her troubles beforehand, and now she had no idea whether they were meant to be together, if this morning was the last time she would see her family, or if Arie would ever see her best friend again. Another thought crossed her mind.

If I don't make it through this, I'll never have a chance to go to Goshen with Lorrina and watch her dance. Arie laughed at the absurdity of being concerned about her plans at this very moment, but the longer it persisted, the more the white horses galloping and her mother's voice from her dream could be heard above the raging winds outside the window.

Now I'll never know for sure if I was really destined to dance, all because I was too terrified of what my parents had to say. I would've simply seized the opportunity to follow my dream if I had known. It's out of reach if the storm strikes, but maybe part of me wishes it would.

The tub was empty of water, yet it felt like it was filled to the brim with frigid liquid, fully submerging her and causing her to sink farther down. *I've spent much of my life trying to mean something to those around me, but what if I never mattered to them? Maybe I should be left alone here. My parents don't really understand me. I'm just a burden. I'm only deserving of their attention when my actions meet the standards they set for me, and I fall short every time. I had many chances, but I wasted them all. I truly want to understand who I am and at last see myself.*

Arie sought to focus on anything but the loud whistling of the wind and the ripping and tearing of what she assumed to be the roof's framework above her. She couldn't hear it over the racket, but Arie could tell her screams were hoarse, as if she'd swallowed a wad of sewing needles, points freshly sharpened. Arie heard a loud thump, followed by the sound of glass rupturing, and she felt the weight of window fragments smacking the shower curtain's canvas.

"Dear Lord," she hollered. "Please help me!"

Chapter 14

With the bathroom window broken, Arie could hear terrifying sounds of the tornado more clearly. As she reinforced her hold on the rim of the porcelain tub, Arie hunched farther down, her heart hammering as she tried to be mindful of the glass on the shower curtain. Arie's back muscles were pricked by the firmness of her spine against the bathtub. Listening to the curtains tearing and sounds of suction coming from the window, Arie wondered whether she would be swept into the vortex.

The wind picked up, and Arie heard branches slam against the exterior of their home. She flinched at the possibility of being lifted from the bottom of the tub. She glimpsed her father stepping into view and pulled herself up as the dots that had taken up all of her vision began to vanish.

Arie collapsed into her father's arms, savoring the inviting embrace as he maneuvered them past the bathroom door and along the hallway. He hadn't held her like this since she was about Rudy's age. Arie felt comforted knowing that her father would carry her at any age if necessary.

"I'm all right, Daed." Arie patted him to get his attention. "I can walk on my own."

There wasn't a trace of him hearing Arie's words until he released his hold, and her toes skimmed the floor. He slung his arm around Arie's shoulders, guiding her down the flight of stairs and into the basement. The walls of the musty room held pronounced images of shadows from the battery-powered light positioned on the dust-covered bookcase in the corner.

"Oh, thank heavens!" her mother proclaimed as she neared them. She craned her head toward Dad. "Where was she, Jerome?"

"Rudy and I had just gotten inside the house, and I'd sent him to the basement when I heard glass breaking in the bathroom. I went to investigate, and that's when I found her."

"Are you hurt, Arie?" Mom asked. "No cuts from the broken glass?"

Arie shook her head, weary and feeling as though her soul was undone. "I—I wonder how bad the weather is."

"Your father claimed that it isn't too bad out there, and I'm praying that he's right."

Arie drooped against the wall and darted a glance to her mother. "From the bathroom, it sounded like the roof was tearing apart."

"Try not to worry. What matters most is that we are all here together, and everything will be fine."

Arie noticed Mom's freckles crinkling up on the bridge of her nose—just as prominent as always, even under the low light.

"Why were you hiding in the bathroom when we'd previously spoken about what to do in case of severe weather?"

At the thought of contributing to her mother's stress, Arie's chest constricted. "I messed up. I should've planned better, but I didn't, and I'm sorry."

"I'm not trying to be harsh, Daughter, but I was concerned

about you and whether you were still downtown in the gift shop." Wincing, she cupped the side of Arie's cheek. "I don't know what I'd do without you, Arie. You matter so much to me. You know that, right?"

Despite her mother's sincere remarks, Arie couldn't help but feel a flicker of bitterness roiling in the pit of her stomach. She hoped that her mother wouldn't tell her how she should feel. Why shouldn't she be concerned about this? They had no idea how extensive the damage would be, and the racket upstairs indicated that the tornado had begun to tear their house apart. But if what her father stated was true—that it wasn't so horrible out there—perhaps she was inflating the severity of it in her imagination.

"Come here, my dear daughter, and stop looking so dour." Mom took hold of Arie's shoulders and brought her in close. "It's all going to be okay."

Arie embraced her mother and muttered, "I love you." Dad gave her a hug as well. Afterward, Arie staggered on shaky legs to the area where her younger siblings sat close together on the other side of the basement. Maggie leaped to her feet and flung her little arms around Arie's lower body as tightly as she could, while Rudy remained seated, not saying a word. Arie knelt down beside her siblings, hoping her presence might make them feel safer and comforted.

After a time, the rumbling of the storm outside began to diminish, leaving them with nothing but the stillness of their world.

Brenda ventured out with her husband to inspect the tornado's devastation. Some of the garden ornaments were no longer pinned to the flower beds, the trampoline had blown over, and the bird feeders, together with the seed mixture, had scattered along the graveled pathway. Their barn, store, and chicken coop had not been disturbed, however. Thus, there were no frenzied hens roaming around the premises.

Even though their house was still standing, the twister hadn't entirely left it unscathed. While they hadn't been in the tornado's direct path, it did remove a portion of the roof's shingles. According to what an English neighbor had told Jerome, the tornado had touched down so abruptly that there hadn't been enough time to issue a warning. Fortunately, most of the homes on their road appeared to have suffered only mild damage. If not, the tornado could have prompted structures to give way like dominoes.

Jerome pointed to the roof. "From what I can see from here, Brenda, it doesn't look that bad."

"Not that bad? Jerome, we'll need to lay down tarps before the roof can be dealt with."

"We can always hire Arie's boyfriend and others who work for his father to do the job. Maybe I can even help out."

"I don't think so. You're not getting up there and potentially falling off, dear." Brenda groaned. "As if we need one more thing to worry about."

"You're right. I will need to lay down the tarps for now. At any rate, I reckon it'd be best to close the store for the remainder of the day."

"I'm on board with that idea. I believe we should all take a siesta—maybe for the rest of the day."

"Siesta Key? I wouldn't mind some Sarasota sun on the beach." Jerome chuckled and nudged her arm.

"Ha! Very funny. I'm all for a vacation, but we should wait until our kids—especially Maggie—are older."

Following their exchange of laughter, silence settled over them like a heavy blanket. The prospect of having to endure the process of reassembling everything in the house sent Brenda's mind reeling. It served as a reminder that all they had established on this piece of property and the years they'd spent raising their kids could be stripped away in an instant.

"So, how are you feeling right now, Brenda?"

"I'm still shaken up, but counting my blessings," she answered, wetting her lips. "Even though we weren't warned about the tornado, I'm glad you listened to me and we went to the basement."

"It could have been so much worse, but we did the right thing by hunkering down in the basement. You know, maybe we should go out for supper tonight, or even order some pizza."

"Oh, no. I'm still set on making supper. I need something to take my mind off everything we've been through."

"Suit yourself." He grinned and walked away from where his feet had been firmly planted.

"Where are you running off to?" Brenda called.

"I'm asking Arie to help me check over the pasture fence. We can't let our horses get out."

Once her spouse was out of sight, Brenda glanced out at the collection of clutter in the side yard and considered rehanging the feeders, assuming they were not ruined. In the quiet of the evening, the finches that flew to their home chirped their afternoon melodies.

Lord, I'm not sure why You've allowed this storm, Brenda prayed. *However, I am grateful that my family is unharmed. I understand that if I want my children to trust You, I must first set the example. Even if I lose everything, I will continue to pray as long as there's air in my lungs.*

"I'm definitely gonna tack on some boards to replace the ones that got whisked into the enclosure. Debris from the pasture fence will need to be picked up in the vicinity. That way, no damaged planks can harm the horses."

"How long will it take to do all of that?" Arie questioned her father.

"Depends on what I have lying around. But at least we know what has to be done out here for the time being. Sometime tomorrow, I'll begin replacing the missing boards."

"I can start clearing the pasture of debris."

"You've been through enough today, Arie. Until I heard the bathroom window shatter, I didn't even think about going in there."

"I know I should've found my way to the basement. I'm sorry, Dad."

"No need to apologize. It was a good idea for you to hide in the bathtub, especially with the shower curtain covering you. You were shielded from the glass by it."

Arie scowled. "It wasn't very safe if I was about to be cut like an onion."

"All I'm saying is give yourself a pat on the back once in a while. You were in a state of panic, which would leave anyone in doubt of what to do. But you sought refuge in an appropriate place." With a soft grip on her shoulder, he said, "You ought to have greater trust in your own judgment."

Arie spun around to face Dad, unabashedly gaping at him. Did he just offer her words of encouragement? Her father's rare expression of praise filled Arie with a sense of tenderness in her heart. "I'm glad the storm wasn't more devastating and that we're all safe."

"Same here, as things could've taken a turn for the worst. I'm gonna go to the shed now and prepare for working on this. That's the problem with unpredictable weather: You have to pick up afterward, knowing that everything could be ripped apart again."

Her father took off, and Arie set out toward the barn to check on Aster and their other horses. She'd heard whinnying from the confines, and if it weren't for the hazardous debris littered about, Arie would let her mare and the other three out in a heartbeat.

A short time later, after making certain their horses were all right, Arie headed for the house. She'd barely rounded the corner, when she found her brother by the garden gate. Right above Arie was the wall where she'd hid in the bathroom, and where the decking and shingles had been torn off. She turned her head away, unwilling to look at the sight of it any longer. For the time being, the worst had passed, and Arie needed a sense of normalcy to carry her through the rest of the evening.

Rudy knelt in the yard, peering at the strewn debris from the row of arborvitaes. Raising a hand, he slipped a ripened grape between his teeth, fresh off the vine dangling from the garden fence. Arie understood that the storm had been a lot for an eleven-year-old to cope with. She joined him and rested her fingertips on his shoulder.

"Rudy, you've been awfully quiet. How are you feeling?"

He scrunched up his nose and grunted, and Arie followed his line of sight to the cavity in the earth near the faucet. His pupils were idle as he stared at the puddle of water, laden with remnants of the morning downpour. It seemed as though the boy was in search of something, but then he shrugged.

"Do you want to talk about the tornado?"

"Not really."

"What we went through was really distressing, and it can be tough to talk about. You don't have to say anything if you don't want to, but if you change your mind, I'm here to listen."

Arie's gaze went to the trampoline, which the storm had toppled over on its side. It had been moored down, but the heavy gusts severed it from its stakes. Thankfully, the trampoline's mat didn't seem to have any gaping holes or tears in it. All it needed was to be positioned back on its legs.

"How about we get the trampoline back up so you can jump on it again? Sound good?"

Rudy rolled his eyes. "You can't move the trampoline by yourself, Arie. It's too heavy for you."

"You're right, but that's why you're going to help me with it. Would you kindly assist your big sister with this test of our strength?" Arie coaxed her brother as she bent over, clutching her knees. "Or we might leave it as is, which means you won't be bouncing anymore this year."

She didn't have to ask the youngster twice, for he rose from the wet grass blades that had drenched his trousers' knees.

"Hold here on this side," Arie instructed.

Rudy did as he was told and thrust where the leg was on the trampoline, but his feet skidded on the muddy grass.

"Carefur, I—I mean careful, Rudy."

Rudy snorted, muttering her mispronunciation with mockery as he wiped his hands up and down his pant legs. They tried again to heave the trampoline, but they only managed to lift it a couple of inches before it slipped from their fingers. Arie tucked a wayward hair behind her ear and let out a strangled laugh.

"We might gain some leverage if we both attempted to be

on the opposing side of this thing," Arie proposed, pushing back her shoulder, resulting in a pop similar to unsealing a jam lid, and then there was a faint rush of ease. "What do you say, Rudy? Last-ditch effort?"

"It's no good, Arie. We need greater arm strength. Can we get Daed to help with this?"

"I can help!"

She whirled around, cutting her eyes to the source, and to her amazement, Edwin sprinted over to Arie with his arms outstretched.

"Edwin!" Arie exclaimed, approaching him midway and bridging the gap between them. Tears welled up in her eyes, and she gave Edwin a peck on the cheek before backing away in order to take him all in. "What are you doing here?"

"The weather had gotten so bad that we had to leave the job in Goshen and quit early today. Plus, your father called and asked us to help tarp his roof, so we'll do that yet this evening."

The mention of Goshen made Arie think of Lorrina, and a slight pang stirred in her chest. *I wonder how her family is managing and if they suffered considerable damages from the tornado?* Although Lorrina was technically her neighbor, she lived half a mile down the road. Arie mentally noted that she needed to call her friend soon.

"We could really use your help with the trampoline, Edwin. But I don't want to trouble you with it if you don't have time right now."

"No trouble. I'm more than happy to help with any fixes your father may need." He winked at her. "It's one of the perks of dating a handyman boyfriend. Now, let's get that trampoline back up."

Their efforts were greatly enhanced by Edwin's upper arm

strength as they labored together to raise the trampoline upward. In less than a few minutes, they were able to reposition it, and Rudy gave a round of applause for their accomplishment. Instead of taking Arie's advice to wait until tomorrow for the sun to evaporate the moisture, her brother retorted that he'd be "carefur."

"It'll need to be refastened to the ground with something more resilient," Edwin stated.

"Thank you for everything. Not only now, but ever since we've been together, you've been an enormous blessing. I can never express how much I appreciate you always being there for me."

"Don't mention it, Arie. It's what we do for those we care about. Also, I heard about what happened with the weather here while we were on the way back from Goshen. Keaton had the radio on in the work van, so it goes without saying that I had to make sure you were safe."

"Danki. We're doing okay. Fortunately, there was little damage, but given that it was just a small tornado, it's understandable."

"The tornado that went through this area wasn't that small, Arie." He motioned with his hands as if he had squashed an invisible ball.

"What do you mean?" Arie tilted her head.

"From what we heard on Keaton's radio, that tornado was an EF2, and although it didn't last long, it caused substantial damage in some places. One of our neighbors really got the brunt of it. Now, don't judge me. I only use this accursed thing for business purposes, and I just want to show you a picture of the house." He dug into his pocket, pulling out a smartphone. Edwin swiped his thumb across the screen in several directions, as if he was having trouble navigating the interface. He then held the phone at eye level for her to see. "Take a look."

Everything on the screen was laid waste. A downed power line leaned in front of the two-story house, and the roofing was severely damaged, with half of it torn from the rafters and trusses. The harrowing devastation brought a heaviness to Arie's heart.

"That's dreadful, Edwin. I had no clue it was that awful. Is the family all right?"

"It seems so. They did have an ambulance and a couple of police cars out front, but it didn't seem like anybody was being carried off to the hospital. Given the extent of the roof damage, I might have to talk about this with Reuben to see if we can organize a charity function for that family."

Her gaze lingered on the image for a time before closing her eyes, offering a silent prayer for her neighbors. When she finished praying and opened her eyes, she saw Edwin slip the phone back into his pocket.

"What about your family, Edwin? Is everyone else doing well?"

"Of course. On the way here, I stopped by the house, and my dad was there, since he's been spending more time with my mom and less time on the job sites. The good news is that the worst of it did not reach us." His eyebrows drew together. "Arie, are you all right?"

She attempted to gather herself to explain the thoughts running through her brain, still blindsided by what Edwin had shown her.

"Yes, I'm fine. I just can't comprehend the gravity of this situation. We could've... I could've..."

"Pay attention to what's in front of you, Arie. There's quite the load to unpack. You're here and unharmed, and I promise I'll be here for you."

Is God allowing me the opportunity to dance? Arie wondered unexpectedly. *No that can't be it. That would be ridiculous.* Arie's thoughts drifted back to the last conversation with her father and his advice to trust her own judgment. Unthinkable as it was to Arie, perhaps she needed to act in accordance with her desires. Dancing ballet in the barn and keeping it under wraps did not fulfill her aspirations. *I want to go, but I'm not comfortable upsetting my parents. That much I know. At the very least, I'll go watch Lorrina's class at the studio, and when I have time to call, I'll ask her about it. I owe it to myself, don't I?*

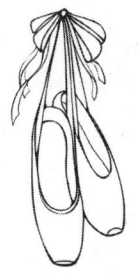

Chapter 15

As Brenda prepared Maggie and Rudy's lunches to take to school, she glanced out the kitchen window at a noisy woodpecker drumming on the trunk of a stately white birch tree that graced the right side of their yard. Meanwhile, two plump robins engaged in a tug-of-war over a worm that had been yanked from the grass by the most aggressive bird. Which robin would win out, Brenda didn't know, and at the moment, she did not care. There were other, more pressing matters going on in her life to be concerned about than which of the struggling birds would win their morning breakfast prize.

A few weeks had passed since the tornado struck their area, and Brenda was pleased that the section of roof on their house that had encountered some damage was now repaired and looked good as new. Other folks in the area had also received assistance in rebuilding and replacing items that had been shattered or destroyed during the devastation. Being part of a compassionate community, where people helped others without expecting anything in return, was a blessing.

Brenda put the finishing touches on Rudy's bologna and cheese sandwich, then took out two more pieces of bread to make

Maggie's favorite—peanut butter and strawberry jam. Today was the first day of school for the children after the summer break, and it was Maggie's first experience of being away from home all day to attend school with her brother. Brenda hoped her younger daughter would be a focused, motivated learner and that she would get along well with the other scholars her age.

It was customary for Amish children to learn the English language when they began attending class at the schoolhouse, but many young pupils, including Maggie, had already picked up a good deal of English by hanging out with their older siblings. Even so, being able to pronounce some English words was not the same as learning how to print or write them in cursive letters. Maggie would learn a lot in her first year of school, and even more throughout the course of her eight years at the Amish schoolhouse, located a short way from their home.

Brenda's gaze shifted to Rudy and Maggie, who were finishing their meal of cereal, banana slices, and glasses of fresh goat milk. She assumed they'd both be dreading the first day of school, but their upbeat demeanors told her otherwise. Maggie had confided in Brenda last night before bed that she was scared about enrolling in school. A brief explanation of what it would be like on her first day, plus a few tender kisses to her forehead, seemed to have put the child's mind at rest, because soon after Brenda had read Maggie a bedtime story, she'd snuggled under her covers and had promptly given way to sleep.

"All right, you two." Brenda crossed the room to stand beside the table. "It's almost time for you to wash up and head out the door, and I've already prepared your lunches. So please clear your dishes and place them in the sink."

Scooping his bowl, spoon, and glass from the table, Rudy replied, "Okay, Mamm."

Maggie sipped on what was left in her glass, followed her brother to the sink, and deposited her dishes after him. "I'm nervous, Rudy. When we walk to school, can I hold your hand?" she questioned, tugging on Rudy's shirttails.

His nose wrinkled, as if a foul odor had worked its way into the kitchen. "No way! No how! Not happening!" Rudy looked up at Brenda. "Mamm, it'll be embarrassing enough to walk with Maggie, but I don't wanna walk hand-in-hand with my baby sister."

"I'm not a baby." Maggie's bottom lip protruded. "I am six years old."

Rudy shrugged. "Makes no difference to me. You're younger than me, so that makes you a baby."

Tears welled in Maggie's eyes, and her chin quivered like a dislodged leaf fluttering in the wind. "Arie would hold my hand, and she's way older than you."

"What of it, Maggie? I don't like holding her hand either."

Warding off a headache with a massage to her temple, Brenda glanced at the clock on the far wall. Brenda was certain that she would have to walk Maggie to school herself if she didn't take immediate action, and she did not have time for that. The most pressing matter was that it would be time to open the business soon, and she needed to be present alongside her husband when the first customers of the day arrived. It wouldn't be fair to expect him to handle everything by himself, and Arie had already left for her job at the gift shop in town, so they couldn't count on her help this morning.

"Listen, Son," Brenda said, lowering herself to Rudy's eye level. "It's your sister's first day. If you walk Maggie to school today, and without complaint, there will be a few extra chocolate chip cookies on your dessert plate tonight. Sound good?"

He offered a wide grin, exposing his front teeth. "All right, Mamm. It's a deal." Rudy turned to face Maggie and patted the top of her head. "Okay, baby—I mean, little sister—before we leave for school, let's go wash our hands, and don't forget your face."

Having a retail establishment to manage and three children to supervise, Brenda was thankful for the moments when her family listened, abiding by what she asked them to do without protest. She exhaled a sigh of relief as the youngsters made their way down the hall toward the bathroom. At least one issue had been resolved today, and Brenda hoped there would not be several more.

Goshen, Indiana

"How did it feel to be working a full shift at the gift shop for the first time?" Lorrina asked Arie, who sat beside her in the passenger seat, as the traffic signal flashed green and she eased off the brake.

"Better than I expected. Barbara has been telling me that I've been really on top of things in the gift shop, and she had previously urged me to work there full-time."

"Will you continue doing it, Arie?"

"My mom wasn't thrilled when I told her I'd be working a full shift today, so I don't believe she'd be pleased if I said I wanted to commit to full-time. My siblings began their first day of school today, so they'll be gone for the majority of the day from now until late spring next year, but my mom still wants me at home when they return from school."

"That's unfortunate." Lorrina compressed her lips.

"It's fine. I'm just glad that the timing lined up perfectly for us to drive over to Goshen today."

Lorrina shot a glance at Arie, then back to the windshield. "So, was that your cover story?"

"C–cover story? No, I was being honest with you."

"Not for me, for your mom. That's the excuse you gave, so she won't wonder why you'll be late getting home—because you had to work longer hours today?"

"Remember how I told you I'd spoken with her?" Arie asked, following a brittle laugh.

"I do remember. And you did mention this to your mom, and from what you told me, she was dead set against it. You didn't tell her you were going anyway, did you?"

"I asked her, 'What if I were to do it anyway?'"

"I knew it. She doesn't know. Arie, you have this habit of not making things up but also not telling the whole truth. I get why you didn't tell her, but you know I don't condone dishonesty." Groaning, Lorrina smoothed her hands along the faux leather steering-wheel cover. "Do you believe your mom suspects you of going to the dance studio with me?"

"She probably doesn't think so, but I'm not sure. Frankly, I didn't think I'd ever go through with this either, yet here we are." With a sigh, Arie went quiet before continuing. "While I don't want to let my parents down, I also don't want to pass up this opportunity. You're right, though. I've been compromising my honesty, but I feel pressured to do so if I want to observe your dance class this afternoon. I know it's terrible."

"Hey, I get it. You're concerned about hurting their feelings. It shows that you care for them. But sometimes you have to ask yourself, do they care about how you feel or just what you say to them? Life is too short to miss out on what actually brings you joy."

The dance studio was sixteen miles from Shipshewana, with a twenty-minute timeframe for arriving there. The roads weren't too congested right now, and the conversation waned while they passed

Norton Lake. As they drove by the houses scattered throughout the expansive countryside, the steady hum of the car's engine filled the silence between them.

They soon arrived in Goshen, and Lorrina glanced at Arie as they drove by the Goshen Theater, aware that she was recalling her visit there with Lorrina and her mother several years ago. They ventured farther into the city until they reached the parking lot in front of the dance studio.

"Well, we finally made it," Lorrina announced as she rotated the steering wheel and slid between the narrow lines of the parking space. Shifting into PARK, she asked, "How do you feel about this, Arie? Any regrets?"

"Maybe a little," Arie admitted. "Even though I'm struggling to come to terms with my choice, part of me is also relieved. It's been a long time since I've seen actual ballerinas with my own eyes. Besides you, of course. Perhaps it isn't quite as beautiful as I remembered."

"Now you're just lying to yourself. Ballet is an immaculate art form, and you and I both know how invigorating it is to frolic around."

Arie laughed, but as she was about to open the passenger door, her hand visibly trembled.

"Arie, are you okay?"

"I don't know if I can follow through with this, Lorrina." She brought her hand to her kapp's ties, clenching them. "If my parents find out that I came here today, they might kick me out of the house. I can't do this. Coming here wasn't a good idea."

"Hang on, Arie. You can't possibly believe that. My mom says that all the time when I do something she doesn't like. If your parents are sincerely concerned about your well-being, they'll eventually understand why you chose to do this. I'm sure your mom doesn't want anything bad to happen to you, but I assure you that I've got your back. I fully support whatever you decide to pursue, as long as you stay true to yourself."

"I know you do. Thank you, Lorrina, for talking me through this, and bringing me with you today."

"Good. Besides, I'd have to miss the first part of my last year of ballet class if I take you home right now. Unless there is an emergency, my dancing instructor dislikes it when her students are running late or don't show up at all."

"Okay. I'm ready to go in, and I'll make an effort to savor every moment."

Lorrina nodded, but she couldn't shake her doubts about this ordeal. *Is it right for me to let my friend do this when she might wind up in trouble? I don't want her to lie, but I also don't want her to be deterred from doing something she wants to do. If only her mother didn't so strongly disapprove of ballet and wasn't so domineering.*

Inside the building, Arie and Lorrina meandered along the corridors, which were lined with numerous portraits, showing dancers of different ages and styles of dance besides ballet, as the dulcet tones of music guided them along.

Halting to take a gander at the walls, Arie's eyes trailed to one specific portrait, and it was of her friend, grinning with lips of rouge and rosy cheeks. Lorrina wore a traditional ballet gown, which featured an ivory lace overlay on the bodice and a tutu accented with a burgundy ribbon. Arie's mind strayed to the innumerable hours she had spent picturing herself on stage, adorned in those exquisite costumes, getting the chance to perform in front of an auditorium full of people. But there was a second individual posing with Lorrina, a young man whose arms were bound around her tutu's flared netting. His costume had the same color scheme as Lorrina's, but it was much more subtle in its design.

"That was from last year's showcase." Lorrina strode over to her. "Definitely one of my favorite costumes."

"Who's in the photo with you, Lorrina?" Arie questioned.

"That's Briar, the only guy in our class. He's a terrific dancer, but a little overconfident."

Arie narrowed her eyes. "You dated this guy, didn't you?"

"Too obvious? He kept bugging me to go out with him and eventually wore me down. We're good as dancing partners, but not as a couple. My mom couldn't get enough of him, though. She thought he was a charmer." Lorrina gave Arie's shoulder a purposeful bump. "We better hurry."

Arie's nerves flared when they entered the dance studio. There was so much to absorb in this new environment. Mirrors covered the walls of the large space, reflecting the dancers as they stretched and chatted with each other. Among the bushel of young ballerinas, a woman stood in the middle of the floor. She must have been the instructor Lorrina had mentioned before. Arie remembered that the teacher's name was Judith, but she was caught off guard by the woman's youthful demeanor. She had platinum curls tucked behind her head in a ponytail rather than a bun, and kindness shone from her brilliant blue eyes, putting Arie at ease right away. Lorrina told Arie that Judith had previously lived on the other side of the United States and had gotten into the Pacific Northwest Ballet in Seattle.

"Nice to see you all back here after a long summer break." The instructor welcomed each of her students and approached Lorrina and Arie. "Lorrina, good to see you again."

"Good to see you too, Miss Judith. I hope you don't mind, but I have a friend with me today. This is Arie Kauffman."

"What a lovely looking young woman you brought with you. And an Amish lady at that. Nice to meet you, Arie." Miss Judith curtsied before rising back up and extending her hand.

Still processing the fact that she was in the company of a seasoned ballerina, Arie shook the instructor's hand. "Nice to meet you too. I hope I'm not intruding, Miss Judith."

"Not at all, dear. Anyone is welcome to visit my class, so feel free to observe. We have chairs along the wall over there." She gestured to the area across the room. Until she'd captured all of the students' attention, Miss Judith clapped her hands. "All right, places at the barre, everyone!"

When the dancers got up from the floor, Miss Judith wandered up to the stereo, changing the track. A couple of the dancers then lifted up what appeared to be a portable barre and hauled it to the center, just like the one Lorrina had used for practice at home. The hitching rail in the barn sufficed, but Arie wished she had a ballet barre of her own, just like her friend.

The ballerinas wore tights and leotards and had their hair put up in buns, reminding Arie a little of Amish life. There were distinctions among the girls, including the colors of their leotards. A couple of them had wrapped skirts, while some donned leg warmers. The pastel hues of their accessories and the pink tones of their slippers were so visually appealing that Arie couldn't get enough of them. The rest of the girls' attire was a huge part of why Arie's mom took issue with ballet, because of how much a dancer's body was revealed wearing such outfits. That's how they had to be, though. Otherwise, their clothes would be too restrictive for the dancers, especially when it came to implementing flexibility in their performances. Taking a deep breath, Arie pushed the thoughts of her parents to the back of her mind and refocused on the class.

"Seven, and an eight. Port de bras forward. Good form, ladies," Miss Judith chirped. "Not bad for missing a few months of class."

Miss Judith led her students away from the wall and into the center of the room after they had been at the barre for about thirty minutes. From there, they moved on to exercises that didn't need assistance from the barre. These were where advanced moves were rehearsed with consistent repetition, and the exertion required for the agile movements left Lorrina's forehead sheening like a lake of ice in the dazzling morning sunlight. Then they lined up in the corner near the entryway, and each dancer moved across the floor in compliance with Miss Judith's directions. Despite how exhausted they must be, the dancers moved with grace and smiles, making Arie stare in awe and envy. They were propelled by adrenaline and dedication, and Arie felt completely involved in it, although anchored in her chair.

Is simply viewing a ballet class enough for me? Arie pondered. Her stomach quivered as she shifted in her seat.

"Balancé, balancé, take up as much space as you can along with the rhythm, ladies!"

After an hour and a half, Miss Judith ended the lesson with a bow and a reverence, dismissing them. Lorrina rushed over to Arie and explained that she had to use the restroom before they returned to Shipshewana. While Arie waited for her friend to return, Miss Judith had left the room and the studio floor was vacated.

The melody of the track continued to loop on the stereo, the piano keys entrancing, and she couldn't stand it any longer. Arie rose from her seat and ambled toward the middle of the floor. Her steps began as usual, but when she skidded gently and flicked her feet up off the floor, as if she were punting a small stone, her toes began to point, guiding her to the room's corner. Then, Arie transferred her feet to fifth position, then to a demi-plié, stretching her rear leg like the ballerinas had done before her across the room.

Normally, as she danced along the bits of straw scattered about the concrete flooring of the barn, there would be no music to coincide with her rhythmic motions. The only rhythm she had was the thrumming of her heart, caused by exertion and the fear of being caught in the act. But all of Arie's shortcomings vanished as she became engrossed in practice, and here there was no sense of worry. No one to criticize her as she spun like a tempest in the turbulent world.

Arie turned her head, and when she saw that the teacher and a few of the other dancers had stumbled upon her spontaneous choreography, she halted.

"That was wonderful, dear," Miss Judith exclaimed. "Simply wonderful. Have you ever taken dance lessons?"

"I actually taught her everything she knows, Miss Judith." From behind Arie, Lorrina appeared.

"It seems like you've done a mighty fine job, Lorrina. Do you plan on taking any classes here, Arie?"

Arie shook her head. "I only came to watch."

"But we'd love having you. Since your friend has been teaching you, and you seem to have a lot of experience already, I believe we may make an exception to the rule that a novice should be placed in a lower level. We still have room for our Tuesday and Thursday classes if you'd like to join us."

"There's no way I could do that. In any case, I doubt I can afford the classes."

"If you took two classes per week, it would only cost you slightly less than two hundred dollars a month. No charge for your first lesson since I need to assess your ability."

"You can easily pay for that if you work at the gift shop full-time," Lorrina stated.

"But some of the dancers take up to five classes a week, right? It'd be impossible for me to keep up with them."

"It's about having fun, Arie. Not all of the students are enrolled in that many classes. Plus, if you think you need a little more practice, I'd be happy to teach you like I used to."

Arie heard the excitement in her friend's voice. "I don't even have the proper ballet attire," she refuted.

"You already have a bun on your head, so you're almost there." Miss Judith grinned as she pinched at the stud that was bored through her earlobe.

"I can help you out with that, Arie." Lorrina patted her on the back. "I happen to have some unworn leotards and an extra pair of shoes."

Arie yearned for this moment, to say yes to Miss Judith's offer right then and there, but she couldn't stop thinking about her parents. She didn't have their permission, and Arie still wondered whether they might kick her out of the house if they found out. Feeling the enormity of these uncertainties setting in, ingrained in her since childhood, Arie's eyes ping-ponged first to her friend and then at Miss Judith.

"Something to think about, dear." Miss Judith smiled. "I hope you'll at least consider the offer."

"I'll think about it," Arie responded. In her heart, though, Arie wished she had answered yes.

Chapter 16

The surge of noise surrounding the contours that Arie laid her back against grew closer. Above the ceiling and through the walls, shaking and fluctuating surrounded her. Wooden framing severed like chopped lumber, all blowing away. The entryway of the farmhouse perished before her. Gaping cracks throughout the home gave way to the atmosphere, obscured by a massive barrier of clouds forming a swirling funnel. As Arie elevated off the ground, the eye of the vortex sucked all the oxygen from her lungs, and furniture revolved about, encircling Arie like the fringes of a gigantic bird's wing.

Gasping for breath, Arie was left in the darkness of her bedroom as the apparitions she'd endured wore away. Her nerves shot back like many pins in a quilt patch as she lay sprawled out on the mattress, struggling to move her arm to brush away the hair that had matted to her face.

Arie's gaze wandered to the ceiling, where the moon's beam, resembling an enormous slug, had left a trail. She wasn't sure what time it was, nor did she even bother to check. Arie would have to be up during the predawn hours, regardless, to begin another long day. Fortunately, it was an off-week Sunday, which meant no church service would be held in their district. But Arie had plans to see Edwin later today, and she shuddered at the thought of bringing up the dancing studio visit with him. If Arie were to follow through with attending Miss Judith's class, she would need to work full-time at the gift shop to have a proper alibi for her parents. She would also need the extra money working longer hours would bring.

Visions of the stirring vortex from her dream filled her mind. As soon as she regained sensation in her arm, Arie swept her tendrils away and lifted the sheets up to her exposed neck. Despite the need to drift off for more sleep, doing so would hasten the arrival of morning and she only had an hour or so left to sleep anyway. Perhaps if it had rained, the droplets hitting the roof might have lulled her back to sleep. Or maybe not, given that more downpours could bring another tornado their way.

"This is ridiculous. It wasn't real," Arie mumbled as she stroked away her stray tears mingled with sweat. "It was only a dream. A dream that could've very well happened."

She was on the verge of throwing the quilt off and going to the kitchen to make some tea, but Arie didn't want to disturb anyone who might still be sleeping in the house. While her eyes were closed, her mind stayed awake, and her incessant worries continued to chafe at her. Rolling onto her side, Arie folded her arms over her bent knees, and tucked her head down. She lacked the energy to reflect on the concerns that had robbed her of peace.

That afternoon during Edwin and Arie's scenic journey, the *clip-clop* of Daisy's hooves reverberated across the thicket of trees. The branches arched above, sheltering them from the brilliant rays shining down on them in the open buggy. As the asphalt rumbled beneath the buggy's axles, Edwin braced himself for the sudden vehicle coming up from behind them. He tugged the reins to steer his mare over to hug the shoulder of the road. Edwin assumed it was a semi-truck, and sure enough, the 18-wheeler accelerated past their carriage. He tasted the smog from the truck's exhaust pipe as it reached his nostrils.

Edwin glanced over at his girlfriend sitting beside him, who seemed to be staring at the schoolhouse with the basketball court and swing set out front. "Something's on your mind, I take it? I've got an ear to lend if you need one."

"I'm sorry, Edwin." Arie yawned. "I had a rough night, so I'm kind of out of it."

Edwin was about to ask her why she'd had a rough night, but Arie shifted her attention to him and said, "There's something I need to tell you, so bear with me."

"Now I'm a little nervous, Arie. Sounds quite serious."

"It isn't really. Sort of. Okay, here it goes." The green rim of Arie's irises caught the sunlight as she tilted her head. "I've been invited to take ballet lessons at Lorrina's dance studio."

"What?" Edwin yelped, resisting the urge to yank the reins. Arie appeared taken aback by his reaction. "I'm sorry for shouting. How'd that come about?"

"Well, you know, funny story actually. I was curious, so I went to watch. One thing led to another, and her ballet instructor saw me dancing at the end of the class."

He looked at her with strained eyes. "You didn't just watch, then."

"See? It's funny since it was a spur-of-the-moment decision that caused this to happen." Arie's back pressed against the upholstered seat. "All right, the truth is, sitting there wasn't enough for me. I wanted the thrill of moving about with the music in front of those studio mirrors."

In an attempt to get Arie to elaborate, he asked, "Was it as you expected?"

"It made me realize what I'd been missing out on. I've actually been wanting to attend lessons for a long time now, but after my parents found out that I went to a dance recital some time ago, I was afraid of upsetting them again."

"But you no longer feel afraid?"

"No, I still am. Despite that, I have a yearning. I've been giving it some consideration. What are your thoughts?"

"It doesn't matter what I think, Arie."

"Of course it matters. You're my boyfriend, and I want to be honest with you, and I want you to feel comfortable with doing the same."

"It's a lot to take in. I thought ballet wasn't going to be an ongoing thing for you." He sucked in a breath. "What about your parents, though? What are you going to tell them?"

"Nothing. I don't want them to find out, Edwin."

"Okay, but I found out. Don't you think it's a matter of time before your parents will too? Once they learn the truth—and especially if it doesn't come from you—they'll probably be angry that you didn't tell them about it."

"No, Edwin. Don't you get it? Before I went to the dance studio, I told my mother that Lorrina asked me to go. I hadn't spoken anything about dancing there, but she immediately scolded me as if I had already gone. I tried to be open and honest, but she was completely opposed to even the thought of me observing Lorrina's dance class." Arie slipped off her head covering and laid it at her feet. "My mother has no idea the toll this has taken on me, or how much I cared about not wanting to hurt her, and part of me doubts that she ever will. It has to be this way if I dance, Edwin. I want to be honest, but I'm put in a position where I can't be."

Edwin exhaled and brought Daisy to a halt at the stop sign. "Jah, that isn't right. My parents have given me and my brother far more leeway to try things out before we make a decision about joining the church. Markel took full advantage of it and continues to do so, but I have no desire to do the same. But I know that if I wanted to take on something I cared deeply about, and my parents said I couldn't, I would be quite *verzanne*."

"I wouldn't say that I'm angered, Edwin."

"It kind of sounds like you are, and why wouldn't you be?"

"I'm just worn out and apprehensive." Arie shook her head. "To tell the truth, when I was twelve, I asked my parents if I could take ballet lessons."

"Really?" he replied, after ensuring that he could make a left turn before gesturing to the vehicle approaching from behind.

"I kept telling Lorrina they were going to say no, but I finally gathered up the courage to ask. As you can imagine, it didn't go well. But my parents decided I should do something with my leisure time, so since I was old enough, they made sure that I learned how to ride a horse."

"You weren't even interested in learning to ride, were you?"

"Not exactly what I'd pick first. As much as I love Aster, there are times when riding with her can be daunting. At least my parents allowed me to do something, although I know they only let me learn horseback riding so I wouldn't bring up ballet again. Since I was still an impressionable kid, they didn't want me to stray from the Amish faith or get into trouble, so I can understand why they forbade me to try dancing years ago. That's probably how they feel about it. But I am an adult now, aren't I? Even as a child, I had to care for Maggie and Rudy when all I wanted was to be a kid." Above Arie's upper lip, her delicate little mole quivered. "I'm sorry, Edwin. I know I'm putting you in a tough position. What's wrong with me?"

Edwin leaned toward her, grasping Arie's shoulder, and planted a soft kiss on her temple. "Nothing's wrong with you, Arie, or the way you're feeling. But like I said before, I am worried about what dancing and not telling your parents could mean for us."

"I understand, Edwin. This is only until next year, and then afterward, we can focus on our future. After what happened a few weeks ago with the tornado, I realized that I need to live my life and can't have any regrets." She brought a hand up and intertwined it with his fingers still resting on her shoulder. "But I promise that you won't lose me, so if you don't want me to do this, I won't."

Edwin hadn't considered it before, but now he understood Arie's steadfast fascination with ballet. It was more than just something she enjoyed. It was about Arie feeling in charge of her own independence and discovering who she was as a person without being told how or what to do. Edwin could tell his girlfriend had been mulling this over and wanted to move forward, yet in spite of that, Arie still sought approval for her decisions.

"I think you should go for it," he said.

"Are you sure, Edwin?"

"Arie, I only recently discovered you were dancing in secret, but you've been dreaming about ballet for longer than we've been together. I'm glad you're being honest with me, and I won't discourage you from trying. You won't get a second chance, and I can tell you don't want to let this slip out of your grasp. Your parents have put a lot on you, and I'm not going to contribute to that. You have no say when it comes to people's choices, and that's why you shouldn't be consumed with what I, or anyone else, thinks. I don't want to stand in the way of your dream."

"I appreciate that, Edwin. Thank you." She leaned over, resting her head on his shoulder. "All right, so it's official. After you take me home, I'm going to tell my parents I'll be working full-time at the gift shop."

"I guess we're staying on the road then for the rest of our lives," he quipped.

"What? Hey, you said I should do this."

Edwin chuckled, "I know, I know. I was only kidding."

He returned his focus to the road ahead, watching Daisy's tail swing back and forth as she trotted. Still keeping Arie close, Edwin massaged his thumb on the rein braiding, but it was difficult to ignore the tingle that ran down to the base of his neck.

Am I doing the wrong thing here by encouraging Arie to do this? What if she prefers ballet over the Amish way of life? Edwin pondered, his heartbeat pounding in his ears. *I can't do this to her. The actual issue isn't her dancing; it's her need to keep it hidden. I've seen how much joy it has brought her, and I can't stop Arie from being happy. But if she fails to keep her promise to me and leaves the Amish faith, I don't see how this will turn out well.*

Brenda had spent her Sunday afternoon sipping iced tea while perusing the latest issue of the *Plain and Simple* magazine. The publication consistently featured a wealth of fascinating articles, not to mention do-it-yourself guides that often included pictures for creating a range of indoor and outdoor home accents and other practical items. Naturally, she'd always looked forward to folding the corner of any recipes that were highlighted, anticipating the opportunity when she would load up her shopping tote with the ingredients from the downtown market and lug them into the kitchen.

When Brenda heard a horse and buggy enter the yard, she got up from her rocker and laid the magazine on the corner table beside her chair before going to peek out the living room window. Sure enough, Brenda saw Edwin's horse and open carriage at the hitching rail.

"Arie and her boyfriend are back," Brenda called, glancing over her shoulder at Jerome.

From his lounge chair across the room, where he'd been dozing off and on for the majority of the afternoon, her husband's sole answer was a single word: "Nice."

"Remember our courting days, Dear?"

"Uh-huh."

"That was a special time in our life, jah?"

Jerome gave a nod. "For sure."

Brenda stepped away from the window and ambled over to stand beside his chair. "We've certainly raised our daughter right. I'm glad Arie has a steady boyfriend who has his head on straight."

"How so?"

"Edwin's a reliable worker, attentive when it comes to his family, and I heard from his mother the other day that he may be preparing to join the church by next year at the latest."

"That's good." Leaning his head against the back of his chair, Jerome closed his eyes and released a noisy yawn.

"If Arie follows in his footsteps, it will be even better. Don't you agree?"

Without providing Brenda a clear answer to her question,

Jerome reopened his eyes, shrugged his shoulders, and stated, "Our daughter will join if and when she's ready."

Brenda started back toward the window from the other side of the room. The hints of autumn peeped through the row of arborvitaes, with golden flecks among the shades of green.

"I despise those arborvitaes." Brenda frowned. "They're like Roman candles on a stick. I wish you would do something about them, Jerome."

"I could get around to it one of these days, but it's a lot of labor, so maybe hiring someone to take care of the dead ones would be good. We could leave a few near the house at least."

"Jah, go for it. I think it'd be fun to have another fruit tree, or a raspberry bush. I like watching the little bees, all fluffy and black and yellow." She dragged her nails along the ridge of her hand. "They're really cute, doing their pollinating."

"Come up for air, Brenda."

"I'm allowed to share my enthusiasm for things," she retorted.

"Why don't you sit back down and relax? I doubt that the young couple would appreciate you spying on them from your position at the window."

Her spine stiffened. "I wasn't spying. I was just—"

"Oh, I know, I bet you wanted to see if Edwin gives Arie a kiss before she comes inside."

Brenda's cheeks warmed. Her husband knew her too well, the unavoidable outcome of committing to twenty years of marriage. If Brenda longed to see her daughter marry a respectable young man like Edwin and join the Amish church, could she help herself? Brenda grudgingly went back to her chair, arms held loosely at her sides. When she heard the front door open and close, she snatched up the magazine she'd set aside and flicked it open to the folded page.

"Hello, Arie. Did you have a nice time with Edwin?" Brenda asked when her daughter entered the room.

Arie nodded. "Jah, Mom. The weather was just right for an open buggy ride."

"Well, don't be a stranger. Have a seat and tell us about it."

Jerome cleared his throat a couple of times. Brenda interpreted that as his indication that she shouldn't put their daughter on the spot.

"Actually, I have something I'd like to say to you both." Arie strode across the ample space between them and plopped down on the sofa.

"What is it, Daughter?" Hope welled in Brenda's soul, anticipating that Arie might reveal to them that she'd made a decision to join the church with Edwin.

With flighty hand gestures, Arie stated, "Barbara wants me to work at the gift shop full-time." She paused and let her hands fall into her lap. "I'm. . .uh. . .thinking about doing so."

Brenda's lips pressed together as she processed this bit of news. After a few more seconds of thought, she glanced at Arie and said, "Absolutely not. I am opposed to that idea. You should be at home taking care of your siblings when they are not in school, and if you worked full-time at the gift shop, it would mean you'd be neglecting the work you ought to be doing around our house while I'm busy working at the store."

Arie blinked rapidly and gave a quick shake of her head. "But, Mom, I—"

"You heard what I said. Your place is here, not at the gift shop all day."

"Wait a minute, Brenda," Jerome interjected. "You can't expect Arie to stay at home all the time. She needs to exercise her independence, and it's not fair that we should rely on her to keep an eye on Rudy and Maggie when they are not in school. Arie needs work experience, especially when she finally moves out of our house and gets married. You want that for her, don't you?"

Arie's eyes flitted her father's way and she smiled. "Danki, *Daadi*, for understanding."

"I see how it is," Brenda said with a huff. "Well, it's obvious I'm outvoted." She folded her arms and pivoted back toward Arie. "I suppose if you insist on working full-time at the gift store, there's nothing I can do about it."

For a moment, Brenda's thoughts turned inward. *But I think it's a bad idea, and now I'll have to either hire someone to watch Maggie and Rudy or take them to the store every day after they get home from school. I wonder how well it will go with Arie working full-time. After the first few weeks, she'll likely become overwhelmed and tired of it and then choose to return to part-time work.* She clasped the arms of the rocking chair. *I sure hope that's how it will go.*

Brenda thumped one foot against the floorboard, then the other, her muscles in both legs tensing as a further notion sprung into her thoughts. *Maybe one of these days, I'll drop by the gift store to see how well my daughter is holding up. If the job of working full-time gets to be too much, I'm sure I would be the last one to know.*

Chapter 17

THE MORNING SUN HAD FINALLY risen beyond the horizon, and Arie was in the midst of preparing to head downtown to the gift shop to officially work full-time. How the summer weeks had flown by! Even though business in the shop had been overrun with unexpected incidents, Arie was both excited and nervous at the prospect of her first dance class. She paced about her room, already wearing her kapp and clutching her handbag. Her heart thumped against her ribcage. She was about to keep this tremendous secret from her parents, and there was no telling what would happen if they found out.

Outside her bedroom door, Arie heard a blood-curdling scream that made her jump. Arie withdrew her hand from her mouth, unaware she'd been nibbling at her thumbnail the entire time. Turning the doorknob and rushing toward the kitchen, Arie spotted her mother slumped over, her fingers gripping the edge of the kitchen counter. Seeing the cutting board out and a knife next to it, Arie was prepared for the worst.

"Mamm, what's wrong? Are you okay? Do I need to call for help?" Arie sputtered.

"No, Arie. I spent some time in the garden, weeding and..."

Mom's voice trailed off as she turned toward Arie. "Tell me, what's crawling on my head?"

"A spider, maybe?" Arie's eyes widened at the green eyesore crawling on her mother's scarf and onto her bun. "Nope, never mind. That's a mantis."

"Get it off of me!" Mom shrieked. Her eye creases deepened at the corners. "Hurry!"

"Hang on, Mamm. Don't harm the poor creature."

"Poor creature? It's on my head, Arie."

The thought of pursuing the insect closer than necessary made Arie a little nervous. A few years ago after one of those little creatures had whipped its protruding eyeballs at Arie and then lunged at her, she'd developed a mild fear of praying mantises. Thinking fast, Arie glimpsed the fly swatter hanging on a nail driven into the wall. She set her purse on the counter and grasped the metal handle.

"Wait, Arie! You're going to swat at it while it's on me?"

"Do you really think I'd do that?" Arie held out the fly swatter. "Now, please hold still."

The mantis was painstakingly coaxed from her mother's bun onto the plastic mesh by Arie's deft hands. Holding onto the swatter, as if for dear life, the insect hooked on with its claws, and Arie towed it away. Astonished that it hadn't flown away yet, Arie carried the mantis out to the front of the house and transferred it to the first plant she came across. The meadowsweet shrub in the pot was devoid of blossoms, but the vivid green shade of the insect hid it within the curved branches.

After seeing it vanish into the foliage, Arie rushed into the house and back to the kitchen, where her mother had some veggies on the cutting board.

As she hung the fly swatter back up and slung her purse strap over her arm, Arie said, "All taken care of, Mamm. The mantis is far away from here now."

"Good riddance." Arie's mother shook her head. "That was *baremlich*."

"As terrible as it was, I thought your new hair clip looked great. Very stylish and natural, don't you think?" Arie chuckled with a smirk.

"No, that hair clip was way too natural for my taste. That little stinker." Mom smiled and threw her arms around Arie. "Thank you for coming to my rescue."

"Glad I could help." Arie stooped into her mother's embrace, and upon release, she cleared her throat. "Well, guess I'd better get going. I'll see you later, Mamm."

"Before you leave, Arie, can I say just one more thing? I know I wasn't very supportive of you working full-time, but I do hope it all goes well and that you have a *gut daag*." Mom's smile wavered, her mouth kneading together like dough. "However, there's no shame in admitting if it gets too much for you to handle."

"I'll remember that, Mamm, and you have a good day too." Arie's stomach sank as she tried to force out enthusiasm.

After a long day of roofing and being irritated with his brother Markel's antics, Edwin was filled with excitement and felt more than ready to perform with the drill team at the Michiana Event Center. Battery-powered lights in various colors were used by each of the eight riders to adorn the saddles and bridles of their horses. They had done this a number of times before, and he looked forward to the audience's approval. Aside from the delight Edwin always felt when he spent time with Arie, his favorite pastime consisted of being a member of the drill team.

Edwin gripped his horse's reins and used the back of his dominant hand to wipe a drop of sweat from his forehead as a man's baritone voice announced the drill team over the speaker system. Edwin and the rest of the squad led their horses under the guidance of their leader, Reuben, all stepping triumphantly, single file, into the arena. They fanned out, two by two, four turning in one direction and the other four the opposite way. The overhead lights in the event center had been dimmed, and the audience welcomed the drill team with a round of applause. Edwin estimated that before tonight, at least half of the audience had never seen the drill team's presentation—although many of the people who'd gathered for this occasion had undoubtedly seen their group perform before. That notion invigorated him even further. It was conceivable that after viewing the team's exhibition, one or more of the Amish youths who were fond of horseback riding might ask about an opportunity to become part of this or some other Amish drill team in the area.

Edwin's mind shifted gears as he concentrated on keeping his horse, Daisy, in perfect form during their choreographed routine done to the upbeat music being played over the loudspeaker. For the next thirty minutes, Edwin and the other team members had to ensure that their horses stayed in step as they weaved in and out, back and forth, making several successful laps around the arena. Every time they implemented a new pattern, the audience members in the bleachers roared more, with cameras flashing. Each rider kept their horse moving by sidestepping here, teaming up there, and maintaining a two-beat gait as the horses galloped from right to left, either in a single line or side-by-side.

Although it wasn't right to brag, which would be regarded as *hochmut,* Edwin couldn't suppress the sense of achievement that emerged within his chest. In addition to the thrill of riding his lovely, dark-haired horse in this manner, he was pleased to hear those watching express such gratitude. Not only that but doing something he was enthusiastic about while contributing to the community made the effort much more meaningful.

As their performance came to a close, Edwin turned to the audience on his side of the arena. Since the building was not well lit, except for the lights on the horses, he couldn't make out any of the faces who sat watching their performance. Edwin wished that Arie could have been present to witness his and the other team members' routine, but he knew she was most likely at her ballet class right now. He couldn't help wondering how things were going for her.

Edwin had not tried to dissuade Arie from dancing, but he prayed fervently that she would grow weary of it and join the church with him. The one thing that bothered Edwin the most was that if Arie didn't give up ballet, she would not become an Amish church member, which meant they could never get married. Edwin was certain his girlfriend understood he was rooted in the Amish way of life and would never feel at ease abandoning it to integrate into modern English society, even if he had not really spoken such words to her.

After the performance, while Edwin and the other team members were preparing their horses for the journey home, Reuben asked if he could speak to them for a few minutes. Edwin reached up and undid the top button on his shirt to better massage his taut neck muscles, thinking that he or one of the other riders might have done something incorrect during their performance. He didn't want to get called out for messing up, but if he had, then he guessed he had a lecture coming.

"What I would like to share with you all," Reuben declared, while ruffling the mane of his horse, Scout, "is that we will be presented with a great opportunity at our next practice."

Oh, right, Edwin thought. *Reuben's probably bringing up what he told me a couple of months back.* He let his hand drop and relaxed a bit. At least Edwin knew now that he hadn't done anything noticeably wrong this evening.

Reuben spoke again. "An Amish rider from Ohio, who is a cousin of my girlfriend, Sarah, will be demonstrating for us the art of Roman riding."

"That's riding two horses at the same time, isn't it?" Katie, one of the team members questioned.

"You'd be correct, and I think it will be fascinating to watch how she does it up close and personal." Reuben clutched his hands together. "Perhaps some of you would like to learn more about it, and maybe one day we'll incorporate Roman riding into our routines. I know it can be the same old same old with our rehearsals, so why not change things up a bit? What do you guys think about it?"

Like a flock of wild geese, everyone started chattering at the same time, but Edwin felt a wave of apprehension spread through his body. The idea of riding with one foot on one horse and the other on another seemed almost unbelievable. Although he had a strong sense of balance when climbing around on the roofs of buildings, Edwin wasn't sure he would ever feel comfortable on two horses simultaneously.

Goshen

As soon as they arrived at the dance studio, Lorrina handed Arie the apparel she had chosen from her collection of ballet attire.

Trying to fit into the leotard and tights had not been effortless. Lorrina's clothing's fabric clung to Arie's physique, so getting into all of it required some yanking and twisting. She may have gotten away with wearing the leotard underneath her Amish dress, but not the tights. Perhaps as the weather became cooler, Arie could conceal the blush-colored tights underneath her stockings.

Arie and a few of the other ballerinas were left in the middle of the floor when Lorrina scurried out to speak to Miss Judith. They were already stretching their tendons and muscles, and Arie crouched down on the outskirts to give herself enough room. She didn't know anyone other than Lorrina and did not feel comfortable introducing herself.

Arie reached out to her extended leg and stretched her inner thigh, examining herself in the mirror. It was a seamless conversion of her outer shell based solely on the attire she wore. *This is surreal. I actually resemble a ballerina. I never expected that this day would ever happen. Now I'm not just a girl wearing an Amish dress, at least for two days out of the week.* Hooking the knotted tie of the shrug Lorrina had lent her, Arie squared her shoulders. *It still amazes me that I did this, and now it's my new reality. However, Edwin is correct—there's a good chance that my parents will eventually find out. For this reason, it's of vital importance that I truly let go and stop worrying about it. No matter what, regardless of the potential repercussions, I will make the most of my dancing experience here. Nothing is going to dampen my spirits.*

"You're Lorrina's pal, aren't you? Can I join you?"

The young man plopped down next to Arie before she could even breathe, let alone answer his question. His forwardness staggered her, but it wasn't like Arie would've known what might have tumbled from her lips in response to his query.

Arie asked, "How'd you find out that I'm friends with Lorrina?"

"Word gets around." His knee brushed hers as he scooted closer. "Funny, I never would've pegged you as a woman living in the bygone era."

She slanted away from him, her cheeks flushing. "You're Briar, right? Could you. . ." Arie curtailed her sentence, wincing at her lack of assertiveness.

"We both seem to be the talk of the ballet class, I suppose. Looks like we have that much in common," he winked. "We probably have a lot more in common. Care to find out?"

"Okay, enough." Lorrina's hands were on her hips, and her lips slapped together as she glared down at Briar. "Please quit being so intrusive to Arie and move along with that little charade."

Briar raised his palms upward. "I'm just welcoming the new ballerina to our circle, taking an interest in her life. I don't see you introducing her to anyone else in here." Brushing away the wavy tresses framing his face, Briar clambered to his feet, grinning at Arie. "It was nice meeting you, beautiful."

Arie exhaled as Briar left, making his way to the grouping of girls by the mirrors. "That was sure. . .unexpected."

"Rude. You're looking for the word rude. Sorry for leaving you by yourself. Knowing him, though, he most likely would've pulled a stunt like that even with me standing right here." Lorrina lowered herself to the floor and rested a hand on Arie's shoulder. "Don't let Briar get to you, Arie. That's his attempt at smooth talking. My advice? Have your guard up and keep a safe distance from him."

It's just as well, Arie thought. *All I want to do is dance, and I'm not really here to make friends. In any case, I'm sure they wouldn't want someone from a "bygone era" disrupting their life.*

Arie followed Lorrina over to the barre and prepared to abide by Miss Judith's guidance. Composing herself, she concentrated on absorbing her newfound reality, determined not to allow the interaction with Briar to stifle her heightened exuberance.

Time went on, and with the repetition of movements, Arie's mind wandered back to Edwin. He had invited her to his drill team performance that would take place tonight, but she'd had to decline due to her dance lesson. Arie felt terrible, but Edwin said he understood. She had visited his practice sessions and seen his drill team's patterns of motion, which were interesting but not as much as dance routines. After so much time devoted to her boyfriend's interests, it was time for Arie to do the same for herself.

Miss Judith had them tendu and plié into fifth position as she strolled past the barre, observing the ballerinas' constant motion of pointing their feet back from side to front.

"Sous-sous, hold!" Miss Judith called out. "Remove your hands from the barre and balance."

Detaching from the wooden handrail, Arie rose from fifth position with a plié to the balls of her feet, elevating her heels off the floor. With her toes pressed together, she raised both arms toward the recessed lighting, mirroring Lorrina, who stood in front of her.

"Very nice arches, Arie. However, make an effort to raise your chin higher and keep your fingers closer together." Miss Judith pointed upward. "Imagine someone above the ceiling plucking your limbs with an unseen thread."

Shifting her stance, Arie envisioned the likeness Lorrina's teacher had offered her. Arm placement and posture were something Lorrina had corrected Arie on during their practice sessions at her house, demonstrating how much her friend valued proper technique. Before turning to face the barre, Lorrina gave Arie a thumbs up.

Following her time at the barre, Arie's entire body was thoroughly flexed from head to toe. She'd never had that much barre training at home by the stables, so simply going with the flow and not worrying about someone walking in on her was liberating. Arie knew what awaited her the next day: stiff calves and hamstrings, which she'd undoubtedly feel when bending down to replenish the lower shelves in the gift shop.

"Well, since Briar is here today, I believe we should do some pas de deux." Miss Judith's honeyed tone carried throughout the room as she positioned herself in front of the class, her gaze swiveling to Arie. "My dear, have you done any ballet with another dancer before?"

"No, I haven't, Miss Judith," Arie replied.

"Are you open to trying it with Briar? It'd be beneficial for you to learn how while taking these lessons with us."

Miss Judith's question hung in the air, and Arie's heartbeat quickened as she subconsciously relived the previous awkward encounter. If appraising eyes weren't on her, she would've excused herself to the restroom, but Arie grudgingly obliged. She stiffened as Briar moved closer without hesitation, his hands on her ribs, as though repressing the urge to swipe his fingers away from her waist. For a brief moment, Arie regretted not having the fly swatter she'd used for the mantis.

On second thought, agreeing to this was a huge mistake. Arie inhaled and drew her shoulders back. *Calm down, Arie. This is strictly professionalism, so no big deal.*

"All right, let's begin with something simple. Échappé, échappé, and then passé, and Briar will steady you as you transition to a turn." Miss Judith demonstrated the combination, then asked, "Do you want me to run that by you again?"

Arie rolled her head in the direction of the floor and then replicated the movements, though Briar's hands touching her hindered Arie's concentration. Hearing one of the dancers snickering behind her, she stumbled forward. Her body felt unbearably warm from her upper torso to her ears, as if vapor would form above her if she was doused with icy water.

"Don't aid him with the movement, Arie. Allow Briar to guide you through the combination. Let's go again, from the top."

Arie was keenly aware that her hairline was speckled with sweat, and the ticking of the wall-mounted clock cut through the piano melody from the stereo. *Breath, Arie. Push back against those wound-up feelings and don't let them get to you. This is something you've dreamed of doing for years.* She lifted her leg back to fix her slipper, which had loosened a bit off her heel. Arie had already resolved to do this, so there was no point in delaying the inevitable.

Allowing Briar to weave his arms underneath hers again, Arie bent her knees and sprung up, then brought her toe up to kiss her leg, then the other side, as her arms followed in unison. She hadn't noticed beforehand, but she felt a lot of support from Briar's toned arms around her midsection. Arie allowed his hands to propel her into a spin, then lowered her heels to the ground. Claps resounded from behind, and as Arie peeked at the full-length mirror, she saw Lorrina grinning at her.

"Much better. Fantastic work, both of you. You two have just met, but with time and practice, you will find your footing with one another." Miss Judith offered Arie a reassuring nod.

"I'd say that I've already found my footing with you," Briar said, mere inches from Arie's ear.

"W–what?" Arie stammered.

"You know, the short routine Miss Judith had us try out. We

move really well together, don't you think?"

Arie was unsure how to react to his comment, so she fiddled with her hands, hoping to control her breathing while concentrating on the floor beneath her feet. Fortunately, Miss Judith's voice pierced through the class chatter as she changed the track on the stereo, revealing the next set of exercises across the floor. Arie was stumped about what to make of Briar and the reasons for his apparent interest in her.

Chapter 18

For the past few weeks, although Brenda and Jerome's workload had increased at their store, things seemed to be going well without Arie's help in the afternoon hours. Since both Rudy and Maggie were at school, Brenda was spared from worrying about who would look after them during the day. The children had behaved well, hanging around the store until closing time and coming straight home when school let out. Sometimes Jerome would find small jobs for Rudy to do, and Maggie was usually kept busy at the office desk, coloring pictures or practicing her ABCs. Given that Maggie had barely written any English letters or words before she attended school, Brenda was astonished by the speed at which she had picked it up.

With so many customers visiting the store to purchase specific sale items, today had been particularly busy. Business was good, and Brenda was pleased about that, but there were times when her back and legs hurt from standing for extended periods of time, and this was one of those days.

"You look *mied*," Jerome said, stepping up to where she stood near the checkout counter. "Why don't you go sit down in my office for a while and take a short break?"

"No, I'm not that tired," she replied with a shake of her head. "Besides, I wouldn't feel right about leaving you up here by yourself to wait on customers."

"The day has been somewhat demanding." Jerome gently patted Brenda's shoulder. "But for now, at least, things have slowed down a bit. Actually, only a few people are in the store at the moment." Rubbing at his beard that resembled a tangle of cobwebs today, he pointed toward the back of the building.

Brenda glanced in that direction, watching two young Amish women browse the aisle where some of the houseware items had been marked down. "I suppose I could go put my feet up and relax for a few minutes," she remarked, stifling a forthcoming yawn.

"Good idea. You'll feel better when you've been off your feet for half an hour or so."

"Ring the bell on the counter if we get too busy again, and I'll sprint out of the office right away," she assured him.

"Okey dokey." Jerome flicked the fingers of his right hand toward their office at the far end of the building. "Feel free to grab a soda or fix yourself a cup of tea and enjoy some well-earned solitude."

Appreciating her husband's thoughtfulness, Brenda hurried away. When she entered the office, she grabbed a ginger ale from the ice chest that Jerome kept stocked with cold drinks for them during lunchtime or breaks. Brenda seated herself behind the desk and propped her throbbing feet on a wooden crate that Jerome kept beneath the desk so that it could be used as a footstool when needed.

"Ahh...that feels better," she murmured before uncapping the bottle and gulping the cool, refreshing beverage.

Brenda closed her eyes and reclined on the mesh cushion of

her chair after consuming half of the drink. It would have been easy to fall asleep if she had a pillow for her head, but there was no pillow. And even if there had been, Brenda would not have allowed herself the luxury of dozing off. She would have to remain vigilant and prepared to go back to the front of the store to assist Jerome in case more customers showed up.

It wouldn't hurt to do a little thinking, though, Brenda told herself as her mind wandered to their eldest daughter. *I wonder how Arie has been doing today. There must be a lot of things for her to do at the gift shop, and I imagine that working there full-time would be exhausting. And no doubt, on a day as nice as this one, there are plenty of people in town shopping for the best bargains. Perhaps people have been looking for gifts to buy for special occasions. Given that the gift store is situated in the center of town, where many visitors and locals love shopping, that building has most likely been far more crowded today than ours. Whereas here, we are not as conveniently located, so we normally get fewer customers than the shops in downtown Shipshewana.*

Exhaling, Brenda ran her hand over the plastic sides of the bottle, causing condensation to drip onto the desktop, where it rested. *I have to respect Arie's commitment, even though I miss having her home and available for support. I detested hearing it, but Jerome was right when he said that she has to exercise her independence. Our daughter had undoubtedly matured and seems to be handling herself quite well these days. Besides, we're doing fairly well without her help, which I'm grateful for.*

Brenda's musings halted, and her eyes snapped open when she heard a familiar cry near the front of the store. Practically leaping out of the chair, Brenda dashed to the area beside the checkout counter, where she found Jerome on his knees and Maggie sobbing in her father's arms.

A ripple of fear spread up Brenda's back and to her neck. *What has happened to my little girl? Has she been gravely injured? Oh, Lord. I hope not.*

Upon seeing Brenda, Maggie pulled away from Jerome and rushed into Brenda's arms when she bent toward the child.

"What's the matter, sweetheart?" Wiping the tears from her daughter's flushed cheeks, Brenda posed the question: "Maggie, are you hurt?"

Maggie shook her head and sniffed as Jerome stood. "Rudy walked home from school and left me to walk by myself." Her chin trembled. "I was scared, Mamm. How come my bruder has to be so mean?"

"Calm down, Maggie," Brenda pleaded as her daughter began to bawl like a wounded heifer. Two more customers had just entered the establishment, and the elderly couple's attention was instantly drawn to Maggie. Brenda was aware that some questions would no doubt be raised if she didn't take action right away.

As Jerome waited on the previous customers, Brenda took her daughter by the hand and led her to the office. If any questions were asked, then Maggie's father would be the one answering them.

When Brenda reached the office, Maggie continued to sob while clutching to her apron strings. In an attempt to soothe her, she patted Maggie on the back and repeated: "Calm down now, Maggie. Calm down. Don't cry. You can do that for me, can't you?"

"I want my big sister," Maggie blubbered as more tears spilled from her eyes. "She should have come to the schoolhouse to walk me home."

"Arie's at work," Brenda reminded the child. "She's no longer here to walk you to and from school, and I'll have a talk with Rudy as soon as he comes into the store."

"He took off for the barn, Mamm. Rudy's not comin' to the store." Maggie took a deep breath as more tears welled up in her eyes, leaving Brenda at a loss for words of consolation. The truth was, someday, when Arie got married and moved out of the house, she wouldn't be available to help Maggie or Rudy anymore, and that thought saddened Brenda. Although she looked forward to Arie having her own family, Brenda was facing one of the consequences of that change right now in front of her.

Maybe my husband was right when he suggested that I consider hiring someone to watch the children after school, Brenda pondered as she continued to pat Maggie's back. *Of course, that won't solve the problem of who's going to walk Maggie to school, but at least she'll have someone to walk her home in the afternoon, and I won't have a sobbing daughter on my hands.*

Brenda handed Maggie a tissue to wipe her nose before getting out a can of soda for the child to drink, causing the tears to subside. *In the meantime, I hope Jerome has a talk with Rudy about leaving Maggie to walk by herself. He must realize that his sister is still a little girl and that, with Arie gone, she needs the support and safety of her older brother.*

Goshen

As Lorrina opened the door to let her friend in, a multitude of scents filled the Electric Brew coffee house, including the savory fragrances of their panini sandwiches and wraps, the delicate aromas of various baked goods, and the predominant roast of the beans. The bustling of patrons had eased off, because the establishment would close in the next hour. It was one of her favorite places to visit for food and drink, especially after a rigorous dance class, and now she had Arie to accompany her there to decompress before returning to Shipshewana. Lorrina offered to pay for the orders they placed when they neared the barista at the counter, but Arie intervened and insisted, digging through her purse for her wallet.

As they waited for their order, Lorrina saw a vacant table and gestured for Arie to join her, but she appeared to be engrossed in the charming ambiance of the quaint space. With an eclectic mix of antiques and plant hangers encircling them, there was no shortage of things to gaze at. The coffee shop had an aesthetic that reminded Lorrina of one of her favorite television shows. Was it a living room or a restaurant? Who could tell?

"Thank you for treating, Arie. Next time though, I'll be sure to make it up to you."

"Make it up to you? You've been so kind to drive me to ballet and provide me with dance attire that it's the least I can do." Before settling into the chair across from Lorrina, she nudged a plate with a piece of cake over to her. "Oops—sorry for your cake being lopsided."

"Eh, no biggie. That's exactly how I want my future husband to be."

"Lopsided or a chocolate raspberry?" Arie chuckled.

"No. It doesn't matter how he looks, as long as he makes me happy. Silent prayer before we enjoy?" Lorrina asked.

Nodding, Arie bowed her head and her eyes fluttered shut. Following suit, Lorrina was amused at the fact that she had only begun praying silently because of her companion and the Amish custom of praying in silence before meals.

"Amen." Lorrina eyed the clear plastic cup that Arie held in her hands, brimming with ice and brew, as she picked up her fork. "You're brave. The fact that you can enjoy coffee so late in the day still astounds me. I'd be up all night if I had your iced cappuccino."

"Caffeine doesn't really keep me awake. It gives me energy, but I still yawn throughout the day and occasionally feel drowsy. Besides, it's mostly sweeteners and syrup anyway, and the day isn't over yet. I have plenty to do before I turn in for the night."

"True. The new school year has just begun, yet I'm already supplied with homework." Lorrina delved into the mound of chocolate with her fork, as if she were tilling soil in a garden.

Taking a long sip of her coffee, Arie's demeanor stilled, and she slid her chair closer to the table. "So, what were you talking about with Miss Judith on Tuesday?"

"Oh, she was asking if I would be interested in taking over teaching one of her classes. It's for the younger ballerinas. While observing Miss Judith's classes last year, I covered for her when she wasn't available to teach, and now she's seeing how I'll do on my own. I'm very excited about it."

"Lorrina, are you officially going to be a dance instructor?"

"Hopefully. At the very least, I'll get some experience under my belt. I could always end up teaching somewhere other than Goshen. I might consider doing that." Lorrina's insides fluttered, and her pulse quickened, yet her cup of tea lay untouched. "After I graduate, I could always move away from here."

With rapid blinking, Arie's lips pinched together as she set down her drink. "Really? You'd actually move from Shipshewana?"

"Maybe even from Indiana." She drummed her feet along the floor beneath the table, but Lorrina noticed her friend's pained expression. "Hey, no need to look so glum, Arie. I won't disappear out of thin air forever. We could write letters to each other and keep one another in the loop, and I'd still visit from time to time."

"Where would you even consider going?" Arie questioned.

"Hard to say for sure. I've just always wondered what a new beginning might be like. I could rediscover who I am, or even meet the person I'm destined to be with." Right after Lorrina swallowed her first bite, a tickling sensation spread down the inside of her nose, reaching to her upper lip.

"Achoo!"

"Bless you, Lorrina. Too dusty in here? Are you coming down with a cold?"

Lorrina reached for a napkin and giggled as she rubbed her nose. "No, it happens whenever I eat chocolate."

"Are you allergic to chocolate?"

"I hope not. I also sneeze when I brush my teeth. Sometimes the sun does it too. Very strange."

"Jah, very strange," Arie said, her brows furrowing. "Don't take this the wrong way, but if it were me, I don't think I could start with a clean slate. There's already so much established. I think it's best to work with what you have."

"Yet you chose to dance." Lorrina ripped open a packet of sugar and stirred it into her decaffeinated tea. She watched wisps of steam rising from her cup. "At times, we have to dismantle what's been established and construct a new sense of belonging. Stepping outside of our comfort zones can help with our unanswered questions."

"Lorrina, don't you fear being alone? What if it's not the right decision to leave everything behind?"

Sighing, Lorrina lifted her tea, blowing it along the rim before responding, "From my own perspective, having those thoughts holds us back from what we feel led to do. Besides, even when we're by ourselves, we're never truly alone. Even when I'm unsure of my course of action, God is guiding me."

"I've already said this to you before," Arie responded, "but you're always so confident and know what you want out of life."

"That's not always true, Arie. I'm constantly questioning stuff. Especially when it comes to my home life. Afterward, I reflect, but in the moment, I fumble and say things I wish I hadn't said. That's why I believe some distance could have advantages for me."

"You're probably right about that." Arie tapped her finger across the lid of her coffee cup before picking it back up. "I need to ask, do you regret having me tag along with you to Goshen?"

"Only if it's not what you want to do would I ever regret it." Lorrina sipped her tea, the delicate flavor with a hint of sweetness easing her spirits. "How do you feel about it, Arie?"

"It's tiring, yet I always feel more alive afterward. That's one of the reasons I'm happy to be here today rather than at home at the moment. To be honest, it's nice not to have my mom watching my every move."

"I hear that. Growing up, as soon as I was criticized for something, it became a glaring issue, and I felt like I needed to rectify it as soon as possible. Otherwise, it's all I can think about, knowing that it makes my mom unhappy."

"Do you still worry about needing to fix whatever gets pointed out?"

Lorrina nodded, her palm resting on the warmth permeating the ceramic cup. "I remember sitting in the family sedan in the parking lot when my mother and I went to the grocery store together. Straight away, she'd comment on people's clothing or how they should change their eating habits as they passed us and made their way to the entrance. In other words, 'since they don't behave or dress like us, we shouldn't like them.' Given that everything I was taught in church goes against that, I felt off about it.

How could my mom judge like that without knowing who those people were? I couldn't wrap my head around it. But then I caught myself acting just like her. It bleeds into your other relationships when you deal with it at home. Because it's all you know."

"I don't understand, Lorrina. You've never behaved that way around me. Every time I have visited your home, you and your mother both made me feel very welcome."

"She knows how to appear gentle and kind, but she passes judgment on how the Amish live. But I pushed past her judgments because, regardless of what you wear, you have a good heart, and that's what drew me in. I gained an appreciation for people's individuality and learned to see past appearances. And I can see that the reason you care about how you're perceived is because those expectations bled onto you. That's why I've encouraged you to be open and honest with yourself, rather than basing your ambitions on what others expect of you."

Lorrina had no idea what else to say. She didn't want to push her friend, especially since she could tell Arie's thoughts were swarming around her like a massive hornet's nest. "Arie, is everything okay?"

Arie flinched, tracing absently on the table with her fingertips. "Jah, I'm sorry. Don't worry about me. I was just thinking is all."

I wish Arie didn't have to continue hiding her love for ballet from her parents, Lorrina thought. *I can relate to Arie's inner turmoil and the struggle to strike a balance between one's own desires and other people's expectations. All I know is, when someone responds to your difficulty by being personally offended rather than showing concern for you, something is wrong.*

"Anyway"—Lorrina picked up her napkin from the table and wadded it in her hand—"I'll drop you off a little ways from your house again so your parents won't suspect anything."

Silhouettes of the buildings lining the sidewalk crept along the easement as they headed for the car. Lorrina thought back on the conversation in the coffee shop. Was it appropriate for her to tell Arie about her mother's judgmental ways or that she was considering moving away from Indiana? Despite her contradictory thoughts about the situation, Lorrina vowed to be the support Arie needed, no matter how bumpy the road ahead might be.

Chapter 19

Shipshewana

As Lorrina prepared for bed that night, her mind replayed every detail of what she had told Arie at the coffee shop. She prayed she hadn't overstepped her bounds or said too much, knowing she had a tendency to do so. But Lorrina had expressed what was on her heart and what she honestly believed.

Hopefully, Arie took it as food for thought and will mull things over thoroughly while deciding what the best course of action would be for her own life. All I want is the very best for my dear friend and for myself as well.

Her shoulders lifted as she heaved a weighty sigh before crawling into bed. Hopefully, a restful night's sleep would give a better perspective on things—for both her and Arie. Lorrina drew up her bulky, cable-knit throw, closed her eyes, said a prayer, and allowed much-needed sleep to overtake her.

Beep! Beep!

The blaring, high-pitched sound blasting from outside Lorrina's door dragged her from the mists of drowsiness and brought her to a sitting position. She felt immobilized, almost rooted to the mattress where she sat.

Beep! Beep!

The aggravating noise continued. It took Lorrina a bit to shake the cobwebs from her brain and realize the smoke alarm was sounding. It wasn't a simple *chirp-chirp*, indicating that the smoke detector's battery was running low. No, this was an all-out warning that there might be a fire somewhere in the house—possibly in the upstairs hallway outside of Lorrina's door.

She snapped on her bedside lamp and blinked when she saw that it was almost 3:00 a.m. Lorrina leaped out of bed, dashed across the room, and removed Quillace from his cage, fearing the worst despite the fact that she had not smelled any smoke. If there was a fire in the house, as Lorrina suspected, she could not bear the thought of her adorable little hedgehog perishing in the flames.

Lorrina opened the door cautiously and peeked out, and with her nose pointed upward, she sniffed while looking up and down the hall. The deafening sound of the smoke alarm overhead continued, and other alarms going off around the home echoed the one overhead.

With only a slight pause, and holding her pet securely against her chest, being careful of the spines, Lorrina rushed down the hall to her parents' bedroom, with the night-lights plugged into the outlets illuminating her way. Their door swung open, and the two of them emerged so swiftly, Lorrina almost collided with her mother.

"Whoops, sorry. What's going on?" she asked, looking at her father. "All the alarms seem to be going off at the same time."

"That's right," he answered. "They're hardwired, and each one connects to the other. So when one goes off, they all do. We need to go downstairs and see if there's smoke anywhere in the house." He gestured for Lorrina and her mother to follow, flipping the light switches as he went.

Between her thumping heart and the nerve-wracking chorus of alarms ringing throughout the house, Lorrina wanted to scream and flee straight out the front door. But she held steady until her father gave them the all clear.

"There's no smoke anywhere," he hollered when Lorrina and her mother joined him in the kitchen.

Mom held her hands over her ears like earmuffs. "Please make that horrible racket stop," she shouted. "It's enough to give me a headache, and while you're trying to figure out what's going on, Peter, I'm going outside!"

Quillace had begun to squirm, and for his sake, as well as her own, Lorrina grabbed a flashlight from the top of the fridge and followed her mother out the back door. At least in the back side of their yard they were not visible from the road or the neighbor's house across the street. Of course, they probably couldn't be seen anyhow, given how dark it was outside in the wee hours of the morning. It was a good thing too, since they were all still wearing their pajamas.

"I detest being woken up in the middle of the night," Lorrina's mother groaned as she fiddled with the ties of her floral robe. "Especially for no good reason at all. At this point, I would've preferred waking up to a small fire that could easily be put out to compensate for my troubles."

Lorrina shivered, even though the nighttime environment wasn't that cold. When she noticed that her throat burned as she swallowed, she realized how worn out she felt from rushing through the home. She wondered if she might be coming down with a cold or the flu.

Dad had presumably identified the source of the malfunctioning smoke alarms, for all was finally quiet. Lorrina's fear had subsided as well, and she felt ready to return to her bedroom, where she could put Quillace back in his cage before retiring to get some shut-eye. Although Lorrina wasn't sure how much sleep she'd get now that the alarms had been turned off, she could probably catch a few extra hours.

Mom grumbled something that Lorrina couldn't decipher as they entered the house. Lorrina thought her mother was complaining about having had her sleep disrupted, and then Dad suddenly announced that he'd located the problem.

"What was wrong?" Lorrina questioned.

"One of the smoke alarms is dead, and it set all the others off."

"We've discussed this before, Peter, but you never listen to me. Maybe you should keep a closer eye on things," Mom griped, pointing at him. "Batteries don't last forever, you know. I suppose I should repeat myself more so you remember to change the batteries."

Instead of rebutting her argument, Dad merely offered a pensive smile and left the room. Lorrina empathized with him but often wondered why he seldom stood up to Mom. Perhaps her father didn't believe it was worthwhile and would rather not go back to bed angry.

Lorrina trudged behind her parents, and every time she shuffled her slippers along the wooden floor, she felt pressure in her sinuses.

"Lorrina, you're not looking too well. You're flushed," Dad said, resting a hand on Lorrina's forehead. "In fact, you seem to be running a fever."

Her mother blew out a breath. "You ought to go get the thermometer and check to see if you do have a fever."

"That's just great," Lorrina muttered. "Guess I won't be going to school."

"For sure," Mom interjected. "If you're sick, the only place you belong is in bed."

"Duly noted. I'm heading there now, so I don't get you both sick." Lorrina staggered past her parents and made her way up the stairs, with her hedgehog nestled in the crook of her arm.

I'll need to call Arie so she'll know that I won't be able to drive her to Goshen later today. It's tough to get ahold of her when she doesn't have a smartphone. She pursed her lips and rubbed the velvety skin on Quillace's chin. *I don't like skipping a dancing lesson, but it wouldn't be fair to risk exposing this to everyone in class. Hopefully, Arie can find another ride, or else she won't be attending ballet class either, and that would be a shame, because I know how much she has enjoyed it so far.*

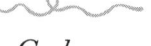

Goshen

It was the outset of another ballet class for Arie, though this time, she'd hired a driver instead of relying on her friend to drive her to Goshen. She'd received an unexpected phone call from Lorrina while working at the gift shop that morning. Learning that her friend was unable to take her to dance class due to illness, Arie had two options: Either head straight on home or call upon someone to drive her to Goshen.

Because she'd been taken off guard by her friend's sudden ailment, Arie hadn't been sure what to do. While serving customers, Arie decided to hire a driver, and she was now settled on the center of the floor in the dance studio, awaiting the routine she'd been following for weeks now.

I have to get used to Lorrina not being around anyway. Arie paused, realizing something was stuck on her skirt. Thinking it was a bug, she batted at it without success. Then she leaned forward and identified a sliver of wood. Picking it off, Arie smoothed her skirt before continuing to stretch. *I should've been happier for Lorrina and encouraged her to follow her heart. She's done that for me this entire time.*

"Okay, ladies, and Briar," Miss Judith announced as she brought everyone's focus to the front of the studio with a clap of her hands. "As you all know, auditions for *The Nutcracker* will be upon us very soon, and I know the majority of you in this class will be going to try out and would like to be in top form. That's why, if you have your pointe shoes, you can wear them for today."

The dancers positioned themselves at the barre as the musical accompaniment commenced. When the ballerinas rolled up onto the tips of their toes, Arie marveled at how seamlessly they executed it. After seeing the advanced ballet dancers' performance at the Goshen Theater, Arie remembered questioning Lorrina about how they held their balance. The shoes provided support, with an oval-shaped platform at the apex and a sturdy box encasing the toes. A common misconception about pointe shoes, according to Lorrina, was that the box had been made of wood, but it was actually constructed from layers of fabric, as well as paper and cardboard.

Even while the shoes provided support, a dancer's strength and technique propelled them from a normal standing position to their toes. It required a lot of resilience, especially when a dancer stood on tiptoes for long periods of time, maintaining their balance and grace without revealing a trace of discomfort. The shoes were both beautiful and treacherous, and rows of them were at the barre, their blush-colored satin shimmering beneath the studio lights. It was in that moment, however, that it dawned on Arie she was the only ballerina not wearing pointe shoes. Canvas slippers could be worn by anyone, regardless of their experience in ballet.

Throughout the lesson, Arie could almost feel the looks of some of the dancers boring into her. Although she didn't anticipate the students to start dancing in them, Lorrina had mentioned to Arie that there was a separate pointe class at the studio. All Arie could do was watch as they pranced and bounded around the room, and while she was astonished by their finesse and proficiency in their movements, it served as a reminder that she fell short of the rest of them.

If I hadn't been denied the opportunity to dance back then, I could be wearing my own pair of pointe shoes right now. This isn't fair. I can't even keep up with the rest of the class. As Arie yanked on her ballet shoe's elastic band and eased it off, her stomach felt as if it had shriveled like a grape sun-drying in the July heat. *If it weren't for my upbringing hindering me, would I be as good as the other dancers? Would it have been possible for me to dance en pointe if my parents had given me the option to take ballet lessons when I was ten? Or would I still be in the same dilemma as I am right now?*

A tap on Arie's arm drew her back to the present moment. "Where's your friend today, beautiful?" Briar asked.

As she gathered up her ballet bag and turned to face him, Arie frowned. "She's sick." Fortunately, he wasn't much taller than her, so she could stare into his dark eyes.

"While we were dancing today, I noticed that you looked less enthusiastic when the other girls flaunted their pointe shoes."

"I wouldn't say they were flaunting them, Briar. Now, if you'll excuse me, I need to call for a ride home."

"How are you gonna do that? Do you even know how to use a phone?" With a wide-eyed expression, he gave an undignified snort.

"Very funny. I'll be using the phone at the front desk. And yes, other Amish and I know how to operate a telephone." Shifting her gaze away from him and clenching her jaw, she forced a smile and said, "Good day to you."

Skirting around Briar, Arie quickened her gait from where they stowed their belongings in cubbies. As she proceeded out of the room and into the foyer, past the portrait wall, Miss Judith waved and wished her good night. A few of the dancers were grouped around and staring out the bay windows, presumably awaiting their rides home. Arie went to the front desk, where the phone sat, unattended, but available for use if necessary.

"You know, I could get you a pair of shoes right now."

Rendered stationary by Briar's words, Arie wondered if she'd heard him correctly. She firmly shook her head. "I don't think so. You need a dance instructor's approval to wear pointe shoes."

"That's true, if you buy them in person. It's easy to purchase them online these days. You really can't do that, though, can you? It still seems weird to me that you are only allowed to churn butter in your spare time." With another snort, Briar folded his arms. "What's that look for? I'm just joking. Don't ruin your lovely face by taking it personally. Based on everything I've seen from you in the last few weeks, I believe you're ready for those shoes. I am a seasoned dancer, so I would know. I could take you straight to the dance boutique and then drop you off at your house afterward."

Arie clasped her hands together, the tips of her fingers tingling. "I don't know, Briar. I appreciate the offer, but I don't need to have pointe shoes."

"You ought to think twice if you want to be taken seriously as a dancer and not be the odd one out. I doubt your friend would be willing to buy them for you, so your best chance at getting a pair would be through me." He winked. "If you put in a lot of effort, you might even become part of *The Nutcracker* production at the Goshen Theater."

Briar's comments inhabited her mind while glancing around at the other dancers. There were only so many months left, and then Arie would return to her usual routine. It was both exciting and frightening to consider slipping on pointe shoes and dancing on stage under those beams of light from above, showcasing her abilities and captivating the audience with her performance as though she'd been doing it for years. There was no way she could accomplish it. Arie was a novice, and while she'd gained a lot of knowledge from her friend, Arie had witnessed Lorrina's steadfast determination firsthand. Arie felt sure that if Lorrina knew she wanted to buy pointe shoes, she would advise against it.

Then again, Arie reasoned, *even if I don't get a chance to wear the pointe shoes on stage, I could still keep them as a keepsake for years to come. It'd be a means of looking back on it all after I joined the church, as bittersweet as that sounds. But what if I don't? These past few weeks have been wonderful. Should I really give it up?*

"I'll consider it at least, Briar, but I really should be heading on home."

"Hear me out. We can go ahead and drive over there today." Briar fiddled with the cuff of his denim jacket, narrowing his eyes. "I'd be doing you a favor by bringing you over when Lorrina isn't there to question it, since I know you're concerned about her finding out."

"I appreciate the offer, but I don't want you to go out of your way for me, especially since you don't even know me all that well."

"No trouble at all. I just don't want to see a talented and gorgeous girl's potential thrown away."

Arie brushed her sweaty hands against her dress. She continued to fantasize about Miss Judith's announcement of auditions for *The Nutcracker*, which intensified the urge to show everyone that she was good enough to perform. Even though Arie was conscious of the opposition, this was her path, and it was about finding closure for the dreams she had long suppressed, still yearning to be released. After all, Arie had denied herself this chance for so long, what was the harm in trying? But why would Briar be so generous to her? Perhaps she was overthinking and misinterpreting the motives of someone she barely knew. Briar had offered to do something nice for her, so maybe he wasn't all that bad.

"You know what, why not?" Arie glanced toward Briar. "I'll do it. Let's go and get the pointe shoes right now."

Chapter 20

Arie had been busy in the sewing room because, as Briar had assured her, he had persuaded the pointe shoe fitter in the boutique to allow Arie to try on the selection of pointe shoes on hand. As she'd stood there, looking at the rows of dancer apparel and accessories and letting him speak, she'd been bewildered by his approach. He had explained to the fitter that Arie also attended his ballet class, and that Miss Judith had requested him to drive her over to the boutique and assist with the whole process of getting her shoes. Since Briar had been in the boutique many times, the fitter said he would take his word for it. And he had.

Arie couldn't believe that Briar could fib with such ease, without even batting an eye. Arie had felt like a frayed cord that day, tugged on and unraveled, just like she had whenever she'd hidden the truth about anything.

She clamped her thumb around the pencil she held and marked the inside of the shoe. Arie then rummaged through the sewing cabinet drawer for thread and embedded the pin along the seam to bind the satin ribbon. The fitter had given Arie all the information she needed about where to sew the shoe's elastics and ribbons. Arie was unaware—or more accurately, she had forgotten—that ribbons were not included, because there was no doubt that Lorrina had brought it up when Arie asked her about pointe shoes.

This process is nerve wracking, she told herself. *I'm simply grateful that my mother taught me the basics of sewing by hand, because I would have to use the sewing machine otherwise.* Arie eyed the wall-mounted candle holder constructed of horseshoes and shook out her wrist. *Hold on, can you use a sewing machine for pointe shoes? I should've asked the fitter, but that entire encounter was all a blur at the time and even more so now. All I know is the price of these shoes is absurdly high.* She dipped her chin, her lips quirking at the sight of them in her lap. *Considering how beautifully crafted they are, maybe the money was well spent.*

With a sewing needle in hand and the first shoe nestled in her lap, Arie wove the needle in and out through the fabric, stitching until the ribbon was firmly latched on. Then, she secured the square stitching with a knot before cutting the remaining thread with scissors.

I still can't believe my mother actually followed through with finding someone to watch Maggie and Rudy for the hours when they come home from school each day. I'm glad she did, since I know Mom might be wary of anyone who isn't related to us. That's why she expected me to be the one to keep an eye on them. I see why Mom still doesn't like it when I'm not at home all day until it's the weekend. That's why I've been making an effort to be around here whenever I can, but I don't think she knows that I also need to set some time aside for myself. Like my mother said herself, having something you're passionate about helps you take your mind off things and avoid feeling overwhelmed. And now that ballet is within my grasp, I must ask myself, have I finally found my flowers?

After Arie had managed to sew the ribbons onto both shoes, she ran her fingertips along the ivory stitching. "They're so stunning," she crooned. "These shoes are nearly too beautiful to become soiled by touching the floor."

"Arie!"

Dumping the shoes straight onto the rug at her feet, Arie kicked them beneath the sewing table's bottom open shelf, her legs knocking the sides of the knee hole as she did so.

"Arie," Mom said, tipping her head as she peered around the doorframe with eyebrows raised higher than normal. "What are you doing in here? I thought you were going to rake the leaves out in the front yard."

"J–just doing a quick stitch on something, Mamm." Arie faltered, her eyes flitting to the ribbon protruding from beneath the table. "I'm sorry. I'll sweep those leaves from the yard in a moment."

"Well, please tidy up the side yard after you're done with the front. The garbage bins are in the shed."

"Okay."

When Mom retracted her head and disappeared down the hallway, Arie sagged forward onto the desktop, burying her head between her folded arms.

Yes, Mom, I know where the garbage bins are. They, along with the rake and everything else garden-related, are always in the shed. Why does she expect me to be responsible even though she speaks to me like I'm a two-year-old child? With a sigh, Arie glanced up at the window in front of her, and gazed at the barn in the distance, with leaves strewn all over the graveled path. She stooped down and gathered up her pointe shoes. *In any event, the sooner I can get those leaves raked up, the sooner I can ride Aster. And maybe,* she thought with a measure of hope, *I can even take my pointe shoes out for a spin. Quite literally.*

Upon entering the arena where the drill team would be practicing soon, Reuben approached Edwin, accompanied by a young Amish woman with ebony hair tucked neatly beneath her kapp.

"Hey, Edwin, there's someone here I'd like you to meet." Reuben gestured to the woman, who didn't appear to be much older than her mid-twenties. "This is Sara's cousin, Esther Troyer. She's from Holmes County, Ohio, and is here visiting all week. The best part is, she has agreed to demonstrate for our group how she does Roman riding and a few other stunts on the backs of one or both of her two horses." Reuben fairly beamed, and the way he bounced from foot to foot let Edwin know that their drill team leader was quite excited.

Edwin extended his hand. "It's nice to meet you, Esther. I'm looking forward to seeing you perform."

"Good to meet you too, and I hope you'll enjoy what you see." She shook Edwin's hand with a firm grasp.

He figured Esther directed her horses with the same rigid hold. Edwin had a hunch that, despite her attractive appearance and stunning, pale blue eyes, she preferred working with horses over sewing or cooking, with how calloused her hands were.

When Esther stepped aside to talk to some of the young ladies on the drill team, Edwin asked Reuben, "Were you aware that your girlfriend's cousin would be visiting this evening?"

"Jah." Reuben gave Edwin a quick shoulder bump before gesturing to the building where their team members had stabled their horses prior to practice getting underway. "As soon as I found out when Esther would be visiting Shipshewana, I made arrangements for us to hold our practice session in this indoor arena."

Before Edwin could comment, Reuben spoke again. "Besides,

with the sun setting around six these days, relocating our practice to the Fox Run Stables made sense. It will also be an excellent place to work on our routines during the winter months when there's snow on the ground."

"That's true," Edwin conceded. "Practicing in an indoor arena like this gives us access to much better lighting as well."

"Yep, for sure. So, what are we waiting for, Edwin? Let's get on in there and see what Esther has to show us before we bring our own horses out for an hour or so of practicing."

Edwin sat down in the main section of the bleachers to observe Esther's demonstration. He wanted a good view but not too near, which could lead him to miss a few things as she circled the arena on her glazed-coated, chestnut horse. No doubt the stallion had been well-groomed and supplied with a proper diet.

He straightened his back and gazed at the young woman, clothed in long black tights under her lengthy, emerald-green dress, as she rode into the center of the arena, perched on the horse's back with both arms outstretched. Several of the drill team members gasped, and Edwin found his excitement mounting. He couldn't comprehend how Esther maintained her balance, as basic horseback riding on a saddle could be dangerous if not done correctly and with caution.

After making it all the way around the arena in that posture, Esther trotted out the way she'd arrived on the scene. Edwin had to wonder what other tricks the talented young woman had up her sleeve. After a few minutes, she showed up again astride two identical horses, down to color and height. Edwin figured they could have been biological twins. Esther, who seemed to have perfected this skill, rode around the ring with one foot on each horse's back, like she'd been doing it all her life.

That's a whole lot of talent right there, not to mention bravery, Edwin thought as Esther paraded past him, grasping both horses' reins in a steady tandem. He held the sides of his head and observed as the horses strolled, trotted, and then cantered beneath her feet, while Esther remained comfortable and seemed quite sure of herself.

Edwin's breath expanded at the sight of those maneuvers, which were unlike anything he had seen before. He paid close attention, noting that each of the young woman's feet appeared to move somewhat independently of the other since, rationally, her horses didn't quite trot in perfect synchronization, even though it seemed as if they did.

After a few roundabouts in the arena, Esther brought her horses to a halt in an overhang of dust, and everyone on the team let loose with cheers and applause. As she trotted the jubilant beasts out of the ring, Reuben stood up from his bench position in the bleachers and regarded the team members behind him.

"Well, what'd you all think of that?" Reuben fairly beamed. "Wasn't Esther's ability to ride one horse without hands, then two horses at the same time, incredible?"

"It was," shouted one of the young women on their team. "But what she did could also be very dangerous!"

"That's true," one of the men agreed. "If the rider made one false move, she could slip between the two moving horses and kiss the floor. That could lead to a potentially serious injury."

Edwin turned to look behind him and saw the fellow who'd just spoken swipe a palm across his brow. His team member was right, but he couldn't stop thinking about how it would set their group apart from others in the area if they had someone who could include Roman riding to their performances.

Reuben steadied himself one foot at a time. "Come on, guys. I'm really excited about the idea of Roman riding and other stunts we can pull. If any of you want to learn, maybe my girlfriend could talk her cousin into spending some more time here to teach anyone interested in learning how to ride in such a thrilling and entertaining manner."

"I'm not sure if the Roman style, or any other kind of trick riding, is a smart idea," said another young woman. "It does seem too dangerous, and we sure don't want any of our team members to take needless risks and end up terribly injured only to make us look good."

With his ideas racing at a rapid pace, Edwin sat in silence. He'd been thoroughly intrigued by Esther's performance, wondering whether Arie would consider joining the drill team if she were to take an interest in Roman riding.

And maybe, he reasoned, *if she was interested and felt brave enough, Arie might even decide to learn a few other tricks on the back of her horse, using some of her ballet training. Now, wouldn't that be something if our drill team could incorporate some exhilarating trick riding into our regular routines? Why, it has the potential to attract large crowds from far and wide. Adding something fresh and exciting to benefit events, rather than just for show, might generate a significant increase in revenue. That would certainly help the person in need who we were raising funds for.*

Edwin lifted his straw hat, scratching the top of his head. *Am I thinking these things for selfish reasons—so that Arie would give up dancing and join the church with me?* He heaved a long sigh. *I'll need to think this one through before saying anything to Arie about it.*

Arie, planted firmly on Aster's saddle, trotted along the fence line of the pasture. She'd been feeling better acquainted, riding her horse without incident lately. That was undoubtedly made possible by ballet, as it gave Arie a healthy way to release her tension. Not being homebound most of the time had contributed to the lessening of those pent-up feelings.

After guiding her mare into the stall, Arie provided her horse with oats to munch on and then used the currycomb all over Aster's head and body. The disadvantage of her full-time job was that she had to catch up on some of the neglected tasks that her mother had handed off to her, although as the weather became autumnal, there were fewer plants to tend to around the property.

After retrieving her hidden pointe shoes from the hayloft, Arie went on to the makeshift barre of a hitching rail and carried out her usual routine. She then sat down on a bale of hay to tie the ribbons around her ankles. It took a few tries to properly wrap the ribbon around, but once she did, Arie tucked the knot into the ribbon along the ankle bone. She strolled to the barre, tightened the drawstrings, and stuffed them into the shoes. Her feet sank into them, and she gripped for dear life with both hands as her toes pressed against the platforms and the concrete slab below. Arie couldn't fathom it. She was up on releve—right on her tiptoes, above the balls of her feet—and even managed to balance for a brief while without placing her hands on the barre.

Roaming around with her arms stretching to catch the dust particles in the sunshine flowing through the crevices, she attempted to roll up on the tips of the shoes. She winced as the tendons in her feet behaved like newly woven cotton shrinking in a batch of hot water.

Perhaps I overdid it with the barre positions. The strain along the vamps of the shoes was too much to bear, so she crouched on the hay bed and undid the ribbons. *But if I stick with it, I might be able to show up at class with them, and if they see me excelling at dancing en pointe, I'll truly be living my dream of being a ballerina. I just wish the shoes weren't so painful.*

Arie sprung up and laid her pointe shoes on the bale of hay. Then, giving herself ample floor space, she glided from one leg to the other and landed in a plié. The relief of being able to dance freely and not having to wear pointe shoes was unparalleled. However, Arie had missed hearing piano music to dance to since she'd begun taking lessons.

As the blood throbbing in her ears subsided, Arie walked briskly to the spot where she had also brought out a bottle of water and tipped it to her mouth, finishing off the remaining contents. Her gaze flickered around the barn before looking directly into Aster's inquisitive eyes. Rising from the bale, she sauntered toward her horse's stall, feeling warmth from the sun's rays and the refreshing autumn breeze that traced about her entire frame. With tented brows and a faint blow from the mare's nose, ears upward, Arie threaded her fingers through Aster's mane once more. As her horse's head gingerly moved toward her, Arie scratched between those large eyes, lined with wispy lashes.

"What was all of that, Arie?"

Arie jumped, eliciting an immediate reaction from Aster from the sudden movement. As the mare's ears pricked up, Aster snorted and threw up her head with a whinny. Glancing over her shoulder, Arie noticed Rudy and Maggie at the breezeway entrance.

"S–sorry, Aster. It's all right, girl," she soothed, trying to keep the horse at ease, then she turned to face her siblings. "Why are you two out here?"

"Mamm's wanting your help with supper and didn't know where you were, so she sent us out to find you." Rudy's lip curled. "Didn't Mom get upset with you about wanting to dance?"

"H–how did you know about that?"

"I overheard our parents talking about it after breakfast on the morning right before the tornado happened."

"Listen, Rudy. Please, don't tell them about what you saw out here. I've wanted to do this for so long, and there's a lot at stake if they find out."

"I dunno. You're usually on our case when we disobey Mom and Dad, and yet here you are doing this. Seems like you're asking for a whole lot without expecting me to get anything out of it."

"Are you really trying to bribe me, Rudy?"

He cocked his head, casting her a penetrating gaze. "Sure am. So, what's in it for me?"

"What is it that you want exactly?"

"Well, I'm in need of a new fishing pole. One that's just like the pole I had before."

"Before what, Rudy? What'd you do with the other one?"

"I might have lost it when I went fishing with Samuel."

"Does Daed know anything about it?" Arie questioned.

"No, but you're keeping secrets too, so it's only fair." Rudy smirked, rocking back on his heels.

Peering past her brother, Arie sighed and saw Maggie toting around her plush-looking bunny. "Maggie, you won't tell our parents about this, will you?"

Maggie shook her head, held up the stuffed animal, and added in an excited tone: "It was so amazing, Arie! Will you show us how to do all of that?"

Unsure of how to react, Arie ran a palm across her forehead, still drenched in perspiration from her exhilarating dancing or her nervousness at this moment that seemed to be smothering her. In an attempt to retain her composure and avoid showing herself in such a state like this, Arie assured her siblings that she would be inside the house shortly.

Really, I'm asking my own siblings to cover for me, putting them at risk of getting into trouble as well? I should be the only one at risk because of this secret, but now everyone is becoming involved. Even those shoes I wanted so badly. I know I shouldn't be wearing them, yet I'm still trying to do so in the barn. What am I even doing here?

Arie was aware of the implications of being discovered, but for the past month, her love for ballet had outweighed those potential consequences, and now she wasn't so sure. Edwin had been right. It was only a matter of time before her parents found out.

Chapter 21

Goshen

"Arie, try not to move your supporting leg as you transition to a turn," Miss Judith commented, detaching from Arie's ankles, and lacing her fingers together. "Don't worry, pirouettes are not easy to execute. It requires a lot of coordination and plenty of practice."

Apart from Arie, everyone had on their pointe shoes. These previous weeks had been rejuvenating when Arie didn't feel like she had to put her all into everything she did. Now, however, even the trifling things seemed insurmountable at times. Worrying about her inferiority to the other dancers, Arie had been waking up more lethargic than usual. Despite having practiced with the dance shoes at home, Arie faced difficulties rolling up onto the platform without the assistance of the hitching post or anything else she'd used for support.

Arie looked to her friend, who had overcome her sudden onset of illness at last. Lorrina brought her back leg up into passé, held it there while spotting the studio mirrors, and twirled on the end of her foot—a flawless movement sequence, with a body in graceful alignment. It was understandable why Lorrina's mother had been disappointed that her daughter showed little interest in pursuing a career in ballet. Lorrina's artistry and devotion to her craft made her an ideal candidate to be a prima ballerina.

After the reverence and the other dancers had scattered to gather up their belongings, Lorrina swiveled toward Arie.

"Phew! Another tiring, yet fun ballet class," Lorrina exclaimed, brushing at a tuft of hair that had fallen out of her bun. "I'll be sleeping hard tonight, especially since I won't have any coughing fits to worry about."

"Jah, being sick is never pleasant." Arie gulped a breath, attempting to recuperate from the rigorous exertion of her dancing lesson. "Hey, Lorrina. Are you planning to audition for *The Nutcracker* this weekend?"

"No, I've done it before, and this year I'd like to take a break from performing in the show. Besides, I still have my final winter showcase to dance in, so that's sufficient for me."

"Would I be able to dance in the winter showcase?" Arie questioned.

"I don't see why not. I think you ought to ask Miss Judith about it, though." Lorrina pointed with both fingers toward the room's entrance. "Be right back. Before we leave for home, we can stop by the Electric Brew and grab something to eat."

"Okay, but please don't take too long."

"No promises, Arie. I only have one speed right now, and that's pitifully tortoise."

Lorrina drifted out of the room, and Arie went over to Miss Judith, who had finally gotten around to shutting off the stereo. When Arie approached her teacher, Miss Judith's face brightened.

"Hello, Arie. Have you been enjoying yourself here, taking ballet in my classes."

"Very much," Arie replied, wringing her hands. "I was wondering, would I be able to perform in the winter showcase?"

"Of course, Arie. We'll be going over the routines for both classes next week, so if you want to learn them, we'd love to have you join us."

"Is it possible for me to wear pointe shoes like the rest of the class?"

Miss Judith's smile grew thin. "Arie, I think you've got lots of flair, especially given what you've learned from your friend. But you must have years of adept ballet training to strengthen your ankles, and I don't want you to injure yourself."

"Oh..." Arie looked away, fixing her eyes on the outer walls of the studio, part of her anticipating when Lorrina would be back. "Is there anything I can do to get myself closer to wearing them?"

"I'm sorry, Arie. At the very least, I would advise a few years of instruction, and we don't offer any adult classes in our studio. I'm assuming you feel obligated to keep up with the rest of the class, but most of them have been dancing in their ballet slippers since they were three." Miss Judith extended her arm to pat Arie's shoulder. "You should feel proud of yourself, Arie. Pointe shoes don't make a performer. What matters is the light from within that they radiate during their performance, and yours is quite brilliant. That's why I wanted you to take my class and gain some experience, and whatever you decide to do with it later is entirely up to you."

There wasn't much for Arie to do other than sit down amid the chairs since Lorrina hadn't gotten back yet. Bouncing a knee, her mind whirled with all kinds of thoughts regarding what Miss Judith had told her. Even though she had foreseen that response, Arie did hope that the teacher might let her dance en pointe while keeping a close check on her. Remembering that she would still be able to dance on stage, even if it wasn't on her toes for *The Nutcracker*, Arie closed her eyes and took a deep breath.

"I'm shocked you didn't bring your pointe shoes with you today."

Briar's face cut through Arie's gaze. "About that, I don't think I should wear them, Briar. Miss Judith said I wasn't ready for pointe shoes."

"Do you doubt me? Because I wouldn't have driven you over to buy the shoes if I didn't think you were ready for them."

"The only thing is that she's the one instructing us, so—"

"You know, teachers aren't always right," Briar cut in. "I said that you're ready, and since I've been dancing considerably longer than you have, I'm the one who knows best. I hope you're not mad at me for pushing you."

Her fingers curled along the cushion of the chair. "D–did I say I was?"

"No. Simply put, the auditions are here this weekend, and there's no real need for me to bring you along if you fail to demonstrate dancing en pointe."

"Aren't there other roles in *The Nutcracker* that don't require me to dance in pointe shoes?"

"Yeah, but they're usually for the non-lead characters. You're too beautiful and talented to try out for one of the lesser roles." Leaning over, Briar brought a finger to Arie's face and raised her chin up to meet his eyes. "You deserve to be Clara, and that's why I've been here—to make that happen for you."

She flinched from Briar's touch as though his fingertips were lit matches. Arie's gut wrenched under the weight of his gaze, which felt like the pounding of a chisel chipping away at her bit by bit.

"I..." Her body rose off the seat of its own accord. "I need to use the bathroom."

Arie hobbled out of the space in a blank daze, the world circling around her. Her throat constricted as she shoved the bathroom door open. Arie's senses were assaulted by the odor of lavender aerosol floating in the air, not calming her nerves in the slightest.

I can't do this. My time to be prepared for the audition is inadequate. My feet tense up so much while wearing pointe shoes, so how can I even expect to audition in them? Releasing a long, ragged breath, Arie looked at her reflection in the mirror. She turned on the faucet, rubbed her eyes, and splashed chilled water on her smoldering skin. *I'm just tired. Briar went to all the trouble of allowing me to have the shoes, and I don't want to upset him. If I prove myself, I might be given the opportunity to play a significant role on stage. Isn't this what I wanted?*

Shipshewana

"I'm glad we could find time to eat together," Edwin said as he and Arie entered the Blue Gate Restaurant on Saturday morning. "Now that you work full-time at the gift shop and I'm usually on the run with my job, I don't get to see you as much as I'd like."

"That's also not being helped much by my ballet lessons." Arie's delicate mole expanded as her lips pressed together. "I'm sorry."

Edwin shook his head. "I've also been preoccupied with the drill team, so there's no need to apologize. We just need to continue adjusting to our hectic schedules."

She leaned closer to him and whispered, "I agree with what you said, and I'm glad we could work it out to have breakfast here together."

After Edwin checked in at the podium, and made sure his name had been put on the waiting list to be seated downstairs for the Saturday breakfast buffet, he'd been informed that it would be at least thirty to forty minutes before they could be seated.

"Why don't we go browse the bakery items while we're waiting?" he suggested.

"I guess that would be okay," Arie replied. "But if they should call your name while we're in the bakery, we might miss out on breakfast."

"Not to worry." Edwin showed her the pager he'd been given. "This will vibrate when it's time for us to be shown to a table."

"All right, let's check out the delicacies they have in the bakery." Arie chuckled and gave his arm a little poke. "But I bet seeing all those pastries will make you hungry."

Edwin put the paging device in his pocket. "Too late for that." He raised his head and sniffed as they got closer to the bakery, which was on the same floor as the entrance. "All the wonderful aromas here have caused my belly to rumble like a cement mixer."

Arie prodded him again, rolling her eyes. "Very funny, Edwin. Just be careful you don't get caught up in the sweets."

When they entered the bakery and Edwin caught sight of all the tantalizing breads, cookies, pies, muffins, and fudge on display, he knew it would be difficult not to buy something sweet. "Maybe we should have waited up front on a bench instead of coming here, where I'm tempted to buy one of these goodies," Edwin admitted.

"I know what you mean. Just looking at those German chocolate bars makes my mouth water." Arie pointed to the items in question. "But I don't think it's worth spoiling our appetites for a hearty, all-you-can-eat breakfast just to eat one of these pastries now."

"You've got that right." Edwin took a step toward the display case. "Even so, purchasing some pastries to take home wouldn't hurt. If we each bought a half dozen or so, we could share them with our families."

"Edwin, you make a great point. I'm sure my parents would love some pecan cinnamon rolls. It might inspire my mamm to bake some herself."

"Maybe I'll buy a Dutch apple pie." Edwin neared the counter and was about to place his order when the pager in his pocket buzzed. He reached in, withdrew the blinking device, and showed it to Arie. "Whoops, saved by the buzzer. We need to go downstairs for breakfast right now so we don't lose our place. I suppose we could always come back here when we've finished our meal."

Arie nodded. "That is, if we don't forget, or if we are too full to consider pastries."

Edwin offered his hand to Arie, and when she entwined her fingers with his, they rushed out of the bakery. Now all he could think about was heaping his plate at the buffet with sausage patties, cheesy potatoes, biscuits with gravy, scrambled eggs, and perhaps, if he had room left over after all that, a melt-in-your-mouth doughnut.

After filling their plates at the buffet and offering a silent prayer once they'd returned to their table, Edwin decided to bring up the topic of Roman riding. He didn't want to rush into it, though, so he waited until they'd both eaten most of the food on their plates.

Edwin hurriedly devoured a forkful of cheesy potatoes, took a swig of water from his glass, and cleared his throat. "I've been waiting for a chance to tell you about something that happened during my drill team's last practice."

Just as she was about to cut into the butter, Arie set down her knife and gave him a wide-eyed stare. "I hope no one fell from their horse or sustained any injuries."

"No, nothing like that, but there was a lot of excitement among the team members when our leader said that Sarah's cousin had traveled from Ohio with her two horses to demonstrate Roman riding."

"I see." Arie snatched up her knife again and scraped a lump of butter. "How'd that go?"

"Watching Esther Troyer stand on the back of one horse with no hands was exciting enough, but when she stood atop two horses at the same time and road around the arena, it was absolutely amazing." Edwin's pulse pumped a bit as he visually relived when he'd sat on the bleachers and watched in awe. "You know, Arie, in some ways that kind of riding could be as much fun as ballet."

Fumbling with the bread on her plate, she asked, "In what way, Edwin?"

"Well, um... I guess you'd have to see it for yourself to understand." Edwin inclined his head toward Arie. "Why don't I hire a driver sometime soon, and we can go to Holmes County, Ohio, to see Esther in action? We could make a full day of it, and I'm sure we'd have a lot of fun. What do you say, Arie?"

Instead of answering, Arie sat peering at her plate. Her silence lasted so long Edwin believed that his girlfriend would remain quiet for the rest of their meal. Before he could tell her she didn't have to agree with him, Arie spoke up.

"Riding on a horse and dancing ballet are not the same thing, Edwin." She swept her hands around in a circle. "Why can't you consider how I feel about that?"

"I'm sorry, Arie. You won't be dancing forever, though, so I'm merely suggesting that idea as something fun you could do once we decide to join the church. Didn't you say that's what you planned to do?"

"Edwin, I—I don't know. I just wish I had more time to think about all of this. Various things are putting pressure on me, and they're all pointing in different directions."

Arie's lack of interest in Roman riding or joining his drill team was as apparent as the petite nose on her lovely face. Pressuring her into becoming a member of the faith or doing anything she didn't sincerely wish to do was the last thing Edwin wanted. He figured prolonging the inevitable wasn't the best course of action for either of them.

"I understand what you're dealing with, Arie."

"Do you really?"

"I believe so, and I already know what I want out of life. For me, I want to stay in the Amish faith, get married, have kids, and spend time with the person I love." He reached over and placed his hand on her arm. "That would be you, Arie. But if you're unsure whether you want to do any of that, I don't want to put any more pressure on you. So, until you decide what you truly want, we probably should not go places or do things together anymore."

"Wh–what are you saying, Edwin?" Arie asked, her chin trembling.

"I am saying that it might be best for both of us if we end things between us."

"You mean, break up?" She clutched the neckline of the matching cape covering the upper part of her dress.

"Jah. I believe it's better for both of us this way. Don't you agree?"

Arie lifted her shoulders as she stared down at her nearly empty plate. "Maybe you're right, Edwin. Under the circumstances, it might be for the best."

To Edwin's amazement, Arie had willingly accepted his

suggestion. He'd hoped that Arie loved him enough that she would set her desire to dance aside and agree to become part of the church with him so that they might someday marry.

But apparently her desire to become a ballerina takes precedence over her desire to live out her days with me. Edwin's arms felt limp as he dragged his thumb down the table covering. *I shouldn't be taking this so personally, but it's hard not to when I honestly thought Arie would fulfill her commitment to me.*

Watching from the living room window, Brenda saw Arie step down from her boyfriend's buggy. Brenda had planned to have a heart-to-heart conversation with her daughter this morning, but when Arie announced that she and Edwin were going out for breakfast, Brenda decided that the conversation could wait. Now, however, she was not about to let the opportunity to speak with Arie slip by.

When Arie entered the house a few minutes later, Brenda, remaining in the living room with her arms folded, called out to her. "Arie, I need to speak with you."

"Can it wait, Mamm? I need to go upstairs and spend some time alone in my room right now."

"No. What I have to say cannot wait a minute longer."

Arie appeared in the living room in a matter of seconds. She scrunched up her nose. "What's wrong? Is someone in the family grank or seriously hurt?"

"No one is sick, nor have there been any injuries." Brenda uncrossed her arms and pointed at Arie. "This conversation I wish to have is about you."

"Oh, okay. Is there something you need me to do?"

"Jah, there is. I want you to be honest with me for a change."

Arie's gaze flickered from Brenda to the rest of the room and back again. "About what, exactly?"

"I know what you've been doing since you began working full-time at the gift shop."

"Have you talked to the manager to see if I've been working hard?" Arie's face contorted, and Brenda saw a hint of moisture below her daughter's eyes.

"I have not talked with your manager about you or your work habits, Arie." Brenda held both arms against her sides. "Your little sister, however, divulged the truth."

"W–what truth?"

"That you've been dancing in the barn, and don't deny it, Arie. Maggie and Rudy were both there, and they witnessed you swirling around and leaping into the air while wearing a pair of dance shoes on your feet. You were practicing ballet like your friend Lorrina does. Am I right?"

Arie nodded slowly in the affirmative.

Brenda's body temperature soared. "I presume that Lorrina has been teaching you ballet for some time and you've chosen to keep it from us. Is that correct?"

"Jah, only recently Lorrina has not been my teacher."

"So, what are you saying?" Brenda questioned. "Are you attempting to teach yourself?"

"No, Mamm. I've been taking ballet classes at the dance studio in Goshen, and I ride over there with Lorrina after I get off work."

Brenda gave a frustrated shake of her head. "I'm very disappointed in you, Daughter. How could you go behind your father's and my back and do something like this?"

Arie opened her mouth as if to respond, but Brenda stopped her short. "This is something we need to discuss, Arie. After watching you dance, your sister will want to follow suit. You should be setting a better example for your siblings. Don't you realize that wearing immodest clothing and dancing is not the Amish way?"

"But I haven't joined the church, I'm paying for my own lessons, and I intend to continue going to class. I didn't tell you because I knew you'd be upset and I was worried you might kick me out of the house." Arie paused a few seconds before continuing. "All I'm doing is trying to figure out who I am as a person. This whole time, you've expected me to always cater to everyone else's needs, and now, I can't think for myself or make my own choices."

"Arie, why would you even think that way? After all I've done for you—"

"I've done plenty for you and this family as well, and I'm tired of my efforts getting overlooked and my passions being discouraged. Even if you disagree with how I feel, I cannot open up to you unless I feel safe doing so."

"You don't understand, Arie. I only want what's best for you and our family." Brenda drew in several deep breaths, hoping to calm herself. "If you choose to pursue ballet, what will happen to your relationship with Edwin, who has plans to become an Amish church member?"

Arie's shoulders drooped as she spoke in short sentences. "That's not an issue, Mamm. Not anymore. Not ever again."

"What do you mean?"

"Edwin ended our relationship this morning." Arie began to sob, and the tears she shed flowed down her cheeks and onto the front of her dress.

"Oh, my..." Brenda's heart ached at her daughter's words. Her fury was lessened when she saw the anguish and dejection on Arie's face, even though she was still upset that her daughter had lied and was taking dance classes without Jerome's or her knowledge. She stepped forward and encircled Arie's quivering frame. "I'm so sorry to hear this, Arie. Jah, so very, very sorry." Brenda gently patted her daughter's back.

As Arie crumbled into her arms, Brenda became acutely aware that Arie's acts of disobedience were also pleas for acceptance. In addition to the compassion she felt, Brenda had a glimmer of hope.

If Edwin broke up with Arie, then he must also know about her dancing lessons, she thought. *That's probably the reason he ended their relationship. And if Arie truly loves him, the way I think she does, then she might change her mind about dancing and set it aside in order to become a church member so they can get married.*

Chapter 22

Goshen

INSIDE THE THEATER, THE MASSIVE overhead arch illuminated the stage with its circular light fixtures. The present moment intertwined with Arie's memories, resonating like the murmurs of people milling about the auditorium as she followed Briar. Her eyes pricked with tears as she lingered in the carpeted aisles, remembering back to when she had been in this same building so many years ago. Arie paused next to one of the seats and traced her fingers along the armrest, pinpointing the spot where she'd been seated next to Lorrina's mother. As much as she would have preferred to relive the wonderful moments of that day, Arie's thoughts kept returning to what had happened earlier today.

Since Briar had made plans to pick her up, it wasn't like she could have bailed out. So, after going upstairs to her room, throwing on her leotard and tights, wrapping her skirt and zipping up a hoodie, and tucking the pointe shoes in her bag, Arie had come downstairs and poked her head in the kitchen to announce that she was leaving. There had been no verbal response from her mother, but Mom's silence said it all. She wasn't happy or supportive of Arie's decision to dance.

"It's so bright up there." Arie gestured to the stage, while squelching her thoughts in order to focus on the here and now. "Wouldn't it be difficult to see with the light in your eyes?"

"The only thing we can't see on stage are the people in the audience." Briar indicated the seats with a wave of his hand. "We still have about an hour or so before auditions, so make yourself comfortable."

After getting situated on the velvet seat, Arie reached into her bag to retrieve her shoes. However, when she noticed some of the pupils from Miss Judith's class in the seats in front of her, she became jittery, realizing she'd be performing in front of them. What if next Tuesday, they told Miss Judith that she'd worn pointe shoes to the audition? What if Arie tripped and sprained her ankle, preventing her from dancing for weeks or even longer? The multitude of *what-if*s crowded her consciousness.

"Briar, if I wear the shoes, someone's bound to tell Miss Judith. I can't go up on stage wearing them."

"You're worried about that? I helped you get the pointe shoes. The least you can do is go up on stage and put them to good use."

"What was that about pointe shoes?" Lorrina asked.

With each heartbeat, Arie's pulse thumped faster in her ears as she glanced away from Briar, aware that seeing Lorrina here only intensified the warmth radiating off her skin. It made no sense. Lorrina had told Arie that she wouldn't be at the audition. *Do I have any right to question it, considering that she didn't know I would be here either?*

"Lorrina!" Arie shot up from the chair, maneuvering around Briar at the end of the row. "What are you doing here?"

"I should be asking you that question, Arie. Although I'm not in the show this year, I'm here to support the students I've been instructing. When I saw you with Briar, I was quite surprised."

Lorrina's eyes narrowed. "Since when have you two become friends?"

"Oh, Arie didn't tell you?" Briar smirked at her. "Here I thought friends were supposed to tell each other everything."

As Briar continued his tirade, he essentially told Lorrina that she was to blame, and shouldn't have been spreading unfounded rumors about him, because he was a nice person who never received recognition for his good deeds. The tension escalated, and as Arie endured the conflict between Briar and Lorrina, her heart hammered in the hollow of her chest. It was quite apparent that her first impression of Briar was exactly what Lorrina had said, and Arie could no longer stand it.

"You listen here, Briar," Lorrina scolded. "I don't know if you're doing this to spite me or for sick amusement, but you've gone too far. If Arie wants to audition, that's fine, but she should not be wearing pointe shoes."

"This has nothing to do with you, so stay out of it. She wants to audition for Clara. That's why she rode with me here. Isn't that right?" He turned to look at Arie.

"No, it's not," Arie said with a shake of her head.

"What? Are you kidding? You can't be serious." His nostrils flared as he glared at her.

"Briar, I appreciate that you took me to get the shoes and thought I could pull this off, even though now, I'm convinced that I can't. So, no. . .I won't do it."

"You're getting a bit full of yourself there. Why are you being so difficult, Arie? I thought you wanted the part of Clara. And now you're backing away from the opportunity?"

"I was afraid to miss out, but this isn't worth it. You ignored me every time I told you that I didn't believe it was a good idea and that Miss Judith had said no. You also understood that I was under pressure, even when I remained silent. All you were doing was putting false hope in my head. Since only I am aware of my limitations, I'm done making excuses and will not take the stage with pointe shoes when I know I'm not ready."

"I never did any of that. You really have some issues," Briar stated with a noisy huff. "You were the one who was envious of everyone else's pointe shoes. Guess that's what I get for rescuing a sheltered woman from a bygone era."

With a scowl contorting his face, Briar stormed off toward the stage's steps, leaving Arie dumbfounded by the whole exchange. Though it had been brewing beneath the surface and would have eventually surfaced, until today, she hadn't seen Briar so enraged and overtaken by his own self-importance. In an attempt to calm herself, Arie inhaled an uneven breath.

She shifted her attention to Lorrina and spoke with a firmer voice. "You were right about Briar. I'm sorry, Lorrina. I'm sorry for not telling you. I just really wanted the pointe shoes. Briar offered to take me to the dance boutique when you were sick, and I stupidly accepted."

"I'm not mad about Briar being a jerk." Lorrina's eyes softened. "I am upset, but mostly because I must have really done something wrong for you not to be honest with me."

"You did nothing wrong. All I do is keep secrets. I already knew how you would react, so I figured no harm done if you didn't know. I'm not a good friend, Lorrina."

"Arie, don't be so hard on yourself. You are exceptionally kind. Always have been, ever since we've been friends."

"No, I'm not. I'm a lenient person," she replied with a shaken breath. "I simply don't want to bother people or make them angry, but I've let down everyone in my life, and they're all upset with me now."

When Lorrina moved closer, and pulled Arie in for a hug, Arie rested her chin on her friend's shoulder.

"Although you offended Briar, you are not a cruel person just because you disagreed with him or didn't do what he expected. Being true to yourself, upholding your convictions, and resisting opposition from others make you a more compassionate person. I'm proud that you were finally able to do that, Arie."

Knowing full well that she had finally had to face a fact she had long repressed, Arie gripped her friend tighter, not even bothering to stifle her tears. Even though the strain of her disagreement with Briar had not gone away, Arie felt the burden of the pressure from his manipulation lift off her shoulders. It would be best for her to return to her parents' house, since that was exactly where she wanted to be right now.

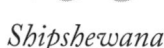

Shipshewana

"That doesn't look very comfortable. Why are you sitting on the hardwood floor rather than on the couch or in a chair?" Edwin's mother asked when she entered the living room, where he sat near the fireplace, legs crossed, and his gaze fixed on the mound of logs that had been placed on the hearth.

As she edged closer, Edwin squinted up at her, noting her protruding stomach under her dress in the shade of pomegranate seeds. She already had a somewhat top-heavy appearance and was around halfway through her pregnancy. He was glad his mother wasn't having morning sickness anymore, but her drawn expression and the dark circles beneath her eyes indicated her significant fatigue. Edwin hoped for her sake that when it came time for the baby to be delivered, things would go smoothly for both mother and child.

Mom interrupted Edwin's thoughts by bending down to rest a hand on his shoulder. "Is something the matter, Son?"

"Jah."

"Want to talk about it?"

"Not really, but I suppose it might help if I get it off my chest."

With a hand cradling her stomach, Mom shuffled across the room and lowered herself to the couch. Then she invited Edwin to join her. After steering clear of the coffee table, Edwin sank into the couch cushions.

"Nothing's right in my world anymore." Edwin groaned.

"Nothing at all? You have a good-paying job, a place to live without paying rent, and you've been blessed with a sweet girlfriend. Something must've really altered all of that for you to be feeling that way."

He leaned forward, both hands on his knees, and said, "It's over, Mom. Arie and I aren't seeing each other anymore."

"Oh, my. Seriously?"

Edwin gave a sluggish nod. "And it was my idea to break up with her."

"How come? I thought things were going so well between you two. What happened, Son?"

Since he was no longer seeing Arie socially, Edwin figured he had nothing to lose by telling his mother the whole story. Besides, it wouldn't be long before the entire Amish community became aware of what had happened. The gossip mill ran rampant sometimes, and the news that he and Arie were no longer a couple was bound to get out. For that matter, she'd probably told her parents by now, and Edwin wondered if they'd learned that their daughter had secretly been taking ballet lessons. He could only speculate on their reception of the news. He told his mother that he had witnessed Arie performing some ballet moves in her family's barn, but had vowed to keep it a secret.

"Unfortunately, Arie later informed me that she was thinking about participating in dance classes."

Mom's brows furrowed. "How would that fit into her plans to get baptized and join the church? That is what she'd told you previously, right?"

"Jah, but things changed, and now. . ." Edwin hesitated and rubbed his wrist while mulling over his next words. "When I took her to Blue Gate for breakfast, Arie made it clear that she wasn't sure anymore, even though she'd promised she would only be doing ballet for a short time. All I know is if Arie doesn't commit to our Amish ways and pursues a career in ballet, there is no way we can have a future together."

"Unless you were to leave the Amish faith yourself." Mom pursed her lips. "Would you ever do that, Edwin?"

"Not a chance. Because, like Arie, I shouldn't follow someone else's path if it isn't aligned with my own."

As Edwin fought to keep his emotions in check, he felt his mother's cool hand on the back of his neck. Even though talking about the situation with his mother helped to lighten his load, it also brought back the pain he'd felt from losing the young woman he had hoped would be his wife someday.

"So, what are you going to do now, Edwin?" Mom asked.

"I'll tell you what our son is gonna do—he will either move on with his life and find a young woman more suitable for him or try to fix the problem between him and Arie."

Edwin's head snapped up, and he sat straight, unsure how long his father had been standing there listening. He shifted on the cushion with his fingers curled into the palms of his hands, unable to think of anything to say.

Edwin's father marched across the room, halting right in front of Edwin. "You know, if you weren't so invested in that all-important drill team you belong to, you could've spent more time with Arie, so she didn't feel the need to get involved in dancing."

"What are you saying, Dad? Do you think it's my fault that Arie doesn't want to join the church?"

"I'm sure your daed didn't mean that at all." Edwin's mother patted his back a few times. "You are not to blame for any decisions Arie chose to make. And in my opinion, you made the right decision by allowing Arie to explore her options for the future rather than rushing into something she wasn't ready for."

"I'm not surprised that you would take his side." Dad glared at Mom while folding both arms tightly against his chest.

Mom tipped her head back and looked up at him with lips pressed together. "I was not taking anyone's side." When her facial muscles relaxed a bit, she added, "If Arie doesn't have any plans to join the church, then Edwin did exactly what he needed to do."

"Okay, then it's Arie Kauffman's fault that this happened."

"Dad!" With his chin raised, Edwin rose from the couch. "We've broken up, but I'd appreciate it if you'd not speak ill of Arie. I'm the one who suggested we should end things, not her. However, she did agree with me."

Knowing Arie, Edwin thought, *she probably wouldn't have taken the first step in ending our relationship, and there's the possibility that Arie only agreed to it because she felt that's what I wanted. I hope she's giving it a lot of consideration now, and when it's time to make the right decision, she'll know what to do.*

With a scowl, Dad went to his beloved recliner and took a

seat. "Why does life have to be so complicated?"

Edwin had been wondering the same thing all day. Never in a million years had he expected things would turn out the way they had for him and Arie.

"I am sure feeling *mied* this evening." Brenda stretched both arms over her head, unable to hold back the impending yawn.

Sitting slouched in his favorite chair across the room, Jerome peeked at her above the pages of the newspaper he had been reading for the past hour. "Today, there was an awful lot of work at the store, so I can understand why you'd be tired."

"This whole thing with Arie hasn't helped." She stifled another yawn with her hand. "My nerves are on edge, and my whole body is feeling the effects of the stress her dishonesty has caused. When she left earlier for some kind of dancing audition, it really hurt me, Jerome."

From the bowl on the side table next to his chair, he scooped a handful of peanuts and popped them into his mouth. "We should have seen this coming, Brenda. Our eldest daughter started acting restless and a bit strange ever since she began working full-time at the gift store in town."

"Something that seemed off to me was how often she made trips to the barn, supposedly to check on her *gaul*. I mean, how often every day does a person need to check on their horse?"

Jerome took a drink from his glass of water and replied, "Well, if Aster was *grank* or something, then maybe. . ."

Brenda cut her husband off. "Be serious, Jerome. Arie's horse has not fallen ill, nor has the mare been injured in any way." She bopped the side of her head. "One of those times I saw her out there, it seemed a bit suspicious. I should have realized that something was off with Arie and called her out on it right away."

"There's nothing either of us can do about it now," Jerome said. "We can't go back in time and change a single thing."

"You're right, but we don't have to look the other way either."

"What are you thinking we should do, Brenda? Arie is not a little girl anymore, and this is the time of her rumspringa, so we can't really forbid her to dance. If it's something Arie truly wants to do, she's going to do it, with or without our approval."

Brenda nodded. "But I will not tolerate her sneaking around behind our backs or keeping the truth from us about anything she does. Lying to her parents is disrespectful, not to mention wrong."

"I wholeheartedly agree. Have you told our daughter that, in so many words?"

"Not yet, but I plan to tell her in the morning. Since Arie excused herself as soon as supper and the dishes were done and went straight up to her room, I figured it would be best to postpone the lecture until after we've all had a restful night's sleep."

"That makes good sense," Jerome agreed. "I'm glad you thought it through."

"I have. Unfortunately, after I confronted Arie about what Maggie and Rudy saw their big sister doing in the barn, I haven't been able to think clearly. Arie has always been fairly obedient, and I hadn't expected that she would ever act out."

"Guess there's not much point in talking more about it now," Jerome said, rising to his feet. "Now that the kinner are upstairs and probably asleep, we both ought to go to our room and call it a night."

Brenda heaved a lingering sigh. "I couldn't agree more."

Brenda didn't know how long she'd been asleep, but she was roused out of her slumber by the sudden sounds of a loud, jarring thud shattering glass. Trembling and disoriented, she sat upright. Her feet hit the floor at the same time Jerome leaped out of his side of the bed.

Her voice faltered, but she managed to say, "That sounded like something hit the side of our house."

"No, it wasn't here. We'd have felt the impact. The noise that woke us was farther out." Jerome flicked on the battery-operated lamp on the nightstand beside his bed, hurriedly slipped into his trousers, and grabbed his flashlight. "I'd better go take a look."

"I'm going with you." Brenda donned her heavy robe as well as a pair of sandals, since going barefoot in the dark would not be a good idea. She assumed that when they got to the back door, where Jerome typically kept his outdoor footwear, he would throw on either his boots or a pair of shoes.

Treading on the heels of her husband as they raced out their bedroom door, Brenda snatched a second flashlight so they could see better once they were outside. They had barely entered the main hallway outside their room when Arie and two trembling youngsters were caught in the beam of their flashlights.

"What was that horrible noise, Daadi?" Maggie asked.

"Jah, what was it?" Rudy ceased talking to rub his eyes. "I was sleeping real good, and the sound woke me up—nearly knocked me right outta bed."

"We all must have heard it at the same time, and it caused every one of us to wake up," Brenda stated, trying to keep her voice calm. The children's alarm was evident, and she didn't want to further their worries. "We believe there has been an accident on our property."

"You mean with a car?" The question came from Maggie.

Brenda shoved her hands into the spacious pockets of her

robe. "Jah, I'm afraid so."

Maggie sought out her older sister for solace as tears poured down her cheeks. Arie knelt, wrapped her arms around Maggie, and whispered soothing words to calm her down.

"Settle down now, children," Jerome said, patting the top of Maggie's head. "Your mamm and I are going outside now to take a look."

"I wanna go too," Rudy insisted, giving his father's elbow a tug.

Jerome shook his head. "No, Son. You need to stay here with your sisters, which will help them feel less distressed." Even though he spoke under his breath, Brenda could hear all he said as he leaned closer to their son's ear.

After a few moments hesitation, Rudy raised his eyebrows. "All right, Dad. While you're away, I'll be the man of the family."

Brenda would have been touched by their son's change of heart to stay in the house with his sisters, if it hadn't been for the dread of what must have occurred somewhere on their property. Although she knew none of her children would drift off to sleep during this unexpected situation, she was tempted to tell them to go back to bed.

"How about I heat some hot chocolate on the stove for you both?" Arie suggested, grasping her sister's hand.

Brenda nodded. "Good idea, Arie. Feel free to get out the cookie jar too."

"Okay, Mamm," Arie responded. "I'm heading to the kitchen right now, so Maggie and Rudy, please follow me."

Brenda kept an eye on her three children while Maggie and Rudy trailed behind their older sister. She often wondered how Arie managed to keep her siblings in line. Whatever Arie's technique was, Brenda was grateful that her daughter was willing to keep the young ones occupied while she and Jerome went outside to find out exactly what had transpired.

She accompanied Jerome out the rear door after he had laced up his pair of boots. Brenda took a deep breath, steeling herself against the cool air as they made their way to where the sound seemed to have originated. They headed toward their general store, and Brenda prayed while gazing up at the sky.

Heavenly Father: If a vehicle struck the building, I pray that no one was harmed and that whatever happened out here, You will provide us the strength to cope with it.

Chapter 23

WHILE MAGGIE AND RUDY WERE finishing their breakfast that morning, Arie walked out with her parents to inspect the damage that had been done to their store during the night. Even though no one had been harmed—not even the elderly woman driver who had collided with the store just before the brink of dawn—the many repairs would leave Arie's family in financial hardship.

According to what Mom and Dad had told Arie when they'd returned to the house last night, it had been a real shock to venture out and discover pieces of wood scattered all over the ground and a full-sized car with the front end wedged halfway through the left side of the building. Arie's father had said that the poor English woman who'd been operating the vehicle appeared a little disoriented and somewhat dazed. She'd been emotional while attempting to explain things to Dad and wound up weeping in Mom's arms.

The woman, who'd identified herself as Selma Gates, explained that she lived in a small town in the southern part of Indiana and had driven herself here to visit an elderly sister, who lived in Shipshewana. The woman further claimed that she couldn't see well on the darker patches of road, since her headlights had gone out and there were no streetlights in the countryside. Believing that she was at her sister's residence, where she'd been expected several hours earlier, the woman had made a sharp right turn, lost control, and crashed straight into the store. On top of that, Selma stated that she didn't know what she'd hit at first but eventually understood it had been a building rather than a tree or fence. Fortunately, the woman had a cell phone in her purse, and when she'd finally calmed down enough to think things through, she'd called for a tow truck and a ride to her sister's house. Before leaving, she'd told Mom and Dad that unfortunately she'd let the insurance she'd had on her vehicle lapse due to lack of funds. Of course, that meant that Arie's parents would have to pay for all the supplies and labor needed for the repairs to the store. The poor woman would also need a new car, but she'd mentioned that her nephew might be able to help her with that.

After hearing Dad's version of the events, Arie felt relieved that he'd insisted that she and her younger siblings stay in the house. The children would have been frightened by the sight of the vehicle wedged partially inside their store, along with the distressed woman crying hysterically.

It probably would have frightened me as well, Arie thought as she clasped her mother's hand and gave it a tender squeeze. The sight of the damaged shelves, the shattered drywall, and goods scattered everywhere drove home the magnitude of the catastrophe.

Arie took a deep breath, remembering how important it was to set her sights on what was truly important and not the results of the tragedy lying in front of them.

"It'll be okay," Arie assured her mother. "You and Daed have been through rough times before, and the Lord will see you through this situation as well."

"You're right, Arie. But the repairs to the store are an added expense we surely don't need." Her mother's lips quivered. "I was so pleased when the flooring was installed. Before, the old floorboards used to squeak with every step, and it was nice to have new flooring put down recently. We put so much effort into making this store attractive to all the customers who come in, but now it's in ruins."

"Not only that," Arie's father spoke up, "but the accident caused such a mess inside the store, we won't be able to open for business until things are cleaned up and the gaping hole where the car came through is at least temporarily patched up." Dad shook his head slowly and spoke in a strangled voice, giving evidence of the emotions he felt. "Trouble always seems to be around, and we're never ready for it when it comes. At a time like this, it's really hard to stay positive."

Hearing her parents' comments and observing their discouragement devastated Arie. Mom and Dad were sincere, diligent people who didn't deserve this kind of misfortune.

The words of Psalm 34:17–19 ran through Arie's mind: "The righteous cry, and the Lord heareth, and delivereth them out of all their troubles. The Lord is nigh unto them that are of a broken heart; and saveth such as be of a contrite spirit. Many are the afflictions of the righteous: but the Lord delivereth him out of them all." Every person would experience trouble in their lives regardless of how wonderful they appeared to be or how hard they had tried to glorify God in their words and acts. But she needed to have faith that God would be with them through all their difficulties.

As she continued with her reflections, Arie let go of her

mother's hand and massaged her forehead. Between what had happened with her and Briar yesterday and this unexpected, middle-of-the-night accident, Arie saw it as a wake-up call for her to refrain from dancing and build a stronger bond with her family. Mom and Dad needed her more than ever right now, and if they didn't have to pay someone to keep an eye on Rudy and Maggie after school, they could use that money toward the repairs on the building and the purchase of replacement supplies for others that had been damaged.

Arie stood in front of them. "Mom and Dad, may I please tell you both something?"

"Of course, Daughter," Mom responded. "What did you want to say?"

"I'm very sorry for keeping my ballet lessons a secret from you two. I regret hiding things and letting you believe I would be working extra hours when I was actually dancing."

As if to reply, Mom opened her mouth, but Arie continued. "I feel guilt-ridden for everything—not working at the store when you needed me and not helping to support our family financially—so I've made a decision."

"What might that be?" her father questioned.

Arie gazed squarely at their faces and said, "I'm going to give up ballet and utilize my income and time to help our family here in the store and at home, looking after my siblings and doing whatever chores need to be done to lighten Mom's load."

For a few seconds, Arie's mother covered her eyes with the palms of her hands. When she lowered her hands, eyes fluttering open, she asked in a near whisper, "You would really do that for us?"

"Jah, I'm your daughter, after all, and it would be my pleasure. Here of late, I've been thinking only about myself. Rather than trying to uphold a pretense of righteousness, I should've provided you with the truth." Holding her hands together, Arie took a moment to catch her breath. "Last night, when you and Dad came back to the house and told us what had happened, I gave it a lot of thought. I ignored Edwin and Lorrina's advice that I should be honest, which put me in circumstances I would never want to find myself in again. The good news is that I now firmly believe that ballet was not my calling. One of our ministers cited Romans 12:2 at church a few weeks ago, and it got me to thinking and questioning what I was doing, although I didn't act upon it soon enough. That verse says, 'And be not conformed to this world: but be ye transformed by the renewing of your mind, that ye may prove what is that good, and acceptable, and perfect, will of God.'"

"That is an excellent passage of scripture," Mom said as tears spilled from her eyes and rolled down her cheeks.

"I believe we all spent some time in introspection last night, Arie," Dad interjected. "My thoughts were about not taking things for granted and appreciating my family more." As he wrapped his arm around Arie's waist and gave her an affectionate hug, she choked up as a torrent of emotions threatened to wash over her.

Mom leaned forward, extended her arms, and firmly embraced Arie. "Thank you so much for your honesty and desire to help out. We love and appreciate you, Daughter."

"I love you too," Arie murmured against the fabric of her mother's dress. For the first time in a long while, she felt loved and appreciated by her parents. One thing was certain: Arie knew without reservation that she'd made the right decision by deciding to give up her passion for ballet. Perhaps someday, Lord willing, she would find something else that would bring her the joy dancing had—something less worldly that would not go against the Amish way she had been brought up to appreciate.

Seated on one of the benches in the youth section, Arie's attention honed in on the beginning of their visiting minister's sermon. Despite the incident at her family's store in the wee hours of the morning, today was Sunday, and they'd left for church bright and early. On the way there, while traveling in the buggy, Arie's mother had insisted that they all needed to surround themselves with the caring people in their community for support. Arie was familiar with how the rumor mill went about, and similar to the summer tornado that struck the community, a vehicle damaging a portion of the store was sure to start some discussion among those who were at today's church gathering.

"Other than how we react to the external influences in our lives, the truth is that our circumstances are far beyond our control." With his eyes sweeping the room like a feather duster, the minister said, "Our words, our bodies—which our souls inhabit—and of course, what we put our trust toward are all under our control. We tend to rely too much on the opinions of those around us, so there's a lack of self-awareness, and as a result, we have trouble identifying our own course of action. First John 3:18 reads, 'My little children, let us not love in word, neither in tongue; but in deed and in truth.' You will find the purpose of your life if you live out your faith in an honest manner that is in accordance with the will of the Lord."

As the minister proceeded to talk about one's own awareness and the pursuit of truth, Arie's eyes strayed to Maggie, who was once again settled next to her on the wooden bench. As much as Arie was taken aback by her sister telling their mother about her practicing ballet in the barn, part of her was thankful the truth had finally been revealed. She thought back to the sermon she'd heard a few months earlier, when another minister had reviewed the scripture in Luke about how even the things we keep hidden from others will eventually come to light. Her sister, in contrast, was being honest, and Arie didn't want to foster secrecy anymore. Like the preacher had declared, she needed to strive for truthfulness in everything.

Although Arie's parents had said they still had some misgivings about ballet, dancing was not by nature wrong. It simply was not in keeping with the Amish practices or what they felt was pleasing to God. And as Arie had figured out, there were certainly underlying pressures from being a ballerina. Lorrina had been born into an English household, so she'd learned how to navigate things of the world and developed discernment; therefore, she'd chosen to teach ballet rather than strive for a career that wouldn't fulfill her life. Arie, however, had idealized ballet, and while it helped her get through some tough times, it also added to the pressure she had been under, knowing that her parents didn't approve. Perhaps if she had not grown up in an Amish home, ballet could have been her calling, but Arie knew deep down that she'd been attempting to live her friend's life rather than her own.

After church, Arie planned to call on her friend and share with her that she would no longer be accompanying her to the dance studio in Goshen.

Arie tried to avoid glancing at Edwin, who sat beside his brother on the other side of the barn. She thought about the times Edwin had been supportive of her, even after discovering her secret about ballet. Arie knew he'd hoped she would remain faithful to her original promise and join the Amish church. Since her decisions had ruptured the bond between them, when she joined the church, it would not be as part of a dating couple.

Even if I've given up ballet, it could be too late to save my relationship with Edwin, Arie thought as she scrubbed a hand against her cheek. *As much as I desire to reach out to him and say that I'm no longer taking ballet lessons, I don't think I deserve to have him back after everything I did and said. I had my chance with Edwin, and I botched it up. Edwin deserves better.*

Eyes fluttering shut, Arie bowed her head and offered up a silent prayer. *Lord, please give me the wisdom and fortitude to embrace the path I've chosen and to live my life in keeping with Your will and not what others expect of me. From now on, I intend to be truthful and compassionate in all that I do, and I will stand firm in my convictions, no matter how difficult it may be.*

Edwin found himself unable to concentrate on the hymns, the reading of the Bible, and the sermon. He wasn't distracted by the uncomfortable backless bench he had been sitting on or boredom. His gaze kept returning to Arie, positioned with her hands folded on the women's side of the barn where church was being held this morning. Oh, how he missed spending time with Arie Kauffman. The truth was, Edwin cherished everything about his ex-girlfriend—everything except the one thing that had driven them apart. If only...

Was I a fool to break things off with her? Edwin wondered. *Might there have been some way we could've worked things out between us?*

He flinched, knowing the answer to his own question. As long as ballet was the most important thing in Arie's life and she had no desire to join the Amish church, there wasn't a single thing Edwin could do about it, and there was no way they could have a future together. It was as simple as that. Edwin rationalized to himself that he could go on without having Arie in his life. But in his heart of hearts, Edwin knew that he would never forget his first love and all of the wonderful memories they'd shared. He also knew that he might never find another woman he'd want to marry. Of course, Edwin's mother thought otherwise, and she had expressed it to him a few days ago when he'd been moping around.

Edwin's lips clamped shut as he made himself direct all of his attention to the sermon at hand. It did no good to speculate on the *what-if*s or *might-have-been*s. All Edwin needed to do was look forward to the future and try to be the best person he could. And he couldn't let anyone—not even Markel—tell him otherwise. Edwin refused to heed the words of somebody who hadn't been in a committed relationship.

The barn, which had been meticulously cleaned for this Sunday's services, brought a burst of fresh air as the crisp autumn weather billowed in through an open window. Edwin inhaled deeply and thanked God for the chillier days of the year. The breeze drifting into the building was a welcome relief, and it definitely made sitting for three hours in the stuffy barn more bearable. Edwin was also glad that he'd been able to unwind and focus his attention on the sermon.

When the service was over, Edwin wandered around outside, waiting for lunch to be served, while taking advantage of the opportunity to clomp through a few clusters of colorful leaves that had dislodged from the trees lining the yard. About that time, Edwin's friend, Leroy Lehman, joined him on his trek among the litter of twigs and yellowing foliage. Edwin always enjoyed the chance to catch up with any of his friends he hadn't seen since their last Sunday service, and Leroy was no exception.

"Did you hear what occurred at the Kauffmans' general store

last night?" Edwin's friend asked him as they plowed through the crunchy leaves and circled around two large white birch trees.

Edwin shook his head. "No, I didn't. What happened?"

"Some woman from out of town drove her vehicle right into the side of their store."

"Are you serious?" Edwin's mouth slackened as he came to a standstill.

"Sure am. I heard Jerome Kauffman telling my daed about it before church service started this morning."

Edwin combed the back of his thick head of hair with his fingers. "What exactly happened?"

"I just told you," Leroy said. "A car crashed into the Kauffmans' store."

"But how? I—I mean how could such a thing even happen?"

"Well, from what I heard. . ."

Edwin spent the next few minutes listening with interest as his friend explained what he knew about the accident, but the details were a tad bit sketchy. Hearing about the ordeal made him concerned. To find out how everyone was doing and whether Jerome and Brenda needed a hand with any repairs that had to be done at the store, Edwin felt obliged to pay a call on Arie's family. He had one concern about going over there today, however. Wouldn't Arie most likely be there? Given that she was still a ballet student, which had driven a wedge between them, Edwin would find it awkward to see her again.

If we hadn't broken up, this wouldn't be a problem, Edwin thought after saying goodbye to Leroy and heading off in the opposite direction, his footsteps guiding him around the birch trees again. *Maybe I should hold off till tomorrow when Arie won't be home. At least that way, I wouldn't have to see her and be tempted to say something I shouldn't.*

Chapter 24

Upon arriving home on Monday, Edwin changed his work clothes and headed out on foot for the Kauffman residence to offer his services in repairing their store. A gust of wind whisked over his body, bringing shivers up and down the middle of his neck. Fall was definitely here and was sure to bring more cold weather until winter took over. In some respects, Edwin looked forward to the changing weather. Without the oppressive humidity that summer brought, working outdoors was a little easier. Although replacing shingles on a roof could be exhausting, Edwin's body never heated up as much in the cooler months as it did in the summer.

When a car whipped by, sounding its horn, Edwin shifted farther to the right on the shoulder of the road and picked up his speed. Every now and then, drivers would honk or veer closer to pedestrians, perhaps hoping to frighten them. But most drivers were courteous and reduced their speed as they approached someone walking on the side of the road.

With horses and buggies, some folks were also impatient. They would come up behind a buggy, blare their horn several times, then veer into the opposite lane and accelerate. This often spooked horses. Edwin had witnessed it happen numerous times and encountered the behavior himself while driving his own horse and carriage.

"Some people can be so inconsiderate," Edwin muttered as he neared the Kauffmans' driveway. "I wish every human being could see the benefit of being polite."

Edwin stopped mumbling and strode up the driveway in the direction of the general store. He hoped Arie's parents were there and he wouldn't have to bother anyone at the house, where they might be fixing supper. One thing was certain: Arie wouldn't be around, since she worked full-time at the gift store or could possibly be at a ballet class in Goshen.

When he neared the general store, Edwin noticed a section on one of the exterior walls where there were plywood sheets, along with a hodgepodge of scrap framing material. No doubt it was the spot where the vehicle had run into the store. Edwin shuddered as he considered the extent of the damage to the store's interior and the contents of any shelves that might have been inside within the area of impact.

After seeing the CLOSED sign in the store's front window, Edwin concluded that Jerome and Brenda had most likely closed the store and wouldn't reopen until the building was repaired. That made perfect sense. It would be impractical to have regular customers mixing with various trades making repairs.

Guess I'll head on over to the house and see if anyone's at home, Edwin thought.

Soon, Edwin found himself on the Kauffmans' front porch. His eyes drifted to the vacant hook that once held the hummingbird feeder. He recalled what Arie had told him about Rudy getting stung by a wasp earlier that year. Jutting his chin, Edwin lifted his hand to knock, when the door swung open and Rudy emerged onto the porch.

"Oh, I didn't realize anyone was here. Just came out to get a rake from the tool shed." The boy pointed to the scattered leaves in the front yard. "My daed said I should get a few piles started before it's time to eat supper."

"Makes sense to me," Edwin responded with a nod. "By any chance, is your father at home? If so, I would like to speak with him."

"Nope. He and Mom went to town to get some supplies for the store, and they're not back yet."

"Wait, so are you and your little sister here alone?" Edwin questioned, raising his brows.

"No, we're not. I'm here with my siblings."

Edwin's fingertips touched his parted lips, as Arie stepped behind her brother, towering over the youngster. "Oh, uh—Arie—I didn't think you'd be here at this time of the day."

She tipped her head to one side. "Why not? I live here, Edwin, remember?"

"Of course I do. Just didn't expect—I mean, I figured you'd either be working at the gift shop or attending one of your ballet classes."

"I'm actually back to working at the gift shop part-time, and I've decided that there will be no more dance lessons for me."

"Seriously?" He slapped a hand against the side of his face.

"Jah. I'm very serious, Edwin."

"Why? How come? What changed?" The words tumbled out of his mouth like a kid at a gumball machine inserting a handful of quarters.

Arie tapped her brother's shoulder. "Rudy, don't you have some leaves to rake in the yard?"

Arie's brother leaped off the porch and raced through the yard, leaves crinkling beneath his feet as he sprinted in the direction of the tool shed.

"If you'd like to come inside, I'll explain," Arie said, never taking her eyes off Edwin.

He scuffed his feet a few times on the doormat, gave a nod, and accompanied her indoors.

"Maggie's upstairs in her bedroom right now cleaning up a mess of papers on her floor," Arie explained, shutting the door behind them. "So we can talk privately in the living room without any interruptions."

"All right," he replied.

Edwin followed Arie down the hall, and she guided him to the living room. Once they were there, he rounded the coffee table and settled on one end of the couch.

After seating herself in the rocking chair and pressing her feet on the floor, Arie gradually built up momentum. "Edwin, I made the decision to give up ballet after the vehicle crashed into the side of my parents' store. Other things influenced my decision too, but..."

Edwin listened as Arie mentioned something about pointe shoes and feeling guilt-ridden. He was on the brink of asking why the mishap had prompted Arie to give up ballet when she went on to elaborate.

"The crash at our store was a wake-up call for me to quit dancing and build a stronger bond with my family. I realized how much my parents needed my help, and if they didn't have to pay someone to keep an eye on Rudy and Maggie after school, they could use that money toward repairing the store."

"I see." Edwin grabbed a throw pillow propped up at the corner of the couch and positioned it behind his back.

"So I feel that it's best if I give up ballet and use my income and time to help my family right here and in the store." Arie paused. "I've also been thinking about the words in Romans 12:2 that reminds us that we should be renewed in our minds rather than conform to the world. Even though I enjoyed ballet, I was not raised in an English family like Lorrina, and the truth is, I prefer the life I have right now."

"That's a good Bible verse," Edwin admitted. "But are you certain that you'd be happy if you give up ballet? You were desperately wanting it before."

"You're right, Edwin, but that was before my eyes were opened. I'm confident that I've made the right decision. And who knows—maybe someday I'll find something else that will bring me the joy dancing did—something that won't conflict with my faith."

Edwin drummed his fingers along the arm of the couch, wondering if he should say what had come to mind. Throwing caution to the wind, he blurted out, "I know what you said before about the drill team, but if you should decide to give it a try, it wouldn't go against our Amish values."

Arie bobbed her head. "I know, Edwin, and I don't think anyone in our church district would see it as worldly. They wouldn't go to the events and encourage the members of the drill team to continue performing with their horses if they did. After all, many of the events your team participates in are for worthwhile causes, and the funds raised benefit those with high medical and hospital expenses. It would be wonderful to take part in the charitable contribution you all give to the community."

Edwin leaned forward, resting both elbows on his knees. "Are you saying that you might consider coming to a drill-team practice to see if it could be something you would enjoy doing?"

Her eyes gleaming, Arie clasped her hands to her chest and said, "I know how my folks will feel about it, but I'm willing to give it a try."

Edwin cracked a grin and nodded, feeling the bridge of his nose twitch. "Great. I'll let you know when our next practice session is scheduled, and we can see how it goes."

Arie looked at Edwin as if she had been waiting for him to say something else, but instead, he rose to his feet. "I'd better go, Arie. When your parents arrive home, please let them know that I stopped by and ask them to let me know if they need a hand with any repairs on the store."

"All right, I'll make sure to do that." Arie led Edwin to the front door, and as he opened it and prepared to go out onto the porch, she reached out and brushed his shoulder with her hand. "Before you go, Edwin, there's one more thing I'd like to say."

He turned to face her. "I'm all ears."

"I'm sorry for not being truthful with you from the very beginning about my interest in ballet."

"I appreciate that." Edwin squinted against the sun's glare.

"Can you find it in your heart to forgive me?"

He nodded. "I don't believe in holding grudges. Not for long, anyway."

"If you did, I wouldn't hold it against you."

Maggie came barreling down the stairs just then and rushed up to Arie, clasping her hand. "Arie, would you come look at my room? I think it's clean enough now."

With a downward gaze, Arie patted the child's shoulder. "Okay, Maggie, I'll go see what you've accomplished."

"I'd better let you go," Edwin said. "My mamm's probably got supper ready by now. I'll give you a call and let you know when the drill team's going to meet up again."

He stepped off the porch and hastened down the graveled driveway. Although Edwin was grateful for what Arie had told him, when she began dancing, the distance between them had widened. He doubted whether their relationship could ever be as it once was.

That evening, Arie joined her parents, who were sitting in their chairs in the living room. She positioned herself so she could see both of their faces and gauge their reactions to the question she was about to deliver.

"Did you wish to say something, Daughter?" Dad asked, lowering the newspaper in his grasp.

"Jah, I do." Arie moistened her lips and swallowed a couple of times. "If it's okay with you both, I would like to participate in a drill team practice with Edwin and his teammates the next time they get together."

"I don't favor that idea, Arie." Mom's voice grew deeper, and her eyebrows furrowed.

"Why not?"

"For one thing, you could get hurt. Our family has been to several of those drill team exhibitions, and some of the things the team members have done with their horses looked dangerous to me."

"Brenda, why don't we allow Arie to decide what's best for her? I believe she's old enough to make her own decision. And while being on the drill team might pose certain dangers, our daughter has the right to forge her own path." Against the mellow light of the gas lamp over his recliner, Dad's comment was firm yet soothing. "Besides, her taking an interest in the drill team doesn't go against our Christian beliefs."

"I suppose you're right, Jerome," Mom agreed. "And I'm thankful that our daughter is being truthful with us and doesn't plan to run off to the next drill team practice without discussing it with us first." She glanced at Dad, then back to Arie. "Even if I'm not entirely in favor of the idea, what your father said is true. You are old enough to make your own choices. I hope that this choice won't interfere with your desire to stay with the Amish faith, however."

Arie shook her head vigorously. "Of course not, Mamm. A number of team members have already joined the church, and I have no doubt that most of the others will follow suit."

"Then you have my blessing, Arie." Her mother offered a pleasant smile. "Just please be careful out there."

"All right then, it's settled." Dad got up from his chair and stretched his arms over his head. "And on that note, I think I'll get ready for bed. Tomorrow will be another busy day as we continue getting our store repaired and open for business again."

Two evenings later, Arie sat beside Edwin in the rear seat of his driver Bill's truck. When she peered over her shoulder at the two-horse trailer being hauled by Bill's vehicle, Arie felt a sense of enthusiasm, even though it was coupled with a touch of trepidation. Edwin had assured Arie earlier that this would be a fun but instructive evening. Nevertheless, Arie experienced a constriction in her chest, questioning whether she had erred in agreeing to accompany him to the team's practice, which would include a demonstration by the young woman from Ohio he'd previously told Arie about.

Arie looked down, watching Edwin's feet jittering against the floorboard. *He's excited*, she told herself.

When Edwin had called to inform Arie that the drill team would be meeting this evening, he'd given her a quick overview of what to expect once the team started practicing. Although she didn't really plan to join them, with Edwin's encouragement, she'd brought her horse along, just in case.

"I'm looking forward to introducing you to Esther Troyer," Edwin said. "As I mentioned earlier, this is the second time Esther has visited us, and I'm sure you'll enjoy watching her ride two horses at a time."

Even though it might be interesting and even thrilling to watch Esther perform, Arie prayed it wouldn't be something she'd be expected to do. The sensation of standing atop a horse, let alone straddling and attempting to maintain balance on two at the same time, was beyond Arie's comprehension. But her biggest concern was the chance of losing her balance and falling off. The dangerous side of Roman riding or even doing the basic drill team moves had no appeal to Arie.

Then why did I agree to go with Edwin tonight? Arie questioned herself, raising a hand to her temple. *Does the prospect of joining the drill team appeal to me in some way, or was it simply so that I could spend time with him again? Oh dear, what have I gotten myself into this time?*

When they arrived at the Fox Run Stables, Arie and Edwin got their horses situated inside a stall to await practice. Once that was done, Arie followed Edwin into the enclosed arena and took a seat beside him, about halfway up on one of the bleachers.

Edwin leaned close to her ear and remarked, "We'll have a good view from here. You'll be astounded to see what Esther is capable of. I guarantee it."

Arie's only response was a brief shrug.

Once everyone had taken their seats, Reuben stood up and said he had an announcement to make. Arie's ears perked up, eager to hear what the team leader had to say.

With a broad grin, Reuben surveyed the group. In a boisterous voice, he said, "I'm happy to say that Esther Troyer is back again and has graciously agreed to show us some of her new routines. Along with her demonstration this evening, Esther told me that she would be sticking around for a week or two and is willing to teach anyone in our group who expresses interest in some fundamental Roman riding maneuvers." Reuben motioned to the arena where, during practice sessions and event programs, horses and riders made their entrance. "Now, sit back, relax, and prepare yourself for some fantastic entertainment. Please join me in giving Esther a round of applause to show our appreciation."

The young woman, wearing a dark blue Amish dress and with black tights covering her legs, rode into the arena with an air of confidence, standing with her arms outstretched on the back of a well-behaved horse. Arie couldn't get over the team members' excitement as they cheered. According to Edwin, they'd seen Esther's performance before, and Arie assumed it must have been spectacular, or they wouldn't all be so enthusiastic.

Arie's own excitement mounted, and she knew Edwin's had too, for when she glanced at him, both hands were pressed against his chest, and his eyes looked larger than normal. She wondered how Esther could maintain her balance as the horse trotted around the arena.

That seems more challenging than any ballet position I've ever tried, she thought. *To accomplish such a feat, Esther must have sturdy legs and outstanding balance.*

Still standing on her horse, Esther exited the arena the same way she had entered. She reemerged a few minutes later astride two horses of similar color and height. Arie speculated on how long Esther must have spent honing this ability. Moreover, Esther's radiant smile as the horses circled around the arena was an indication that she thoroughly enjoyed Roman riding and wasn't the least bit afraid.

Arie's stomach clenched. *Even standing on a horse, let alone allowing them to trot around an arena like this while only grasping the reins would be terrifying.*

Following the exhibit with two horses, Esther departed once more and returned a short time later riding only one horse, but with an alternative kind of saddle with a reinforced steel horn. This time, the young Amish woman executed a maneuver in which she hung from the side of her horse with one hand raised over her head. A thunderous chorus of applause from all the team members seated on the bleachers reverberated throughout the arena. Arie presumed they shared her sense of amazement. Nothing Esther had done was anything like dancing, but it had a certain allure, and Arie reasoned that the act of trick riding would raise anyone's adrenaline while providing the rider with an air of accomplishment.

Is this something I would enjoy doing? Would I even be capable of it? And if I could, what about Aster? Wouldn't my horse have to be specially trained too? Arie had a lot of questions for Esther, and she hoped for the chance to have a private conversation with her before the evening was over. *Maybe I can do it while Edwin and his drill team members practice for their next event. I can join them later in order to learn some of their moves, but not until after I've spoken with Esther. That might also give me some insight as to whether I would fit in or even be accepted as another team member.*

Chapter 25

ONE MONTH LATER, DURING A group practice, Edwin was taken aback when he saw Arie guide her horse to the arena exit and vanish. She'd been practicing with the team faithfully and had seemed to enjoy the drills. Seeing her leave so abruptly made Edwin wonder if she was disheartened and missed ballet or perhaps wasn't feeling well. He was inclined to hurry out of the arena as well to make sure she was okay.

Maybe I'll wait a few minutes, Edwin told himself. *Then if she doesn't come back, I'll go check on her.*

When Reuben blew the whistle and requested everyone to bring their horses over to the side, Edwin wondered if someone had done something wrong. Occasionally that happened, and their team leader had always dealt with it by having everyone stop what they were doing and gather around for further instruction.

Edwin squinted toward the in-gate of the arena, hoping Arie would return soon with her mare, as it would be unfortunate if she didn't get to hear what Reuben had to say.

"Well, team," Reuben announced, cupping both hands around his mouth, "kindly turn your attention in that direction." He pointed to the exit. "There's something exciting I'd like you all to see. In fact, if everyone's on board with this, we'll incorporate it into the exhibition we'll be doing at the charity event this coming Saturday afternoon." Reuben paused and blew his whistle again.

Moments later, Arie trotted into the enclosure, holding the reins of two horses. The one she sat upon was her own horse, Aster, and Edwin suspected the second horse, which appeared to be roughly the same height as Aster, might be her mother's mare.

That's sure strange, Edwin thought as he fiddled with his reins. *Why would Arie have brought her mom's horse to practice?*

It wasn't long before Edwin discovered the reason. As Arie rose up on her knees, pulled up to a standing position, and planted one foot on each horse's back, his mouth opened wide and his breathing became more rapid. Arie got the horses moving, while standing on the bareback pads that had replaced her saddle and grinned widely. First, it was a modest, gradual pace, and then she directed them into a steady trot. It was an amazing sight as she stood with her knees slightly bent and both horses held together with the proper room between them so they wouldn't bump into each other but also weren't too far apart. Edwin would have thought that Arie had been doing Roman riding for a number of years if he hadn't known any different.

How long has she been doing this? he wondered. *And how come I didn't know about it?*

Edwin continued to watch along with the other team members. They sat with rapt attention, observing this unexpected display of courage by their newest team member. He leaned forward in his saddle, struggling not to hold his breath as Arie continued to guide the horses halfway around the arena. Once she'd circled with the horses twice along the fencing, Arie brought them to a halt.

Amid a round of applause from Edwin and the rest of the

team, Reuben rode Scout to the middle of the arena and proclaimed that he had another announcement to make. "In case you haven't figured it out, Arie began training with Esther when she was here a month or so ago. After Esther returned to Ohio, Arie kept practicing with her own horse as well as her mother's mare. Only I knew about it, because we wanted it to be a surprise for the rest of the group."

"It was sure that all right," one of the young women on the team hollered.

Once practice was over and everyone had dismounted and secured their horses, most of the team gathered around Arie. As they commended Arie on her outstanding display of Roman riding, Edwin stood some distance apart and observed as her face brightened. In spite of his yearning to contribute to the team's outpouring of support, Edwin remained silent and felt an ache in his chest ebb and flow. Arie's gaze locked with his, and he quickly avoided a prolonged exchange by looking to the rafters above them.

"So now, let's take a vote." Reuben walked quickly over to Arie. "How many of you would like to see this brave and talented young woman's demonstration added to our team's programs? Personally, I reckon she should begin by doing it at the event we're participating in this Saturday afternoon, if everyone agrees."

It only took a few seconds for the murmur of voices, nodding heads, and hands to begin lifting. "I think it's a great idea." "That was awesome, Arie!" "Yes, definitely." "I believe it would be a great addition to our routine." Each team member voiced comments of approval, and everyone's heads bobbed like stalks of corn in the breeze.

"All right then—it's unanimous," Reuben stated, gesturing to

Arie. "What do you think? Are you willing to do what you did for us here today in front of a whole crowd of people on Saturday?"

Edwin moistened his dry lips with the tip of his tongue as he waited for her answer and tried to imagine what it would be.

Arie responded to Reuben's question in a matter of moments. She'd expected it, in fact, since he'd told her in a message left on her parents' answering machine that if her presentation this evening went well, he'd ask the team members how they felt about Arie incorporating her Roman riding into their practiced routine.

"Yes," she answered, speaking loudly enough for all to hear. "I would very much enjoy riding Roman style on the horses my driver trailered here for me tonight. Thank you all for agreeing to let me perform this Saturday. I will certainly give it my all."

There, it was out in the open—she'd agreed to do it, and there was no turning back. All Arie needed to do now was invite her parents to Saturday's charity event so they could witness what she was capable of. Even though she hoped that her folks would support this new endeavor and grant their full approval, if they didn't, Arie couldn't abandon her passion for the drill team. Of course, they'd seen her practice with Esther the first week she'd visited, and they knew Arie had been training with both her horse as well as Mom's.

What Arie hadn't told them, though, was that she had become a full-time member of the drill team Edwin belonged to and would hopefully be performing Roman riding during part of their routine. She'd wanted that part to be a surprise, hoping that seeing her in action would allow her parents to see not only that she was having fun but also that she had joined a group of young Amish men and women who performed for others in their community as an act of giving back.

Edwin hurried up to Arie after practice concluded and saw that her horses were led up the ramp into her driver's trailer. He didn't want her heading out until he'd had a few minutes to speak with her.

"That was some big surprise you pulled off," he said, joining her near the driver's truck. "I'm curious why you never told me what you were up to. I thought we were—"

"You broke up with me, Edwin. Remember?"

He swallowed around the thickness in his throat. "Well, jah, of course I remember, but I believed we had worked things out between us."

"We did, and I apologized, so there are no hard feelings on my part, Edwin."

"Nor mine, Arie. It's just that—"

"I'm sorry, Edwin. My intention was to surprise you, not to hide anything." Tugging on the ties of her kapp, Arie cleared her throat. "So, what did you think when I came out to the arena with two horses? Were you expecting a little Roman riding demonstration?"

"You really caught me off guard, and I thought you were fantastic, Arie. I'm sure as time goes on and you continue to practice, you'll get even better."

"Thank you, Edwin. Although that type of riding doesn't reflect the same emotions as ballet, I've discovered something that not only gives me a great deal of pleasure but also provides me with the confidence I've needed to finally be myself." Arie touched Edwin's arm for a moment and went on. "You know, after several weeks of practice, I began to realize that spending more time with my horse and Mom's mare was a lot of fun and quite gratifying. I'm grateful to Lorrina for introducing me to ballet, since it not only helped me gain self-assurance, but it was also a great way to exercise and strengthen my legs and other parts of my body. Without even knowing it, those weeks of attending ballet classes actually prepared me for Roman riding. I never thought I'd feel this way or be willing to admit it, Edwin, but being part of your drill time has been exhilarating. Danki for encouraging me to give it a try."

Edwin touched the spot on his forearm where Arie had grazed his wrist. "You're welcome. I'm happy to hear all of that."

Arie's driver informed her that he had to be somewhere in an hour and asked whether she was ready to leave.

"Yes, I'm ready to go," Arie responded. She turned to face Edwin and said, "I'll see you Saturday afternoon, and I hope everything goes well for all of us on the team."

He nodded and watched as she climbed into her driver's vehicle. A knot formed in Edwin's stomach as the vehicle pulling the horse trailer left the parking lot. There was so much more he'd wanted to tell Arie, but apparently it wasn't meant to happen tonight. Maybe after the charity event on Saturday, he'd get the chance to tell her what was on his heart. He hoped so because it was difficult to keep his feelings bottled up inside.

At the event on Saturday, Arie and the other young Amish women in the group wore their traditional Amish dresses with either a pair of jeans or black tights underneath for modesty. Before the team's turn to present their program, a buzz of excitement surrounded the girls as they readied their horses, ensuring they were prepared and looked their best. Meanwhile, the guys on their team were doing the same. The plan was for Arie to ride with the drill team as they did all their intricate maneuvers. Near the end of their performance, Arie would leave the arena and enter again, riding two horses, Roman style.

As Arie lifted her foot into the stirrup and settled on Aster's saddle, her heart hammered against her ribs. Although it was undeniable that she was on edge, the adrenaline she was subjected to was more a result of excitement than nervous energy. She'd spoken to Lorrina earlier, who was out there somewhere in one section of the bleachers. Her dear childhood friend had come here to offer Arie support and cheer her on.

Arie reached over and patted her horse's neck, remembering how Lorrina had said she was glad Arie had found her true calling. Arie had thanked her friend for introducing her to ballet and stated that dancing had opened the door to her independence. Even so, part of Arie had known deep inside that she was meant to join the Amish church, which she could not have done if she'd continued to dance.

"Are you ready, Arie?" Reuben's girlfriend, Sara, asked, looking over her shoulder at her.

"Jah, I'm more than ready."

Those seated on the bleachers clapped when Reuben led the team into the arena. They started with a mini sweep, where each team member rode along the rail of the arena in an oblique pattern. Next came the pinwheel, where two riders positioned their horses so they were side by side in the center of the arena, facing opposite directions. The other team members lined up, facing the same direction as their center riders. Then the whole formation rotated around the two pivot riders, who circled their horses in place. The team also did some other maneuvers, such as the full team crack, single file cross, figure eight, inner-locking circles, and flank turns. Arie liked the pinwheel pattern the best, but it could pose a challenge at times.

At Reuben's signal, Arie departed the arena while the other riders performed a few more patterns. When it was time for her to reappear, the music that had been playing slowed way down, and as she entered with two horses, the tempo of the music picked up again.

Reuben and the other team members spread out against the rail on both sides of the building as Arie knelt, then stood, with one foot on each of the horses. Keeping up with the rhythm of the music pouring forth from the speakers, Arie went from a slow walk to a full trot, remembering to keep the horses close enough, as she'd been taught by Esther. She managed to keep her balance until close to the end, when Aster flicked her ears back, causing Arie's mother's horse to veer to the right. But Arie took control and quickly guided the mare back in place. At that moment, the musical arrangement grew louder, and each of the team members joined Arie for one last trip around the arena, single file.

As the riders exited the arena, Arie heard a roar of applause from the audience. Knowing that they valued the team's work was encouraging, and it was even more satisfying to know that the funds raised for this benefit event would help a member of their Amish community who was in dire need.

As soon as Edwin climbed down and stabled his horse, he hurried off to find Arie. She wasn't with any of the female team members, and he worried that she might have left already. In addition to wanting to congratulate her on a job well done, Edwin had plans to invite Arie to go on a horseback ride with him tomorrow after church. Although the winter months were closing in on the late fall weather, they hadn't been blessed with any snow yet. The temperatures were fairly mild for the first part of November, so in his mind, it wasn't too cold to go riding.

Edwin stepped back into the main part of the arena and looked around, hoping for a glimpse of Arie. He spotted her about halfway up the bleachers, talking to her parents and younger siblings. Edwin held back until Arie's parents gave her a hug and headed out the door with Rudy and Maggie.

When Arie stepped down from the bleachers, Edwin rushed up to greet her. "Wow, just wow! You did an amazing job."

"Thank you, Edwin," she responded. "I had a lot of fun, and I'm looking forward to more opportunities to incorporate Roman riding into any programs our group has during the rest of the year and next year as well."

Edwin bent his head and spoke close to her ear. "I was wondering if you'd be free to go horseback riding with me tomorrow after church."

"I—I guess so," Arie stammered. "Don't you think it's a little chilly outside for that?"

"It's not that cold out yet, and I think both we and our horses will enjoy the ride. What do you say?"

"Okay, sure." She bobbed her head. "As soon as we get home from church, I'll get Aster ready."

The Pumpkinvine Nature Trail was the perfect place to go riding, and Edwin was super excited to be spending the afternoon with Arie. They'd ridden side by side for quite a while, and then Edwin suggested taking a break and letting the horses rest. While Aster and Daisy nibbled on grass growing along the trail that they could reach from where they'd been tethered, Edwin pulled a saddle blanket on the ground and suggested that he and Arie sit.

"What'd your folks think of you riding two horses at the same time yesterday?" he questioned.

"They seemed to be impressed with my accomplishment, and to my surprise, my mother didn't try to dissuade me from Roman riding. She actually said she was pleased that I'd found something to do that brings me joy and fulfillment."

"That's great, Arie." Edwin reached out a tentative hand and placed it on Arie's shoulder. "I'm pleased about that too, and there's something else I want to tell you."

"Good, because I have something to tell you as well. Do you want to go first or shall I?"

"You can start."

Arie swiveled around so she was facing him directly. "Edwin, I want you to know how much I appreciate your friendship."

"Is that all I am to you—just a friend?"

She lowered her gaze. "You're more than a friend, Edwin. So many times since we started seeing each other, you've offered me your steadfast devotion, and even though you broke up with me, I've never stopped loving you."

He reached for Arie and drew her close, tenderly rubbing her back. "I made a huge mistake breaking things off, Arie. I love you so much, and if you'll have me, I'd like to be your boyfriend again."

"Of course, I'll have you. I never wanted to break up, Edwin."

She pulled away far enough that he could see tears spilling out of her eyes and trickling onto her cheeks. Edwin reached out to wipe them away with his thumb.

"There's something else I'd like to ask you." Edwin's voice sounded strained, even to his own ears.

"What's that, Edwin?"

"Do you feel ready to take classes in preparation for being baptized and joining the church?"

"Jah, I do."

Edwin's heart soared with joy as he leaned close and kissed her lips. Someday, when the time was right, Edwin would ask Arie another important question. But that would happen in God's timing, not his, and Edwin was certain that the Lord would reveal it to him at just the right time.

He felt something wet on his nose and tilted his chin. "*Schnee*," he muttered. "Look, Arie, God has blessed our time together with some beautiful white snow."

She giggled and extended her tongue to catch a snowflake. "I love snow, and this is a perfect ending to a wonderful day."

After returning home, Arie dug her pointe shoes out of her ballet bag for a final glance while preparing for bed, touching the satin ribbons she had sewn on weeks before. Even though ballet was no longer a part of her life, she would hold on to the pointe shoes as a reminder of when she'd been an Amish ballerina.

With a smile on her lips, Arie laid the shoes inside her cedar hope chest and shut the lid. Strolling back across the room, Arie stood by the window, watching the snow descend to the yard, glinting like an abundance of gemstones under the glow of the full moon. She whispered a prayer, expressing gratitude to God for an unforgettable day.

Epilogue

Two Years Later

THE BALMY WINDS SWEPT THROUGH the trees overhead, their limbs spanning over Arie as she sat beside her boyfriend, resting after another lengthy day of practice. Arie and Edwin had made considerable strides with their drill team. Although Reuben had been the one who founded their team, he'd officially resigned and asked Edwin to take over leading the team. Edwin wholeheartedly accepted. Of course, he had asked Arie for help guiding the team's rehearsals, as she'd gotten so immersed in preparing their performances for benefit functions as well as providing outstanding entertainment for the residents of LaGrange County and beyond.

"I have a serious question, Arie. Is it normal for two-year-olds to get grumpy and refuse to eat strawberries, of all things? Olivia loved strawberries before, so what changed?"

With laughter, Arie tipped her head back and said, "A toddler losing their taste for things they used to love eating is common. I've seen it firsthand, twice. And when you think about it, your little sister can't properly communicate her needs, and that becomes very frustrating for anyone, much less a two-year-old."

"That's true, but I'm starting to see why my older brother didn't like me as much when we were kids. It was reasonable in those days, but not so much anymore."

"Welcome to the role of being an older sibling, Edwin. It's what to be prepared for if and when we have children of our own someday. But your little sister is really adorable," Arie added.

"Olivia is certainly cute, which makes her antics forgivable, I guess." Chuckling, Edwin turned his head to face Arie directly. "I'm amazed at how quickly time has gone by. Not too long ago, you surprised me and the other members of the drill team by standing atop your mare. Since then, you have increased your skill with remarkable leaps and bounds."

"Edwin, I have you to thank for that. You opened my eyes to my purpose and potential. I do occasionally miss dancing, but I feel like I've found a great feeling of belonging on the drill team and in our community."

He tugged along the collar of his olive-green, buttoned-up shirt. "Indeed you have. It still amazes me how you can retain your balance on Aster, especially given that you were having concerns about riding horseback with her a couple of years ago."

"I suppose I needed to let go of the reins and put my trust in Aster. I sometimes worry that I won't be able to perform anymore, or that something will go wrong with what I do. But seeing you and the other drill team members showing such passion has kept those worries at bay. I'm grateful to be able to live out my life rather than being afraid to do so."

"I'll keep encouraging you, Arie. Although you were unsure of yourself and your choices when we first met, I knew deep down that you aspired to be the person you are now."

"Edwin," Arie sighed as they reached out to embrace each

other, "I'll be sure to do the same for you."

"You already have, in a lot of ways, actually." He squeezed Arie before drawing away. "There's something I've been meaning to ask you for a while now."

Arie pressed a hand against her chest, wondering what that question would be. She had a suspicion he might do this and had been waiting for Edwin to do so for quite some time. Arie's heart hammered, knowing her boyfriend's next words could change their lives forever.

He touched the side of Arie's face, gently pulling his fingers down to her chin. "There are no words to express how much I love you, Arie Kauffman. But I will be doing my best to show you every day for the rest of our lives if you agree. Will you marry me?"

"Yes, of course I will." Blinking back tears, Arie grasped his hand, a feeling of warmth radiating over her cheeks. "Edwin, you have my unconditional love."

Edwin leaned forward and kissed her, and Arie closed her eyes as tears seeped from under her lashes.

Brenda's Tomato Soup

2 tablespoons olive oil
1½ cups chopped onion
3 cloves garlic, minced
2 stalks celery, chopped
2 carrots, chopped
2 cups vegetable broth
1½ cups chopped tomatoes
½ cup chopped cherry tomatoes
1 tablespoon coconut sugar
1 teaspoon salt
¼ teaspoon pepper
1 cup coconut milk

Place large pot on burner set to medium. Add olive oil and heat until it shimmers. Place onion and garlic in pot and sauté until translucent. Add celery and carrots. Continue sautéing until tender. Add vegetable broth, tomatoes, cherry tomatoes, coconut sugar, salt, and pepper. Bring to boil, then simmer for 20 minutes. Add coconut milk and stir.

Optional: Before adding coconut milk, use immersion blender to achieve smooth and creamy texture. Include additional herbs and spices if desired.

Richelle Brunstetter lives in the Pacific Northwest and developed a desire to write when she took creative writing in high school. After enrolling in college classes, her overall experience enticed her to become a writer, and she wants to implement what she has learned into her stories. Richelle's first published novella appeared in *The Beloved Christmas Quilt* beside the writings of her grandmother, Wanda E. Brunstetter, and her mother, Jean. Since then, she has written several other novellas and short stories. In her free time, she likes composing poetry, outdoor photography, and doodling in her sketchbook. Richelle enjoys traveling, her favorite destination being Kauai, Hawaii.

New York Times bestselling and award-winning author **Wanda E. Brunstetter** is one of the founders of the Amish fiction genre. She has written more than 100 books translated into four languages. With over twelve million copies sold, Wanda's stories consistently earn spots on the nation's most prestigious bestseller lists and have received numerous awards.

Wanda's ancestors were part of the Anabaptist faith, and her novels are based on personal research intended to accurately portray the Amish way of life. Her books are well-read and trusted by many Amish, who credit her for giving readers a deeper understanding of the people and their customs.

When Wanda visits her Amish friends, she finds herself drawn to their peaceful lifestyle, sincerity, and close family ties. Wanda enjoys photography, ventriloquism, gardening, bird-watching, beachcombing, and spending time with her family. She and her husband, Richard, have been blessed with two grown children, six grandchildren, and two great-grandchildren.

To learn more about Wanda,
visit her website at www.wandabrunstetter.com.

SISTERS BY THE SEA

4 Short Romances Set in the Sarasota, Florida, Amish Community

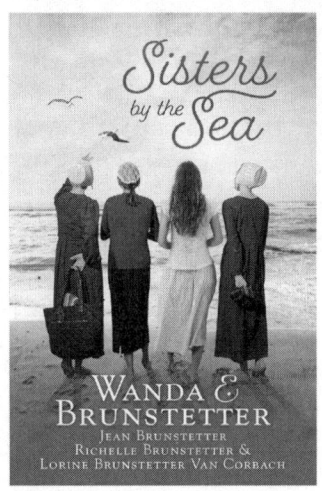

NEW BEGINNINGS FOR FOUR AMISH SISTERS

Journey with the bestselling Brunstetter authors to the unique tropical Amish community of Pinecraft in Sarasota, Florida, along with four young sisters originally from Indiana.

The Seashell Cake by **Wanda E. Brunstetter**

Leora Lambright is the first to leave home for Florida where she decorates cakes in a bakery and meets John Miller, a roofer on winter holiday. They are instantly attracted to each other and spend several days together. But when Leora makes it clear she'll never again live up north, without explaining why, has the romance ended before it could even blossom?

The Beach Ball by **Jean Brunstetter**

Violet moves to Florida to seek her independence and considers leaving the Amish way of life. She works as a waitress and drives her own car. Her beauty and free spirit attract a lot of male attention like Levi, who was also raised Amish, and Dan, who was not. Can she settle on who should have her heart and how to live out her faith?

Fragments of a Sand Dollar by Richelle Brunstetter

Francine Lambright is heartbroken that her longtime boyfriend, Matthew, is thinking of leaving the Amish faith, and they have broken up. She is ready to join the church, but her sister invites her to Florida for an extended visit before taking the pledge of faith. While shell hunting at Lido Beach, Francine meets Lucas Hayes, and they soon begin seeing each other, despite him being an Englisher. When Matthew shows up in Pinecraft unexpectedly, how will Francine's heart respond?

A Sarasota Sunset by Lorine Brunstetter Van Corbach

Alana Lambright has a traumatic past that left her plagued by anxiety. She turns to art for peace and healing. While visiting her sisters in Florida, she meets James Fisher, who invites her on adventurous outings. Alana tries to tamp her anxiety to try new things, but she fails and feels like it pushes James away. Can they each deal with the heaviness in their pasts to embrace a future together?

Paperback / 978-1-63609-660-5

Find This Book and More from Barbour Publishing at Your Favorite Bookstore or at www.barbourbooks.com

Christian Fiction for Women

Christian Fiction for Women is your online home for the latest in Christian fiction.

Check us out online for:

- Giveaways
- Recipes
- Info About Upcoming Releases
- Book Trailers
- News and More!

Find Christian Fiction for Women at Your Favorite Social Media Site:

 Search "Christian Fiction for Women"

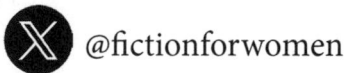 @fictionforwomen